HEAVEN SENT

Amanda Bews

SIGNS
PUBLISHING®
Established 1885

Proudly published and printed in Australia by
Signs Publishing
Warburton, Victoria.

This book was
Edited by Nathan Brown
Copyedited by Lindy Schneider and Kerry Arbuckle
Designed by Ashlea Malycha
Cover photo by Jetrel/Shutterstock
Typeset: Sabon 10.5/14 pt

ISBN   978 1 921292 83 5 (print edition)
        978 1 921292 84 2 (ebook edition)

DEDICATION

For Brendan . . . thank you!

"For I know the plans I have for you, says the Lord. They are plans for good and not for evil, to give you a future and a hope."

—*Jeremiah 29:11 (The Living Bible)*

ONE

They were at it again. I turned up my iPod to drown out their voices. Unfortunately nothing could mask the slamming doors. How could two people who once loved each other enough to get married and have kids feel so much hate now? I tried to ignore the gnawing in my gut and concentrate on the material I was reading for the chemistry test in the morning.

They were an odd match, my parents. Dad was from old money. After spending years "serving his country" as a Liberal Party senator, he had "retired" and now spent his time flying around the country sitting on the boards of big corporations. He earned way more money now than he ever did in politics. Not that we ever had any shortage. There was always plenty to make up for the attention he never gave us. I was sure Dad only stayed with Mum because it would have looked bad to leave her and—above all else—things had to look right.

Mum—well, what can I say? She was a lost soul from a strange bygone era, a modern-day hippie a few generations too late. She'd left her country town many years ago to backpack across the world to become "at one" with mother earth and discover the great universe's plan for her life. She'd spent time living with Incas, monks, swamis . . . you name it, she'd been there. After receiving a vision, she returned to the evils of Sydney to share her talents in the material world. In other words, she spent her days painting unremarkable pictures in a studio Dad built for her behind the pool.

They'd met on George Street, Sydney. She and her dread-locked companions were protesting against capitalism. While members of her group banged tambourines and chanted the evils of the modern world, she sketched sidewalk drawings of animals endangered by deforestation. She must have been hot or something—and Dad had somehow been intrigued and it had gone on from there.

I have no idea how they managed to have my sister and me. But our names reflect their differences. Mum named me. She wanted to call her first daughter something beautiful and idealistic. Something beyond this world where perfection reigned—that's what she tells me, anyway. So what did she call me? Heaven! Can you imagine what it was like grow-ing up with a name like that? The sniggers, the backward glances, the teasing—and that was just in primary school. High school was, and is, so much worse, even though most of the boys have known me since we were five. Hormones do stupid things to boys.

When I'd asked to change my name, Dad told me it was character building. It was the agreement they had come to so Dad could name the second of their offspring. I guess he hoped it would be a boy. When my sister arrived, she got a much more normal name. Katherine—after Katherine the Great. Though, to Dad's disgust, Mum shortened it to Katie. Dad hates shortened names. He believes it is a sign of disrespect to shorten the name your parents gave you and Dad is all about respect!

The ironic twist of it all is Katie is all artistic and alternative like Mum. And I'm the straight-A, athletic, public-speaking school captain like Dad. Go figure that one! So here we are. To the world we look like this perfect family. But if we were to tell anyone what was really going on . . . well, that would be to break the family code of silence and air our dirty laundry in public. That would mean loss of respect and—like I said before—Dad is all about respect. So every morning, we walk out the door smelling like roses. But underneath we smell much worse.

The yelling and door slamming finally subsided. I guessed Dad left again. Mum would be sobbing in her studio. We wouldn't see her until sometime after school. That's when she'd come looking for sympathy. *She is so pathetic and I can't help giving in to her. I wish he'd just leave and break the monotony of it all.*

I checked the clock and sighed, 11.30 pm. It didn't feel like much of the chemistry had made it into my head tonight but I was still confident of an A. Unlike most of my friends, I never crammed at the last minute. I've had a goal: Sydney University Medical School. The second hardest course to get into in the country. And why not the hardest course, you ask? That's Political Science and although I loathingly take after Dad, both physically and mentally, I am *not* doing the same course as him! Some of my mother's blood runs through my veins. I want to save life, not waste my time taxing it.

* * *

The bell rang as I finished checking over my test. I placed it confidently on top of the pile on the teacher's desk and met my best friend Kelly Harris at the door.

"So how'd you go?" she asked.

I smiled and ignored the question. We'd been friends long enough to know the answer and it's rude to boast. At least something in my life could be planned and organised, since my home life was in a constant state of turmoil.

"Fine, thanks. How was Sociology?" I redirected the conversation.

Kelly rolled her eyes. "I bumped into Jarrod in the hall. He says practice is cancelled and can we eat with them. He didn't try to message you because he knew your phone would be off. You know you're the only person I know who turns their phone off in class?" she scowled.

"Yes, and I'm the only person who hasn't had their phone confiscated this year. Besides, I'm in class to learn, not socialise. Gotta keep your eye on the prize, Kelly!" I said, offering my usual pep talk as we headed for our usual tables.

Kelly rolled her eyes again. We viewed school quite differently. She was all about cute boys, parties and having fun and me . . . she tells me I'm 17 going on 30.

Engrossed in conversation, we rounded the corner and crashed headlong into Alex Collins, the football legend himself and with the ego to match. It was like hitting a brick wall. My books tumbled to the ground. Fortunately, my new laptop was well secured in my backpack. I looked up at Alex. Though I'm tall, he still dwarfed me and everyone else. He eyed me up and down leeringly. I'd pick up my books when he moved.

"Hey Heaven. You're looking . . . heavenly today. You wanna come to the game this weekend? I'll save you a seat in the front row. We can study afterwards . . . maybe

4

anatomy?" He followed up his lewd remark by running his tongue across his teeth.

I shuddered with revulsion. I couldn't believe half the girls at school thought he was hot. He was nothing but an oversized Neanderthal.

"Wow, Alex, four syllables! How did you manage that?" I spat.

"Come on, Heaven, you know you want me!" he taunted, stepping closer.

"In your dreams, Collins," Kelly yelled shoving my books back into my arms and dragging me around the mountain of footballer in our path.

"Oh, stand up, Harris!" Alex piped over his shoulder as we cut around him.

"Is that the best you can do with the five brain cells you have left, Alex?" Kelly hurled back.

A chorus of laughter echoed down the corridor. What Kelly lacked in her height, she made up for in spunky retorts. Alex snorted and marched off toward the gym. I pitied whomever he would be matched up with for tackling practice today.

* * *

Jarrod and his friends were waiting for us at the table. Our table was the farthest from the canteen under the ornamental olive trees. He smiled when he saw me and reached over to take my books. He brushed a quick kiss across my lips, wiping away the chill from my encounter with Alex. He slipped his fingers through mine and we dropped onto the bench seat and leaned against the table.

Jarrod and I had been together for six months. I hadn't wanted a boyfriend. My parents' marriage was enough for me to think dating was a waste of energy. But Jarrod had done it all: notes in my locker, late-night text messages wishing me a pleasant sleep (when I'd finally agreed to give him my phone number), movies, dinner, picnics at sunset on the beach. How could I possibly say no? The other girls had been positively green with all the adoration he'd lavished on me. My sister Katie had just about died with frustration at the three times I turned him down.

"Heaven—he's a god! I'd give anything to be you. You've got it all. Stop thinking for once and just live. He's not asking you to marry him. He just wants to be your boyfriend. Give him a break!" she'd yelled in exasperation, holding fistfuls of her hair. It had been quite humorous at the time.

But Jarrod was no quitter. He was as used to getting his way as I was at getting mine. So he'd quietly and persistently worn me down, even after I'd insisted on bringing him home to meet my parents. I thought that would have been enough to put him off. But he'd put on quite a show. Dad had been impressed and Mum was almost flirting with him by the end of the evening.

I'd walked him to his car and was just turning to go back inside when he took my hands and said, "Heaven, what are you afraid of?"

I had frozen as he ran his hands up my arms and cupped my cheeks. That was when I made a fatal error. Instead of turning away, I looked into his eyes. Those wonderfully rich chocolate-brown eyes . . . I lost my train of thought for just a moment, but that was enough.

He didn't wait for a reply; he just leaned in and kissed me. When his lips touched mine, I thought my heart would stop with the shock. But then this burning began. Like the butterflies in my stomach all simultaneously burst into flames. A floodgate opened inside me. The fire swept through my whole body and, to my complete surprise, I kissed him back. When he finally pulled away, I was breathless and he was smiling. He gently stroked my cheek with the tips of his fingers and brushed his lips across my forehead before whispering, "And now . . . you are mine."

With a smile on his handsome face, he waited for me to walk back to the door before he left. I felt euphoric—until he drove away. As I stepped back inside the entrance hall, I was filled with a sense of foreboding. There was now a crack in my ivory tower. I'd let him in. *Would he hurt me? Would he be just like Dad?*

He'd sensed my doubt and had been the model boyfriend. Meeting me after class, carrying my books, driving me around. I began to relax but that was when it started:

"My parents are going away for the weekend. Would you like to come over and spend the night?". . . "What, don't you love me?" . . . "Everyone else is doing it!" . . . "The guys are laughing at me 'cause I'm the only one not getting any."

TWO

The more he pushed, the more resolute I became. It's not that I had any problems with sex before marriage. It wasn't like I was a Christian or anything. It's just . . . I suddenly felt like I was being bullied and I wasn't going to be bullied into this, no matter how good a kisser he was or how beautiful his eyes were.

He'd issued a challenge—and I could do challenges! He'd backed off for the present. We'd called a temporary truce. I think he and his buddies had got together and discussed it, deciding perhaps I just wanted to wait and surprise him after the end-of-year formal as some kind of graduation gift. I was happy to let them think that.

The truth was I was afraid. I didn't want to be that vulnerable with anyone—not even Jarrod Beckette. The crack in my ivory tower was widening.

"What have you got after lunch?" he asked.

"Sorry . . ." I stammered and flushed. I'd missed an entire conversation, lost in my musing.

Jarrod laughed softly and stroked my hand. "I was just asking what you had after lunch."

"Ummmm, errrr . . ." I was getting lost in his eyes again.

"We've got PE," Kelly piped up.

I heard one of the guys mutter in the background something about Jarrod wanting to get physical with me. *What? Was that the only joke guys knew? First Alex, now . . .* I felt the flush rising, a gift inherited from Mum.

Kelly grabbed my arm, "Come on, Heaven. I need to go to the girl's room."

I untangled myself from Jarrod's grasp. He winked at me as I backed away. My heart fluttered. *Why was I saying no again?*

"What is it with girls? Why do they gotta go to the bathroom *en masse*?" Gavin asked, shaking his head.

"Oh, but it's so much more than a biological need, Gav. It's a bonding experience!" Kelly replied, with a flick of her hair and a flashing smile.

Kelly had liked—no strike that, *loved*—Gavin now for two years, eight months and one week. Since the day he'd transferred from interstate. Being athletic, he'd immediately fitted in with the football boys and soon made himself indispensable on the team Jarrod captained. Kelly had been thrilled when Jarrod and I'd gotten together. Suddenly it meant spending most lunchtimes with Gavin.

And she seemed to be making an impact. Kelly was small, quick and very cute—though she kept telling me that she was the girl-next-door, while I was the Italian supermodel, which was a huge exaggeration. Besides, modelling was for the vain and conceited. A long way from treading the hallowed halls of Sydney Medical School.

* * *

We squeaked open the door of the empty bathroom, coming face to face with a row of ageing mottled mirrors and cracked enamel sinks. Kelly whipped out her lip-gloss and began re-applying.

"I thought you needed to visit here," I said.

"No," she puckered her lips, "I saw where the conversation was headed and felt it was a good time to have a break." She straightened her hair with her fingers and squashed her lips together to even out the gloss she'd just applied, then spun around.

"Now tell me again why you don't want to sleep with that gorgeous boy?" she demanded with her hands on her hips. "If that was Gavin asking, I'd be swooning like in one of those old movies."

She dramatically leaned on one of the bathroom sinks, with the back of her hand to her forehead. Unfortunately her hand slipped on the soap-smeared sink ledge. She slumped to the floor, bumping her head as she went. It must have hurt but she remained in character, finishing with a deep sigh and a feigned faint.

I laughed and shook my head as I helped her up. "We've already had this conversation. You know why. Just because you don't get my reasoning doesn't mean my decision changes."

"But he's so hot," she whined.

"Yes . . ."

"And he wants you." Her eyes twinkled as she bit her thumbnail. "And he hasn't cheated on you this whole time. He's told you he loves you and talked about a future together."

"Yes." I rolled my eyes.

"So why not?" Kelly demanded, stamping her foot.

"Kelly, does Jarrod have you on the payroll or something?" I smirked.

Kelly melted her arm over my shoulder and sighed. "I just want you to be happy, that's all."

"Euuwwo, now you're sounding like my mother! Though I don't think she'd be counselling me to sleep around." I laughed.

"It's not sleeping around. Jarrod's your boyfriend—your very long-suffering boyfriend . . ."

"Six months is hardly long-suffering. I've already told him I'm not ready," I cut in defensively.

"Oh, Heaven . . . Your parents are nuts. Just because they're in some weird codependent relationship doesn't mean you'll end up that way. Besides, I'm sure you'll have lots of guys before you decide to settle down."

"I'm not so sure I want lots of guys."

"What? Do you like me or something?" Kelly sassed with a flick of her hips and a grin.

"No, silly, it's just the idea of sex. It makes me feel too vulnerable. Too exposed—too disposable. I don't want to be the topic of locker-room conversation. I don't want boys discussing what I'm good at and not good at. Or how my breasts look in the moonlight. What if I'm bad at it?"

"He wouldn't do that to you!" she said, patting my arm.

"You better believe he would. All guys turn on you in the end. It would likely end up in some cheap gossip column. Some anonymous source filling in the morning commuters about the ex-senator's daughter's first roll in the hay."

"You read too many newspapers," Kelly hurrumphed.

"You read too many romance novels," I countered.

Kelly sighed. "Oh fine, I don't want to debate the joys of virginity with you anymore. Keep it if you want to but it's entirely over-rated. I can't wait for Gavin to . . ." She grinned wickedly but her comment was cut short.

The bathroom door squeaked open and three juniors walked in. We waited for them to choose a stall each.

Then I whispered, "How do you know it won't be a monumental disaster? Most first-time sexual experiences are not pleasant at all. Often they're downright painful!"

"Only if you're uptight!" Kelly scoffed.

"No, that's not it at all. I've asked around and every girl I spoke to just laughed it off as a given. They're all like, 'He was so sweet but I just wanted him to hurry up and get it over with!' That will ruin everything," I said, turning to face the stalls.

There was silence for a moment. I swung round to face Kelly again.

"How would I ever face him again? . . . How?" I asked almost desperately.

Silence again. The toilet flushed.

"Come on," I said. "It must be almost the end of lunch-time. We'd better go get our books."

The guys were just packing up when we got back.

"I'll walk you?" Jarrod asked, picking up my books. I watched his biceps ripple as he moved. He really did look good with his sleeves rolled up.

"No, it's OK. I'll catch you after practice," I replied, taking my books. I didn't want him to be late for class.

He leaned in, his lips tickling my ear, and whispered huskily, "Looking forward to it."

My heart did somersaults. Then he kissed my cheek and was gone. I stood unable to move for a moment as he and his friends disappeared around the corner, laughing and joking together. *He truly is incredibly hot—did I mention that? It might not be that bad after all . . .*

"Close your mouth, Heaven, you'll catch flies," Kelly laughed, slapping me on the back. "You say no—but you act like a girl who sooo wants to say yes!"

I snapped my mouth shut, rolled my shoulders and took a deep breath. The answer was still no!

* * *

We changed into our gym clothes. Mr Higgins hollered for us to hurry up.

Kelly snorted. "Doesn't matter how quick we are, they seem to think it's their right to complain about how long we take," she said, hauling up her shorts.

"My mum told me when she was at school the teachers used to give them five minutes, then come in," Sandra added, as she carefully pulled her top over her head, trying not to mess up her hair.

"I'm sure they would have shut their eyes," exclaimed Rachel, still in her underwear. She always took longest.

"Not likely," Kelly giggled, "unless maybe Braille was involved."

She shut her eyes and staggered toward my chest, hands outstretched, making exaggerated grabbing motions with her fingers. I clipped her on the side of the head and everyone burst into laughter.

"Come on, you girls," called the muffled voice of Mr Higgins from behind the door.

"We'd better get going before he has an aneurism," I said, pulling my brush through my ponytail.

It was track. Running was something I enjoyed doing. Nothing like the monotonous drumming of feet on turf to help focus the mind and get things in perspective.

I lapped Kelly twice. As I came around to do it a third time she hissed, "Some friends run together and keep each other company."

I slowed and looked down at her purplish face. "Now who's having an aneurism? Perhaps I should call Gavin and ask him to come down and give you mouth-to-mouth?" I huffed.

I watched her face change from purple to scarlet. She was too tired to come up with a retort. I laughed and powered through to the finish line.

As I stretched and prepared to go back to the showers, Mr Higgins came over carrying his stopwatch. I stood up and smiled. Most teachers were unnerved by my height. Since Grade Nine I'd been able to eyeball them all and now most of them were forced to look up to me. Mr Higgins was confident enough not to care. I really liked him. He was always kind and never picked on the heavier kids like some of the other Phys Ed teachers did.

"Great time, Heaven. I reckon you've got a really good chance of doing more than just a place at State this year." He smiled, handing me my water bottle.

"Thanks, Mr Higgins. We'll have to see. I've got a lot on this term, but I'll try to fit in some extra training." I took a swig from the bottle.

"You could train with the football team. I'm sure Jarrod wouldn't mind you joining in, though you might show up some of his boys. Probably be good for them," he laughed.

I smirked and felt my competitive spirit ripple. I was

pretty sure I could beat a good portion of the team. It could be fun! "Sure, Mr Higgins. You're on!"

"I'll make the arrangements," he said, heading for the gym.

I dropped on the grass to wait for Kelly. It was one thing to desert her on the track, but she wouldn't forgive me if I left her on the field. Eventually, she huffed across the line and collapsed on the ground next to me, feigning death.

"You can call Gavin now," she gasped, puckering her lips. We laughed until our sides hurt.

* * *

Back in the changing rooms, Cathy Davis greeted me. She was already changed and looking a million bucks. I instinctively stood up. This girl was like a lioness and I needed to use whatever advantage was available. We'd competed for everything since primary school, Jarrod included, though I never really thought of her as that much competition with him. As Kelly had said so many times regarding Cathy, "He only ever had eyes for you." The thought brought a smile to my lips, rather than the usual scowl she was probably expecting.

"What can I do for you, Cathy?" I asked coolly.

"You wanna borrow her maths homework?" Kelly piped up from below.

Cathy ignored the quip and leaned in to whisper menacingly, "Hmmmm, I hear through the grapevine that Jarrod is getting tired of waiting, Heaven. You better watch out. If you don't, he'll just find it somewhere else."

"And I'm sure you'll be first with your hand up, won't you, Cathy?" Kelly interjected.

Cathy was unmoved. "Just thought I'd let you know, that's all. You know, all's fair in love and war. The walls between my brother's room and mine are quite thin. You'd be amazed at what I hear them discuss."

And there was the slam-dunk and the reason she was captain of the debate team. She swept away before I could formulate a good reply.

"Forget her, Heaven. She's still sore that you got Jarrod and she didn't, even though he's been practically living at her house since Grade Six." Kelly patted my arm. "But I hate to admit it . . . you know she has a point," she added quietly.

I felt my competitive spirit flare for the second time that hour. *Would he?* The thought of him and Cathy together was horrifying. I chastised myself inwardly for my response to Kelly's words and my ivory tower quaked a little more. *Was everyone doing it but me?*

It seemed like sexual pressure was coming from everyone and everywhere. Music, books, movies, magazines, advertisements—all telling me if I didn't I was just not normal. Maybe I was just making a big deal about nothing? But then the usual haunting vision came into my mind. It was of Jarrod and his towel-clad team mates in a steamy locker room after a game, all discussing our first intimate encounter. Suddenly they burst into raucous laughter slapping Jarrod on the back, a couple offering him a high five. I would not be the butt of their smutty change-room conversation.

I set my jaw. "He can just wait until I'm good and ready!" I huffed.

* * *

16

The rest of the school day rushed by in a blur. Last period was General Studies, which Jarrod and I shared. Kelly relinquished her usual seat next to me in favour of Jarrod. To her delight, Gavin filled the empty seat next to her. She turned and gave me a wink and a thumbs up.

Jarrod slid into his seat and locked his fingers through mine under the table. Ms Renolds, our 40-something single teacher, was very strict about PDAs (Public Displays of Affection). Kelly always said it was because she never received any herself. I smiled at the thought.

"How was track?" Jarrod asked, tracing figure eights across the back of my hand.

"Great. Mr Higgins wants me to join the team this week for training. You guys had better watch your backs," I smiled.

"I'd be more than happy to watch yours." He winked back seductively.

I giggled and cleared my throat nervously. It was time to change the subject. "So what's with Gavin? Do you think he's interested?" I asked, throwing my gaze in Kelly's direction.

Jarrod laughed and held up his free hand in defence. "It's like I already told you, Heaven. I'm not getting involved. If it turned out badly, Kelly would make mince meat outta me. They're going to have to work it out on their own."

"But you must have talked about it? He must have given you some idea about what he thinks of her? I know what you guys talk about in the locker room," I persisted, jabbing him in the ribs.

Jarrod's smile disappeared. He was about to say more when Ms Renolds called us to attention, ending our conversation.

The bell rang. It was a long class and didn't contain anything of much value. I'd spent too much time dwelling on Cathy's words. As we packed up our books, I glanced across at Kelly. Things seemed to be going well on the Gavin front. Neither looked to be in a hurry to move off.

"You wanna study for the Math test together?" Jarrod asked as he shouldered his bag.

"Yeah, sure," I replied.

"Yours or mine?"

My mind raced back to last evening's fight. Mum would still be in a snivelling heap. We couldn't go to our house.

"Yours," I answered with a smile.

"You wanna lift?" He slipped his index finger around mine. Ms Renolds could handle that.

"Nah, I'll walk with Kelly and come round later."

"OK," he replied as he quickly leaned forward and brushed his lips across mine. I inhaled a laugh. Jarrod was too quick. He was already gone before Ms Renolds could react.

She waddled, gasping, to the door and called futilely up the hall. "Jarrod Beckette, we'll have none of that in my class, you hear me?" she squawked waving an angry fist.

Kelly and I left by the other door before Ms Renolds could turn her wrath in my direction.

"OK, tell me everything! That looked promising," I squeaked as Kelly and I ducked around the corner and away from Ms Renolds's roving eye.

"Eeeeck!" Kelly jumped up and down with her eyes closed. I thought she might burst.

"I am sooo, sooo grateful to you for getting together with

18

Jarrod. Gavin is sooo quiet and shy there is nooo way this would have happened unless you had. I pledge a lifetime of servitude to you for this," she danced.

"OK, can you get on with the story please?" I pressed. "The suspense is killing me!"

"Well," she began, pulling a folded piece of notebook paper from her folder as we headed to our home room, "read this!"

As I read, she jumped about like a frog with an energy drink. It was very distracting. Eventually, with several interruptions from Kelly, I managed to get through the page. It started out innocently enough. Asking to borrow a ruler, commenting on how boring Ms Renolds was.

Finally, Gavin had written. "You want to catch up Saturday night? There's this movie Jarrod and I've been wanting to see. Maybe we could all go?"

My heart pounded with excitement for my friend. I flipped the page over. "SURE!!" Kelly had written. She'd been waiting so long I guess she couldn't bring herself to play it a bit cool now.

I grinned. "That's super, Kell. Did you want Jarrod and me to come, or would you rather go it alone?"

"No, definitely come. I don't want him to get scared off. He's so shy that I might only get one chance. I bet I'll have to be the one to hold his hand and do the old yawn-and-drape trick on him." She faked tiredness and rested her arm across my shoulders. We both laughed.

"Oohh, Saturday is still such a long way away. I wish he could have made it sooner," Kelly stamped.

"He can't. You know he works every night after school.

He's saving up for that car his parents said they'd go halves with," I reminded her.

"True, guess that means once we're a couple, I'll only see him at school and on Saturday night," she pouted.

"Let's not get ahead of ourselves. Let's start with the date and see what happens," I smiled.

"This is so exciting! What am I going to wear?" she bubbled.

"I was wondering when that would come up. Quick, we'd better hurry now. The bell is about to ring and we are going to be late!"

* * *

Kelly and I had walked home from school together since we began school. From Prep to Grade Six, we'd been closer to her house, but as the high school was on the other side of Bakersfield Road, it was now closer to my house.

Kelly chatted all the way home about her wardrobe and what she needed to make the date perfect. I had to promise three times that I would go shopping on Thursday night to help her pick out a new pair of boots.

"So, you'll come?" she asked for the fourth time.

"Of course, I'll come. Now go on, get going. I've got to meet Jarrod at his house in an hour and I'd like to change first," I said, shooing her from my doorstep.

"Something a little more comfortable?" She cocked her eyebrow and grinned wickedly.

"Ohhh, you hussy!" I threw a bark chip at her from the garden beside the door.

"Was just checking," she piped as she ducked out of the way.

"You go home and daydream about Gavin and forget about my love life," I called after her.

"I will, don't worry," she giggled back.

I let myself in. The door was always locked, even when everyone was home. Mum was paranoid about burglars ever since she saw a guy on TV that hit homes during the day and tied up the occupants. They were only found when the rest of the family arrived home from work. Not that it would be likely for him to strike in Sydney when he was serving time in Brisbane. But that was Mum, as neurotic as she was flaky.

I decided against telling Mum where I was going and settled on filling Katie in instead. After freshening up and changing into my favourite jeans and white shirt, I tucked my head round the corner of Katie's room. She was sitting on her bed listening to her iPod and flicking through a magazine. She was always the one to do her homework "later."

"I'm off to Jarrod's. Can you tell Mum I'll be home in time for dinner?"

"Hmmm?" she asked, pulling out an earphone.

"Wow, that's loud Katie. You'll burst your eardrums," I added, shaking my head.

"Lucky I'm going to have a whiz doctor for a sister, who'll be able to fix 'em up for me then, hey?" she replied flatly.

"Was just asking you to tell Mum I'm going to Jarrod's," I repeated.

"In that case, you'll be needing this then, won't you?" she said, flinging a small packet toward me.

I caught it instinctively.

THREE

It was a condom—and I dropped it in surprise.

"Well, don't act like you don't know what they are, Heaven. Relax, I didn't buy them. We got them today in sex ed. You should keep it handy—you know, with all the gossip about you and Jarrod going around, I thought maybe you'd need it," she said, waggling her eyebrows with a smirk.

"What gossip?" I screeched.

"Keep your voice down. Mum's in the kitchen," Katie hissed. "Well, it's just what I heard from Trinny."

Trinny was Cathy's best friend's sister—*was that as difficult to follow as it sounded?* Anyway, she and Katie were friends. Trinny was a snoop and liked to read other people's Facebook accounts. She guessed Cathy's password easily—it was "Jarrod".

I frowned. "Well, you tell Trinny that it takes two people and one of those two hasn't set a date for it just yet."

Leaning over, I dropped the condom in the wastepaper bin.

"OK, OK," Katie replied, rolling her eyes again. "Whatever you want. I was just trying to be helpful. You know, if I were dating someone as hot as Jarrod Beckette, I'd . . ."

"Ewwhoo, enough already. Don't talk about my boyfriend like that. I don't need the visuals!" I said distastefully, as I backed from her room.

"Just trying to help you get things in perspective, that's all, Heav," she called back.

"Fine, duly noted—but no more day-dreaming about

Jarrod. That's almost . . . incestuous!" I said, pulling her door shut.

"Whatever!" she called in a muffled voice from behind the closed door.

I grabbed my keys off the entrance table and locked the door behind me. *What is it with everyone? Next my parents will be wading in on my personal life,* I thought as I crunched down the driveway.

* * *

Jarrod lived only a couple of blocks from our house. His family had moved a few months before we got together. It was most convenient—and sometimes I wondered if it was part of Jarrod's master plan. It seemed nothing was outside the realm of possibilities with him.

I knocked and let myself in.

Jarrod was playing a video game against his brother—not something I was interested in. But Jarrod leapt over the back of the couch and planted a playful kiss on my lips.

"Hey, beautiful!" he grinned.

"Ohhh, get a room," his brother, Jeff, fired over his shoulder. He was already engrossed in another game.

"We intend to!" Jarrod shot back with a wink. "Come on, Heaven. Let's go make out over some mathematics." He shepherded me toward the door.

"Oh, cute . . . very cute!" Jeff replied, as some foul beast tore his character's heart out.

Jarrod laughed and led me to his room. He dropped down on his bed and I pulled out the chair from his study desk and turned it to face him. I was pulling the text book from my school bag when he stepped around behind me and began massaging my shoulders. He was good at that!

I closed my eyes and leaned back in the chair. "Mmmmm, that feels nice." I said with a smile I couldn't suppress.

Jarrod leaned down and his lips connected with the skin on my neck. I felt goose bumps prickle up my spine. He spun the chair around to face him.

"Jarrod, we're supposed to be studying . . . remember?" I rolled my eyes up toward him slyly.

Jarrod dropped to his knees and touched his forehead to mine. He still hadn't let go of my neck. His hands slipped to my cheeks and then he was kissing me. Gently at first but it was becoming more forceful.

It was time to stop—besides, Jeff was at home. At any moment, someone could walk in and I'd be incredibly embarrassed, even if he wasn't. I placed my hands on his chest and began to push.

Between kisses, I managed to get out, "Jarrod . . . please . . . your brother's . . . in the next room!"

Jarrod sighed and sat back on his bed. "OK," he beamed. "I was overcome for a moment—let's study."

I giggled. I was feeling a little giddy. I turned to the practice test in the book.

"But just for the record . . ." he said leaping up to kiss me one last time.

I gave him a playful push.

"My brother would never come in without knocking," Jarrod reassured me with a wink, before tapping my cheek one last time with his lips and dropping back on the bed.

He crossed his arms behind his head and leaned back on the pillow.

"OK, hit me with the first question, babe."

I sighed and shook my head. It was time to make a game plan. I needed to work out what I was going to do. If I didn't have something sorted in my head, this could all happen without me being prepared. The last thing I needed was something unplanned. There was too much at stake. Or so I thought. It seems guys never really plan much ahead of "OK, let's do it!"

* * *

When I got home, Dad was back, which was unusual. Katie was setting the table. My jaw hit the floor. We never ate around the table. Filled with a strange sense of foreboding, I caught Katie's eye.

She just shook her head. "Mum's cooked!" she mouthed.

"Cooked!" I squeaked. I was going to have to prise my eyebrows from my hairline! Mum never cooked.

"Is Grandma here?" I asked.

Sometimes Mum made an effort when Dad's mother came to visit. But Katie just shook her head. I went to my room to put my bag down. I needed a minute to collect my thoughts. Mum's cooked, Dad's home early. Something was definitely up and I guessed fairly soon we'd know.

The food was unappealing, some kind of "all-in-one" hotpot of organic produce and lentils. We never ate meat. I'm sure Dad did when he was away but I never ate it. It wasn't that we weren't allowed, it's just I never did. I'd

25

tried it once but thought it was pretty tasteless and took too long to chew. In the end, I'd waited until no-one was looking and spat it into a napkin. It was nasty stuff, even apart from Mum's "Meat is Murder" sentiments.

No-one spoke for ages. It was quiet except for the scraping of cutlery on crockery and the occasional gulp and gurgle. I wondered which of them would break the silence. If I hurried, I might get away by beginning the dishes and they'd put off whatever it was until some other time—like maybe after my graduation or something! I rose to take my plate out.

"Just a minute, Heaven," Dad said, pressing my hand.

Slowly, I slipped back into my seat. There would be no escape now. I glanced across at Katie and noted the dread registering in her eyes. Dad cleared his throat. He almost looked uncomfortable, which was unusual.

"There is something I need to make you all aware of . . . ummm, I received a phone call from the *Herald* this morning asking me to comment on a 'situation.' A young lady on my staff has . . . ummm, has alleged we have been . . . involved."

"Involved?" Katie asked, not quite allowing her brain to register what she was hearing. Mum looked pale, like she might faint.

Dad's face twitched. "There is a possibility the media will contact you . . . or perhaps come to the house. It's important we keep a united front. By this, I mean . . . if you are asked any questions just say, 'No comment'. There is no need for you two to become embroiled in this. If we don't say anything, all they will have is speculation and it will probably just blow over. I've asked the media to keep my family out of this and I trust they will honour my request."

My blood began to boil. "What, you mean like you honoured Mum?" I hissed.

Silence stung the air. I counted my heartbeats awaiting the repercussions. 1 . . . 2 . . . 3 . . .

Dad stood, his face flushed with rage: "I beg your pardon. I will have none of this . . ."

But it was too late. He'd unlocked the vault. It was one thing to cheat on his snivelling wife—but he'd been caught. All bets were off.

"No, Dad, I beg your pardon. So you want to hide behind us now you've been caught with your secretary . . ."

"Heaven!" my mother squeaked. But I continued as if she'd said nothing.

"And you want us to cover for you? I got you loud and clear." I turned to walk from the room but Dad grabbed my arm.

"It's not what it looks like!" he insisted. But I refused to face him again. He'd broken the facade. The stench of my family choked my nostrils. Nothing could keep it in now, no matter how much Mum and Dad tried to sugar-coat it.

"Whatever, Dad. Whatever," I replied, flicking free from his grasp.

I stalked to my room and slammed the door. Grabbing my iPod from the night stand, I selected my "Angry" playlist and cranked the volume. Throwing myself on the bed, I buried my face in the pillow. Wishing again what I had wished so many times before. Wishing this was not my family. Wishing I had been adopted and any moment my real parents would knock on the door and ask to have me back.

* * *

The door opened and I felt a hand on my back. I swung around and opened my eyes, expecting to see Mum coming in for sympathy. But it was Katie, looking grim. I pulled out my earphones and sat up.

"Wow, Heaven!" she whispered. "I thought Dad was going to have a heart attack when you walked out."

Katie dropped onto the bed next to me. I instinctively put my arm around her. She was my little sister. I wanted to protect her—but, of course, I couldn't. This was Dad's doing. Only he could have protected her from this one.

"It will be alright, you know . . . without him, I mean . . ." I began.

"He's not leaving. Mum said she forgives him. They are going to get counselling. At least that's what they told me after you . . . left."

"What?" I said, leaping to my feet. "Mum's going to what?"

"Shhh, Heaven, keep your voice down," Katie hushed. "Dad's already furious with you. You want him to come in and ground you until forever?"

"On what grounds?" I hissed. "Dad's got no authority to . . ."

She grabbed my hand. "Calm down, Heaven. There is nothing either of us can do about this. If Mum keeps him, it's up to her. Anyway, she'd probably only be staying with him for the money . . . and after all these years with him, I don't think she could manage on her own, anyway," Katie said, shaking her head.

I looked down at my sister. Suddenly she seemed older. Like the weight of our mother's misery had somehow aged her.

"So what do you know about this?" I asked, sitting back down on the bed.

"Not a lot. Mum has suspected it for a while now. And this is not the first time. I overheard her talking to her friend Charlotte about it a week or so ago out in the studio. I was working on my art project and Mum . . ." she stopped. I thought she was going to cry but she just shrugged and paused for a moment. Then she got to her feet. "What does it matter anyway? It's how it is. Just be grateful you'll be out of here and off to university in a few months." She moved to the door.

I didn't know what to say. She was right. I would be gone soon. Then she'd have to face it on her own. She paused for a moment, as if hoping I'd offer her some kind of consolation. But I had none to give. She left, closing the door behind her.

My phone buzzed with a text message. It was Jarrod. Suddenly the misery of the evening thawed a little:

See you tomorrow, sweet dreams! xx

I glanced at the clock. It was already past 10.30. Jarrod would be up early tomorrow to go for a run—and so would I! I set my alarm for 6 am and sent a quick text back about him running past my house in the morning.

* * *

The alarm seemed to go off as soon as I closed my eyes. I pulled on my running clothes, dragged my hair back into

29

a rough ponytail and grabbed a banana. Slipping silently out the front door, I did some stretching while waiting for Jarrod to arrive. It didn't take long. I recognised his familiar gait from a distance. He picked up the pace when he saw me. He was showing off and I was smiling.

I fell in beside him when he came past. We had done this many times since we started dating. The unwritten rule was you didn't stop. His pace was quick but it felt good. The cold morning air burnt my airway and numbed my muscles and brain. It would take a few blocks for them to warm up—or less if we kept up this speed—but it was good to feel numb.

By the way Jarrod kept glancing across at me, I could tell that he knew something was up. He slowed for a couple of paces and I powered ahead. He took it as the cue I didn't want to talk and quickly regained the lost ground. Instead he pushed me harder. We made it to the park in record time. We powered through the circuit and the last of the sprints, before falling on the ground breathless.

"So?" puffed Jarrod, propping himself up on an elbow. His eyes asked the rest of the question.

"Dad's finally been caught out . . . and Mum isn't going to kick him out," I replied, moving into the first of the leg stretches. He didn't reply straight away.

"Wow," was all he said. But his silence spoke volumes and confirmed my sentiments. My mum was a flake!

"She's pathetic!" I spat as I pushed against him to stretch my calves.

"Look, you don't know what her reasons are. Don't be too hard on her. Have you asked her about it?" He braced as I stretched my other leg.

"No—and why would I? I'd just get angry."

Jarrod snorted, "You're already angry. Give her a break and go ask. She might surprise you."

* * *

When we got back to my house, Jarrod walked me to the door, which was breaking the "no stopping" rule. But I guess he figured these were extenuating circumstances. We were both too sweaty to hug, so he settled for a quick brush across my lips.

"It's going to be OK, Heaven. You're tough—the toughest girl I know. We'll get through this . . . together. I'm here for you." He stroked my cheek.

I paused. He seemed so sincere.

"I'll see you at school," I said, turning to go inside.

"See you at school," he called back. He was already halfway up the driveway. I turned to watch him leave. It was always worth the effort.

I considered Jarrod's words as I showered and got ready for school. Maybe talking to Mum was a good idea. But it was something I rarely did. Mostly we'd just end up in a fight or I'd leave as one was escalating. I decided to give it a crack if she was in the kitchen when I went for breakfast. She wasn't.

Dad's newspaper was already neatly refolded, declaring he'd gone to work. Katie wouldn't rush through for a piece of toast and glass of milk for another 30 minutes yet. She never ate a proper breakfast. No wonder she never had the energy to exercise. I sighed and read the newspaper headlines as I ate: a war had broken out here; a murder there; a tsunami warning. My life could be so much worse. I needed to see things in perspective. So my dad was a cheating dirt bag and my mum wasn't going to send him packing. As Dr Phil always said, "People don't do nothing for nothing." There must have been something they were getting out of staying together.

* * *

I was early, which was unfortunate because Kelly was always late.

"Won't be a minute," she called from the bathroom with her head still wrapped in a towel. I dropped onto her lounge chair to wait. This must be how guys felt. I flicked through the channels until I found the *Today Show*. I was listening to the "Hollywood Wrap" when Kelly emerged from her room. *How could someone so little take so long?* There was like a third more of me and I was still twice as fast in the bathroom.

"You ready?" I asked flicking off the TV.

I filled Kelly in on the walk to school. She was unusually quiet as I recounted the previous evening's events.

"I'm so sorry, Heaven," she said linking her arm through mine. "It must be really painful for you."

I wasn't sure how it felt. Mostly I think I was just angry.

The day progressed uneventfully. We caught up with Jarrod and his mates at lunchtime. He didn't press and I didn't offer anything. He just sat with his arm around me and kept the conversation going so I didn't have to contribute much.

He was perfect! Mostly I just watched Gavin and Kelly. They seemed absorbed in one another. Kelly had probably hoped to spend the whole walk to school talking about what we'd wear on Saturday night. I was really raining on her parade. By the time lunch ended, I felt convinced they'd be a couple by the end of Saturday night. Usually I would have mentioned something like that as we headed off to our afternoon classes, but not today.

* * *

The rest of the week rolled through in pretty much the same way. Thursday night was fun. It didn't take long to find the boots Kelly wanted—and they were on sale. She ended up buying a cute new top as well. She was so excited about Saturday night. I managed to catch some of her energy for the evening, but it left me as soon as I walked in the front door.

Dad had gone away on one of his "trips" again. It did take some pressure off, but it also meant Mum was more likely to be in the house than in her studio. I tiptoed in, hoping to avoid her but she caught me coming out of the bathroom.

"Oh, Heaven. I have been wanting to talk with you since . . . the other night, but . . ."

"It's OK, Mum. You do whatever you need to," I replied, turning to leave.

"No, I want to tell you why. I want you to understand," she pleaded.

She was truly pathetic. "I'm never going to understand, Mum. I can't believe you would . . ."

"Please listen. Maybe one day when you are older, you will be able to see that . . ."

"No, Mum, I will not," I cut in. "If you think staying with him will make us feel better, you are wrong. You shouldn't stay with someone who treats you like dirt."

"But there is more to this than you know."

"What?! What more can there be? He cheated and you had him back. God only knows how many other times there have been, Mum. He's always away on 'business.' What's more, you should probably get yourself tested, who knows what he's given you!" My anger bubbled into every syllable.

"Heaven!" she recoiled in disgust. "He'd . . . at least be careful. He wouldn't make that mistake again."

"Again, what? He's given you an STI before?" I shrieked in shock.

"No, that's not what I meant . . . I . . ." Mum stuttered.

Katie popped her head round her door. I knew she would be listening.

"Did Dad give you AIDS, Mum?" she asked matter-of-factly.

"No . . . not at all . . ." She was getting confused. She'd give up and leave us alone soon. "What was it then? Chlamydia . . . the Siff . . . gonorrhoea?" Katie pressed.

"No, no, it wasn't like that . . . ohhh!" The tears were starting and that was Mum's cue to leave. I could hear the sobs before she got to the door. She'd hide out in her studio right though the weekend over this one.

I smiled sourly. At least I wouldn't have to deal with her again before Kelly's date.

"Thanks, Katie," I called as she backed into her room.

She tucked her head back into the hall. "Don't mention it," she smiled grimly.

We tag-teamed well: confuse, divide and conquer. It worked every time. It's not like we enjoyed it—who really enjoys reducing their mum to tears? It was just necessary so we could get on with our lives without having to listen to her ridiculous suggestions or excuses. She was so incredibly out of touch, poor thing!

* * *

I spent Saturday with Jarrod's family. It was easier than being at home. Jarrod's mum was great. We spent the morning in the garden, pulling weeds and talking about the future. She told me about her parents and their break up. It hadn't been pretty and she thought maybe staying was for the best for my mum. I just nodded and smiled but, deep down, I was unconvinced.

In the afternoon, Jarrod and I went to the markets. We wandered around the stalls and looked at all the trinkets and toys. I tried on a couple of T-shirts. I wanted to buy the one that said "I'm with Stupid" but Jarrod wouldn't let me.

"I'll only wear it when I'm with Mum!" I joked.

"Don't you think you should cut her some slack now? She's your mum, after all," he said, slipping an arm around my waist.

"I don't see why. As my mum, shouldn't she be setting a good example for me? Shouldn't she be trying to instil in me the 'I am woman hear me roar'-type values?" I joked halfheartedly.

We were passing a jewellery stall when a cute necklace with a locket caught my eye. I picked it up and looked at it. It was sterling silver and shaped like a heart. It had "Mine forever" carved into it, with lots of vintage-type swirl patterns. I loved it. I weighed it in my hand. The Asian stallholder was at my side almost immediately.

"You like? It yours . . . just 80 dollar . . . so beautiful . . . one of a kind." She waved her hand for me to try it on but I put it back. Bet she'd said that plenty of times before. I saw the light go out of her eyes as she slid back onto her stool and muttered something inaudible. She went back to reading her book.

"Glad you put that down," Jarrod laughed. "Did you see what was written on it? You can't buy something like that for yourself. What would that be saying?"

"That I'm my own person and I will never belong to anyone!" I replied seriously.

Jarrod stopped laughing. "Is that how you look at it? Do you see relationships as some kind of weakness?"

I didn't respond. He was quiet for a moment, then looked across at me sadly.

"I see . . . but maybe, I hope someday you might see it differently." He linked his fingers through mine and said no more. It felt like he was holding on more tightly than usual, but maybe I was just imagining it.

FOUR

I went home late that afternoon to prepare for our night out with Kelly and Gavin. The boys were picking us up from Kelly's house. I threw on a little mascara and lip gloss and was good to go. When I arrived at Kelly's house, every outfit she owned was strewn around her room. It looked like a rainbow had thrown up.

"What's going on, Kelly? I thought we'd already decided what you were going to wear," I uttered in surprise.

"Ohhh, I put it on and I just didn't know . . . I want everything to be perfect. I can't blow this, Heaven. He has to want me!" She was so flustered that I thought she might cry.

"News flash, Kelly. He already does or he wouldn't have plucked up the courage to ask you. Girl, he sees you every day in your school uniform that makes everyone look pregnant." I turned her around to face the mirror and held the outfit up in front of her.

"See, it's perfect!"

She sighed and threw it on.

"You look great. Now let's get going!" I grabbed her hand, dragging her to the bedroom door.

"No, I just have to fix my hair," she said, pulling back. I sighed and dropped on to her bed.

She took another 15 minutes before I heard Jarrod pull up outside.

"Come on, Kelly, they're here! You look beautiful, so let's go!" I grabbed her hand again.

"OK, OK, just let me get my bag," she replied.

I scowled. "If you ask me to choose which one, I'll scream."

Kelly laughed and picked up her little black backpack off the floor. "Ready!"

"At last!" I growled.

"You know, Heaven, you'll make someone a wonderful husband one day!" She giggled and followed me out the door.

I slipped into the front seat of Jeff's car and Kelly coyly slid into the back next to Gavin. Jarrod leaned across and kissed me. It always felt wonderful.

"Um, what time does the movie start again, Gavin?" Kelly asked pointedly.

Jarrod gave me one last quick kiss. "Kelly, just take some notes for later," he scoffed.

The back seat went silent and I jabbed Jarrod in the ribs.

"Hey, what did I do?" he asked with a mockingly injured tone.

"Just drive, Jarrod, just drive!" I whispered.

* * *

The movie was forgettable but it was an action-packed thriller, giving Kelly plenty of opportunity to bury her face in Gavin's arm. During the opening credits, I noted how strategically Kelly placed her hand on the armrest for quick collection. By about halfway through, he had taken the plunge and her fingers were tightly laced through his just in case he tried to let go.

I made eye contact and Kelly winked. She couldn't wipe

the smile off her face. Gavin looked pleased with himself, too. It was nice to be out and enjoying the thrill of new love with my friends. It certainly beat the reality at home. I nudged Jarrod and gestured to the newly locked hands. Instead of being cool about it, he clipped Gavin on the back of the head and grinned.

"About time, Gav," he said in a hoarse whisper.

After the movie, we ended up at a burger place, one of the few chain stores that provide for vegetarians. My friends didn't even ask anymore. After all, as Jarrod says, "Fast food is just junk food—doesn't matter where it's from." After we'd had our fill of greasy fries and over-sauced burgers, we headed to the park to hang out for a while. We'd often go there to sit on the swings and chat. I also thought it would be a good place for Gavin and Kelly to get a little more comfortable with one another before they had to face the gossip and commotion of school on Monday.

I stood up. "You wanna take a walk?" I pulled Jarrod to his feet.

"Why?" he asked, looking a little perplexed. I glanced across at Gavin and Kelly. They both looked at me shyly.

"Just 'cause I said, alright?" Smiling sweetly, I tugged on his arm.

He looked across at Kelly and the light came on: "Oh, so they can make out?"

Both Gavin's and Kelly's faces turned a matching shade of beetroot.

"Does that mean we can, too?" he added hopefully.

"Ohhh, just get moving would you," I said, slapping him on the butt. Jarrod hooted with laughter.

We ducked around behind a clump of trees and I pulled Jarrod out of view. Jarrod backed me up against the tree and leaned in to kiss me.

"Well, this is better, isn't it?" he whispered slyly.

"Cut it out, Jarrod. I'm trying to see," I replied, peering round the edge of the tree.

"I thought we were supposed to be giving them a little privacy?" Jarrod asked with a raised eyebrow.

"Yeah, but I wanna know how it—you know—if things turn out OK," I whispered.

"OK, fine," he said crushing up behind me and peering over my shoulder. "Let's be voyeurs, then we can make out."

Kelly and Gavin were sitting side by side on the swings. They had ceased swinging and were now creeping sideways toward each other. They were just talking and holding hands. Kelly was looking a little coy—not making too much eye contact with Gavin. He'd gotten quite close now. Their knees were touching. He must have made some kind of joke because Kelly looked up and laughed for a moment. Before she could look down again, Gavin had grasped her chin and tilted her face upward. He leaned in and kissed her gently on the lips. My heart fluttered for my friend. I wanted to leave them in their moment of first love but not Jarrod.

"Whoopa, go Gav!" Jarrod yelled. I clapped my hand over his mouth, laughing.

"Shhh, they'll hear you. You'll spoil the moment," I laughed.

"Well, if you wanna shut me up now, babe, I can think of much more pleasant ways," he said, circling his arms around my waist.

"Well, if that's what I have to do," I replied, slyly leaning into his chest.

"Oh, it is—it most certainly is," he whispered huskily. Then his lips were on mine.

* * *

It was late when we finally left the park. Making out in the park worked for me. I knew Jarrod would never try to take anything too far there. He knew there would be no way I'd offer up my first time out of doors on the grass. In fact, he was quite reserved. Maybe he felt I was already under enough pressure at home and didn't need anymore at present.

Gavin and Kelly looked quite comfortable with one another now. Though they did look pretty funny together, with her so much shorter than him. By contrast, Jarrod and I were exactly the same height and he hated it when I wore heels.

They dropped me home first, allowing Gavin and Kelly a few extra minutes together. They wouldn't see each other tomorrow like Jarrod and I would. Gavin worked Sundays in his father's garage. Even though with his marks he could have his pick of most uni courses, it was a foregone conclusion he would begin an apprenticeship next year. Gavin loved cars—especially the classic ones.

"See you tomorrow," Jarrod said with a kiss, after walking me to the door.

"Looking forward to it," I replied, giving him a quick peck back.

He kissed his index finger and pressed it to my nose. "See ya, beautiful." He smiled and crunched back down the driveway to his car. He opened the car door and cleared his throat loudly.

"OK, boys and girls—random hand check," he laughed, leaping into the driver's seat.

I shook my head and went inside. It wouldn't be long before Kelly would be on Skype giving me a moment-by-moment rundown of the evening's events. I needed to hurry in, take off my mascara and get into bed.

It was a long conversation and almost 2 am when I stifled my fifth yawn. I had to go to sleep—but Kelly was just too wired. I didn't think she would sleep for a week. She just kept squealing and bouncing on the bed. I was happy for her and there weren't many things to be happy about these days.

"I can't believe Gavin and I will be a couple for my birthday—did I mention that? Oh, Dad said I could have the party at his place," she beamed.

Kelly's parents broke up before she was born. They still got on OK, probably better than when they were together, but they were like chalk and cheese. We had no idea how they ended up together in the first place, a bit like my mum and dad. But Kelly's dad was a bit of a kid and related to Kelly more like a friend than a father.

He'd told Kelly he'd have an open bar for her and her friends. We weren't officially old enough to drink but that never seemed to stop anyone. She thought everything would be perfect now. I was less convinced. I was worried she'd lose her head and rush into something too soon. Kelly was an all-or-nothing type of girl. But it was too late to start a conversation like that now.

I yawned again. It was definitely time to sleep.

* * *

It was a relaxing Sunday. I spent all day at Jarrod's house. Jarrod's brother had bought a new video game so he and Jarrod spent a good deal of the morning playing it, while I curled up in the corner on the day bed and read a book. I'd just started the last chapter when a cushion flew through the air and caught me on the back of the head.

"Coming for a ride to the bakery? Mum wants me to get some bread rolls for lunch."

Jarrod was grinning at me. I hurled the cushion back in his direction but missed. I knew he'd be too quick for that.

He pulled me to my feet and wrapped an arm casually around my waist. "Come on, if we hurry we can take Jeff's car before he realises I haven't given him his keys back yet."

It was only a short drive. We could have walked but Jarrod loved driving that car. He cranked up the music as we drove away, wound down the window and tapped out the rhythm on the driver's side door. Jarrod was in high spirits.

"So it's Kelly's party next weekend," he smiled. "Is she having it at her mum's or at Ted's place?"

"Ted's," I replied. "She was telling me about it last night," I added stifling a yawn.

"So what time did you finally get to bed then?" Jarrod's eyes twinkled.

"About 2."

"Wow, 2! And I dropped you home just after 12. What did you talk about for that long?" he asked.

"No, she talked, I listened. There was a good deal of bouncing and shrieking involved. She's really excited about the party. Especially as Ted is going to supply all the alcohol."

"All the alcohol? How many kids has she got coming?" Jarrod asked in surprise.

"I don't remember. I think she handed out about 50 invitations. But I'm not sure how many will turn up . . ."

"Lots—if there's free beer!" Jarrod suggested.

I felt uneasy. She'd been pretty free with that information. What if there were gate crashers? There had been a few reports in the paper about teen parties being gate-crashed by unwelcome over-aged visitors. It would be tragic if Kelly's party was hit.

Jarrod cut the engine and we walked inside to collect the bread. Mrs Lee gave us her usual broad grin.

"What I get for you, Jarrod? Nice ham and cheese scroll?" she said pointing her tongs at the cabinet.

"Not today, Mrs Lee, thanks. I've got Heaven with me. She doesn't do meat."

"You no like meat?" she asked accusingly. "How 'bout spinach pie? I got some in warmer."

"No, thanks. We'll just have a dozen multigrain bread rolls, please Mrs Lee," Jarrod explained politely.

Mrs Lee looked disappointed as she tonged the rolls into the bag. Perhaps her business had been a bit slow since roadworks had begun outside her bakery, making parking difficult.

Jarrod handed her the money and we jingled out the door.

"See you next a-week, Jarrod," she called after us with a wave of her tongs.

* * *

I helped Jarrod's mum fill the bread rolls, while Jarrod went back for a rematch with Jeff. I could hear the sounds of warfare in the background, and the cries of dying men and beasts.

"How are things at home, Heaven?" she asked as I loaded a bread roll with mashed egg. I hadn't really told her much last week but I could see she sensed something was wrong. I often wished I had a mum like Yvonne, who noticed what was going on with me rather than just what she was doing.

I cleared my throat. "Ummm, OK, I think Dad will be away this week." I handed her the flattened bun. I'd been a bit too forceful with the egg on that one. She just smiled and nodded. I wasn't really in the mood to get into it right now.

After we had eaten lunch, Jarrod wanted to go back to the markets. It was noisy and crowded. The fruit and vegie section was full of vendors promoting their fresh produce. I bought a large organic apple and chomped away while I waited on Jarrod, making my way through the stands to the permanent pet shop. There were a few chickens and a couple of puppies tumbling over each other in a wire cage. They were cute. I poked my finger through the bars and one of them bounded over and chewed it with its little needle-sharp teeth. I smiled.

We had never been allowed a dog. Dad had said a resounding "No!" when I asked for one for my eighth birthday.

45

Dad always got his way both at home and at work. Clearly everyone said "Yes" to my dad—including 24-year-old blonde secretarial staffers.

Jarrod found me at the pet stand as it was where I usually ended up. I looked around for his bags but he just tapped his nose and led me over to the hot nuts. We bought a bag of pistachios, sat down at one of the tables and crunched our way through half the bag.

"We got any tests this week?" he asked as I cracked another open.

"I've got Physics and we've got Calc."

He chucked a nut into the air and caught it in his mouth. "When?"

"Tuesday third and Friday last," I replied, breaking another. "You want me to come over tomorrow and quiz you?"

"How's about you just come over and I'll worry about what we do," he winked, cracking a nut in his teeth. The innuendo was back. I guess he wasn't feeling too sorry for me any more. I cleared my throat and arched an eyebrow. He just winked at me a second time.

"Sooo, Kelly and Gavin. That was a long time cooking," I said, trying to change the subject.

"Yeah, he's looking forward to the party on Saturday night. Think he's hoping to get some action on her birthday."

My sharp intake of breath sucked a pistachio down the wrong pipe. I coughed loudly and it dislodged. I couldn't believe he'd just said that. "What!? What would make him think that?" I squeaked between coughs.

Jarrod looked taken aback. "Well, it's worth a try, isn't it?"

"They've only been together for five seconds. I'm sure Kelly's not going to give it up that quick," I replied grabbing a sip of his Sprite. Jarrod just shrugged.

He was making a point. He was getting tired of waiting. Maybe it was time to go home. I stood up. Jarrod grabbed my hand.

"Come on, Heaven, can't we talk about this?" he pleaded.

"Why, so you can say you want to and I can say I don't?" I pulled free. "Talking about it isn't going to change my mind, Jarrod."

Jarrod got to his feet, "Well, I just want to know . . ."

"I've told you: I'll tell you when I'm ready."

"And when is that likely to be?" he asked with an edge in his voice.

"I . . . I'm not sure," I stammered.

Jarrod grimaced, ran his fingers through his hair and sighed.

"Look, don't worry about it. It's just . . . well, never mind. Come on. I'll take you home," he said, shaking his head.

FIVE

It was a tense drive home. I couldn't believe he was being like this. When we pulled up outside my house, he wouldn't even look at me. I leaned over to kiss him but he shied away from me.

"Jarrod, I don't plan to make you wait forever, you know. Just let me do this on my terms. It'll be my first time and I want it to be special," I pleaded.

Jarrod sighed. "I know all that, Heaven—but can't you give me like a time frame or somethin'?" he pleaded, still not meeting my eyes.

What was it with guys? Why did they have to be so obsessed with *it*?

"OK, OK!" I said exasperatedly. "Let me think about it and we'll talk about it tomorrow."

"Tomorrow?" He grinned, leaning toward me. I pushed him in the chest.

"No—talk tomorrow, not *it* tomorrow!" I rolled my eyes.

Jarrod grinned. "I knew what you meant, but I can still live in hope!"

I shook my head and sighed. Maybe it would just be easier to be single. But he was wearing his cute, cheeky smile that always made my heart leap. *How can he still do that after he'd made me feel so bad?* I sighed again and went to get out of the car.

Jarrod grabbed me by the shoulders and turned me to face him. Gently, he cupped my cheek and looked into my eyes. "It's just I really care about you, Heaven, and I want to show you how much. I don't understand why you don't feel the same way."

He didn't give me a chance to reply. He leaned in and kissed me. It was a fierce kiss, deep and desperate.

I almost felt sorry for him—but I pulled away.

"I'll see you in the morning, Jarrod."

He released me and leaned back. "OK, Heaven. See you in the morning." He didn't look at me again.

I climbed out of the passenger seat and watched him drive away. *Why did love always have to hurt?*

* * *

It took her five rings to answer. "Hello?"

"So, is it true?" I asked. "Are you going to sleep with Gavin on Saturday night?"

There was a long pause. *How could she not have told me?*

"Well, I already know what you think," she replied coyly.

I was angry with her. "How can you consider giving it up that fast? You only just got together. How is it that Jarrod already knows about this? What if he's only just dating you to get into your . . ."

"Stop, Heaven . . . Look, I might have told him that I might sleep with him after the party—but it isn't for sure or anything," she said defensively.

"Well, all you've done is given Jarrod ammo to use on me. How could you even think about doing this now, when he's already gone and told all the guys?" A vision of my locker-room nightmare flashed in my mind. I shuddered.

"Look, Heaven, I'm not as stuck on all this as you are. It's really not that big a deal to me. I like Gavin. I've liked him for a long time. It's not like we don't know each other. We've spent most of the year getting to know each other, so I don't see why I have to wait any longer." She was hanging me out to dry.

"Fine! Do whatever you want, Kelly." I hung up the phone.

I couldn't believe I was fighting with my best friend over sex. Grabbing my iPod, I shuffled to my favourite playlist and jumped onto the bed. *It was her body. If she wanted to, was it really up to me to tell her otherwise?*

* * *

I got up early on Monday morning. Dad had already left again for the week. His paper was neatly folded on the counter.

I went for a run on my own, making sure I ran a different route to the one I knew Jarrod would use. I didn't want to see him yet. I would've avoided him all week, if possible. Unfortunately, this was the week I was to join the football team for training after school.

I finished my run in record time. Katie was just getting out of the shower when I got back. I raced through breakfast and got ready for school. Throwing another set of gym clothes in my bag, I grabbed my lunch and reminded Katie to lock the door when she left.

I considered not waiting for Kelly. After our fight the night before, I wasn't sure I wanted to see her. I felt alone in my decision, like I was the only one in the world who wanted to be cautious, who didn't want to hurry through it like the cheap wrapping paper at Christmas.

Maybe I was the one who was wrong? Maybe I should just get it over with. Then I wouldn't have to worry about it any more. It wasn't like Jarrod wasn't deserving of it. Unlike Gavin, he'd been waiting for a long time. Should I just give him a break?

Kelly pulled open her front door. Our eyes locked.

"I wasn't sure if you'd be here this morning," she said quietly as she joined me on the front step.

"I wasn't sure either," I replied as we turned back to the street. We walked along, saying nothing for a while. The issue hung between us.

"Kell, I'm sure if you wanna sleep with Gavin this weekend . . . I'm sure it will be great," I offered.

She sighed, "I don't know. I just said it 'cause I knew it would make him happy. I really want to make him happy, Heaven. He's just so . . ."

There really wasn't much point discussing it further. Maybe when it was all over I would be able to talk to her about it again. In the meantime, it was now a no-go zone. I didn't want to fight anymore.

* * *

When the bell rang signalling the end of the last class of the day, I couldn't avoid Jarrod any longer. He would be waiting at the gym for me. After all, where else would he be? It was his team's practice.

"Hey, Babe," he greeted me with a kiss on the cheek.

51

I was waiting for the continued guilt treatment, but it didn't seem to be coming.

"How was the last class?" he asked, taking my bag and walking me to the girl's change rooms. I kept up the defence. Maybe this was just a ploy.

"A total snore, of course. How about yours?" I replied edgily.

"Yeah, fine, but Mr Jenkins gave us a pop quiz," he said as we came to a stop outside the door.

Suddenly a whistle erupted through the gym. I jumped and turned around.

"That's Coach. You'd better hurry. If you're late, he'll give you 50,"

Jarrod flashed the smile that made my heart melt, as Mr Higgins came into view.

"Come on, Beckette . . . unless you plan on joining Heaven in the lockers. I always thought you were a bit of a girl," he laughed good-naturedly.

"If only," Jarrod groaned. All the guys laughed.

I felt my skin begin to change colour, so I quickly ducked through the door.

Even for a fitness freak like me, it was hard going. Mr Higgins worked us until I thought I might puke. I tumbled to the ground next to Jarrod and his teammates, and took a long drag on my bottle of water. They all went quiet when I joined them. I tried not to let my mind wander onto what they may have been discussing.

"So are we all invited to Kelly's party on Saturday, Heaven?" Ben asked. All 12 pairs of eyes fastened on me. I guessed they'd heard about Kelly's dad's free alcohol.

"I dunno," I replied, taking another mouthful from my water bottle.

"Well, can you put in a good word for us, Heav? We need a good party, you know . . . to help us de-stress before the big game. You want us to play well for Jarrod now, don't you?" he continued with a twinkle.

"Ahhh, whatever, Ben. The only thing you need is an adrenalin shot—didn't you notice she almost lapped you?" Gavin cut in.

The guys all laughed. Ben tried to hide the colour creeping up his neck.

"I had a hard weekend, that's all!" he said defensively.

"Well, maybe you should lay off the bottle for a while!" Jarrod laughed.

I knew Jarrod drank when I wasn't around. It had never really bothered me as I figured boys would be boys.

I didn't though. I couldn't bear the idea of not being in control of myself. I'd heard so many stories of people doing really dumb stuff while under the influence. Brenda Harper had gotten so drunk one night that she'd agreed to let one of the guys from our class take naked photos of her on his mobile phone. At the time, she'd thought she'd been really sexy but when they turned up on the net and on all his friends' phones the next day, it just made her look cheap.

I still remembered the whispers in class. One of the geeks had snuck in and made it the wallpaper on all the computers in the IT room. He got suspended but I guess he thought it made up for all the times she'd teased him in primary school. She transferred out the following term. But those pictures would always be out there waiting for her in cyberspace.

"What about you, Heaven? Gonna have a drink at your best friend's party? You like strawberries don't you?" Gavin joked.

"No thanks, Gav. My mind is a well-oiled machine and I want to begin uni with all my brain cells intact, thank you. After all, when you come in with your pickled liver at 35, you don't want your doctor to be suffering from withdrawal, do you?" I asked, vibrating an imaginary knife in front of his stomach and moving it slowly downward.

The guys all hooted with laughter.

"Well, I guess it wouldn't matter really. Not like you'll ever get to use it anyway," Ben crowed.

"At least I gotta girlfriend, Timmins. Guess you'll be playing 'Only the Lonely' in your room again," Gavin bit back, an edge in his voice.

I wondered if anyone else noticed it. I looked around. It didn't seem so.

"Nah, I'll be right, thanks Gav. I look better to the ladies after every glass. I'll just sit myself down by the bar and wait," he winked. "I know I'm a three-glass man, but you—without Kelly, that is—well, you're more like a 10-glasser!"

All the guys fell about laughing. Ben was clutching his side. Gavin sat stony quiet. I hoped he wasn't going to take this as some kind of macho challenge. I held my breath.

Time for this girl to exit the party—it was getting rough. I stood up to leave and brushed the grass from my shorts. I wasn't quite quick enough.

"So, Heaven, how many is Jarrod?" Ben inquired.

"Ay?" I froze.

"You heard—how many would it take for you to give

54

Jarrod a break?" Ben asked. Clearly he didn't realise he'd just stepped beyond the joke.

"Ben!" hissed Jarrod.

All the guys went suddenly quiet. I could feel my temperature begin to rise.

"I refer you back to my earlier statement, Ben. You know, the one where I said I don't drink. Guess that means we'll never find out then, huh?" I turned to leave hoping that would be the end of it.

"Hey, I should ask Cathy—think she'd do it for a milkshake," Ben hollered.

A few guys sniggered. I heard someone stick the boot in and Ben let out a cry.

Next thing, Jarrod was beside me. He tried to take my hand but I flicked it away.

"Just go back to your Neanderthals, Jarrod. Maybe you can find some unsuspecting girl walking past to beat over the head and drag into the bushes," I spat.

"Oh, don't be like that, Heaven. Ben's just being dumb. He never knows when to stop . . ." he began.

"Yeah, but you must have given him the material. Just leave me alone, Jarrod. I'm going home!" I stalked off, leaving Jarrod halfway between me and his teammates. As I left, I wondered which loyalty he'd put first, me or his teammates and his pride.

* * *

I was surprised to see my dad's BMW in the driveway when I got home. It was only 5 pm and I'd expected him to be away all week. His suitcases still stood in the hall. I emptied my sports bag in the laundry and went through to the kitchen to get a glass of water. Dad was leaning on the sink, looking reflectively out the window. I backed out of the room, not wanting a confrontation. He'd still be sore from our last conversation.

The phone on the wall jangled into life and Dad stirred. I made a move to it, when he spoke. "Don't answer it, Heaven. It will just be a reporter. One of the gossip magazines managed to get an exclusive and she's talked. It will be all over the papers by the morning. I've come home to try to salvage the situation."

He didn't even bother to face me as he filled me in on the shame he'd brought on our family. I could imagine what tomorrow would be like. Cathy Davis would enjoy slagging us off. The pictures were probably being plastered all over the internet as we spoke. Part of me wanted to offer him some words of comfort, but I managed to suppress the urge.

I don't know what made me do it. Call it morbid fascination but I fired up my laptop as soon as I got back to my room. I googled my dad and sat disgusted as image after image came up of him and a busty young bimbo. There she was getting out of his limousine, sitting laughing with him at a dinner party, leaving his hotel room looking dishevelled.

There was a knock on my door. I snapped my computer closed as Katie entered my room. She looked disappointed. "It's OK, I've already seen them . . . cheap tart. I can't believe this. School is going to be unbearable tomorrow."

She slumped down on the bed next to me. Sighing, I slung my arm around her shoulders. We would face this alone.

Mum would slink into her studio and wouldn't resurface until the whole sordid thing had blown over.

"Did you check Facebook? Cathy Davis has already posted the worst of them," Katie continued.

"I can imagine!" I replied.

My phone beeped with a text message. It was Kelly. Katie read it over my shoulder. Usually I would have gone off at her but tonight wasn't the night for it. Kelly told me she was sorry and if I wanted to talk she was on chat.

But I wasn't in the mood. I shut my computer down and picked up my iPod. Giving Katie one of the earpieces, we lay back on my pillow and listened to my favourite playlist. Every now and again, she changed songs or hit repeat. Both of us were lost in our own thoughts. Hers were probably about our family. Mine were more about me and Jarrod.

The pressure for sex seemed to be everywhere. People were either having it when they shouldn't—like my Dad—or feeling entitled to it—like Gavin and Jarrod. The question I had to answer was, *Would I? And if so, when?* I didn't know how much longer Jarrod would be willing to wait. How would I feel if he dumped me for Cathy Davis? It was clear she was willing.

* * *

I thought about taking the day off. Katie did—but I would have had loads to catch up on. I saw all the glances and smirks in the hall. Their parents must have been discussing it. Cheating wasn't a big deal normally, but splashed all over the newspaper and discussed on *The Morning Show*, it became big news. My dad had once been a big campaigner for "family values" and the whole thing stank of double standards. People could handle cheaters but not cheaters who actively pointed the finger at others.

I decided to spend lunchtime in the library. Kelly would be off with Gavin somewhere and I still wasn't in the mood to talk to Jarrod. He'd messaged me a couple of times between classes to see how I was but I ignored him. He could just assume I'd forgotten to turn my phone on. I chose the reference section because not many students went back there. I interrupted a couple of juniors making out. They hurried off as soon as I showed up. In their embarrassment, maybe they hadn't made the connection as to who I was.

I grabbed my iPod and an apple and turned to the math homework we'd just been given. There were only a few questions and I'd have them knocked over in 20 minutes. Halfway through the last question, I sensed someone behind me. Dislodging my earpieces, I turned around. Jarrod was coming along the bookshelves beside me. He wasn't smiling. I probably should have responded to his messages. He dragged up a chair and took my hand.

"Thought I'd find you here," he said matter-of-factly.

"Guess you win the prize then," I replied flatly, taking my hand back to finish the problem.

"Homework at lunchtime. Things must be bad." He slouched back in the chair.

"Just wanted to avoid the stares. I've had enough already," I said without making eye contact.

"And me, too?" He raised his eyebrows.

"That's quite possible," I whispered.

"Look, Heaven," he said, taking my hands and turning me around to face him. "I didn't mean to put the pressure on the other day—honest. Is it 'cause I already did it before?" he asked.

I felt a twinge of guilt. That did have something to do with it—his being with someone else. This would be my first time. How would I compare with his first? She'd been much older and—well—more experienced. I swallowed.

"Heaven, it will be beautiful 'cause it will be you and me. I wish my first time could have been with you but I can't change the past. Just tell me what I have to do and I'll do it . . . anything!" The *anything* almost sounded like a whine.

Thankfully, the bell rang. I had no idea what my answer would have been. I thought of the juniors making out. Maybe if I hadn't held onto it for so long I could have shared my first time with someone who was equally inexperienced. Maybe then the whole process would have been less embarrassing. If I held out much longer, I might be the only virgin in the whole year. Virginity was starting to feel like a burden to bear, rather than a gift to share.

"I'm not staying for practice tonight. I've gotta get home," I said as I shouldered my bag. Jarrod didn't try to take it from me. He just sighed.

"Alright, I'll let Coach know. I'll message you later, OK?" he called. I was already halfway through the reference section. I just waved in response.

Unbelievable! I thought. *He didn't even ask how I was doing. All he was interested in was when I was going to give it up.*

Shaking my head, I marched off to English class.

* * *

We were studying *Romeo and Juliet*, the star-crossed lovers who both killed themselves because they loved each other too much to live apart. Seemed an oxymoron to me, to love so deeply yet choose to die. Talk about codependency!

The teacher was going on about true love having no boundaries. Even feuding families couldn't keep them apart. Only death could end the romance *blah blah blah*. It was truly sickening.

Had my parents ever been truly in love? Surely it was never like that? But after all, it was just a made-up play. I thought of Jarrod and his less-than-patient waiting. Romeo and Juliet hadn't waited. They met each other and were at it by the next act.

I frowned. *Had love really destroyed them or was it lust? It was certainly lust that had ruined our family.*

Kelly met me at the door of English.

"You OK?" she asked as we headed to our next class.

"Yeah, fine," I lied.

"Do you think you could drag yourself away from Jarrod on Saturday to help me at Dad's with the decorations?" she bounced. "It's going to be super fun. Dad's bought all these Christmas lights for us to put up and he's hiring a DJ. I messaged everyone last night and have only got back a couple of no's. The only downer is we'll have to be all done by 12. I can't believe it—this will be the first time I've managed to coincide a boyfriend and my birthday. It's gonna be great . . ."

Kelly rabbited on all the way to our next class. It was

General Studies—and I'd have to sit next to Jarrod. How was it someone who was supposed to care about me could make me feel so bad?

Class was uncomfortable and long. Jarrod kept glancing across at me. I could feel he was sorry. I guessed he'd planned to try to patch things up in the library but somehow it had backfired. He'd been writing furiously all through class and I wondered what Ms Renolds had said that he found so noteworthy. I stood to leave but Jarrod grabbed my hand and pressed something into it.

"I'm sorry," was all he said. "Can we talk later?"

Nodding, I looked at the package wrapped in lined paper. I was dead curious. He refolded my hand around it.

"For later," he added and then left.

The last two classes went super slow. I felt the package burning a hole in my pocket and was tempted to open it between classes. But if I opened it now, I'd have to show it to Kelly and I wasn't sure what lay inside or if it was something I'd want to share. So I just followed Kelly to the bathroom to touch up my lip gloss, fluff my hair and listen to her jabber on about the party. Normally I would have been there with her—but not today.

When I got home I'd psyched myself up enough to open the package. The lined notebook paper was a letter and inside was the locket I'd admired at the markets almost two weeks ago. I flipped it open, there were pictures inside, his and mine. He'd also had it engraved. It simply said, "I love you." My heart flooded with warmth. He'd never said that to me in person. I fastened the locket around my neck and turned to the letter.

> *Dear Heaven,*
> *This wasn't the way I'd planned to give this to*
> *you. I knew things would be bad for you when I*
> *saw your dad's pics on the net. I'm really sorry,*
> *Heaven. It must be really hard. When I came to*
> *the library, that's all I wanted to say and tell you*
> *how I feel about you, but it all just got messed up*
> *somehow.*
> *I care about you. It hurts me that you don't want*
> *to but I'll wait until you're ready 'cause I love*

you. I don't want to be with anyone else but you.
I wish I could make you see that.
Text me when you're ready to talk.
Love,
Jarrod

I picked up my phone:
Thanks for the locket, I love it! Don't worry you
wont have to wait forever! xx

* * *

The fighting started again that night. I guess Mum had
seen the pictures and come out of her studio to let Dad
know what she thought of them. The walls shook with
the slamming doors and the clatter of chairs being pushed
across the floor. They were having a real ho-down! Usually
I'd tune out but tonight I was interested in hearing Dad's
excuses. But it was Mum who was doing all the screaming.
I wished I hadn't tuned in when I did. I wished I just turned
up my iPod like usual and left them to it.

"I wish I'd never met you," Mum screamed.

"But where would you be without your girls?" Dad spat
back. "You're always saying they are the only decent thing
I've ever given you."

"I'd trade them for a life free of you!" she shrieked.
"Besides, your blood runs in their veins. They'll probably
end up just like you! You cheating . . ."

That was enough. I didn't need to hear anymore. I felt
the foundations of my tower begin to wobble beneath me.

I saw a couple of photographers outside our house during the remainder of the week. But since my dad had retired from politics, he wasn't front-page news for long. Everything blew over at school by Friday but after what I'd heard my mum say, my insides were in turmoil! *Could she really wish I'd never been born?*

"She doesn't mean it, Heaven. She was just angry at your dad. Those words were never meant for you to hear," Kelly soothed, putting her arm around my shoulders.

"Maybe not," I shrugged her off. "But she still said them—so she must have thought about it!"

"Parents do it all the time. She was trying to make *him* feel bad, not you! Besides, what your dad did is really bad!" she added, checking her hair in the mirror.

We were back in the bathroom at the end of D block. It was the quietest bathroom in the school, where we had our most secret discussions. There was the Year 12 common room but that was usually crawling with students, so no privacy there.

My phone beeped.

"It's Jarrod. He wants to know if he's going to see me this lunchtime." I checked my watch. It was almost 1 pm. I'd kept Kelly from seeing Gavin and I felt bad. He would work all day tomorrow and Kelly wouldn't see him until the party. I had to let her go now.

"You go, Kelly. Catch up with Gavin before the bell. I'll see you this afternoon."

Kelly looked almost guilty. "I can't. Mum's picking me up after school to go shopping for stuff for the party. I would have told you before but you were so . . ."

"It's OK." I smiled. "I'll be fine by myself. I need to catch up with Jarrod anyway."

Kelly perked up. "OK. Well, I'll see you bright and early at Dad's tomorrow. We've got a lot to do!"

* * *

Jarrod was lounging against the fence beside the gate, waiting for me to arrive. He chatted to a few of the guys as they walked by. Every girl passing took a second look. I smiled. *I really was very lucky he loved me!* His face lit up when he saw me. He threw his bag over his shoulder and came over.

Reaching to take my bag, he asked, "So how was your day? I missed you at lunchtime." His free hand linked through my fingers as he walked me to his car. He threw our gear in the back seat and we jumped in. It was just a short drive home but I told him what my mum had said the night before.

"Wow, Heav. I guessed you must have been discussing something pretty important to keep Kelly away from Gavin," he said sadly. "If it makes you feel any better, I think you're fantastic!" He smiled.

It did make me feel better. At least someone wanted me. I'd known for years Dad didn't think much of me, but this was the first time I'd heard Mum felt the same way. I put my head on Jarrod's shoulder. At least I had Jarrod.

He dropped my bag at his front door and carried the other to his room. I felt exhausted from all that had been going on. I dropped down on Jarrod's bed and curled onto my side. Picking up his iPod, I scrolled to the playlist I'd loaded on for him and hit play. Jarrod climbed up behind me and I offered him the other earpiece.

"Don't know why you like this music so much. It's very depressing. Shouldn't you listen to something else when you're in this kind of mood?" he asked, stroking my hair off my face. I smiled as his lips brushed my cheekbone and slid round to my chin. His attention made me feel warm inside. He made me feel wanted.

"No, it's perfect for the mood I'm in! Didn't you know girls like to wallow in misery?"

I giggled as his lips shifted to the back of my neck.

"I can think of a better way to improve your mood—and mine, too," he whispered huskily into my ear. His breath sent tingles down my spine.

I rolled over to face him, slipping my arms around his neck. "Tell me how."

He smiled wickedly. "Well, how about I show you instead?"

Then his lips were on mine.

* * *

I left just after his brother arrived home. Truth was I was feeling embarrassed. Things had gone a lot further than they ever had before. We had stopped short of *it* but still . . . *it* could have happened if Jeff hadn't turned up when he did. It was like I craved Jarrod's attention all of a sudden.

It was certainly pleasant to be wanted and touched like that. But the worry began creeping back in. I'd opened a door and wondered if I had the strength or the will to close it again. The locker-room conversation was playing out in my mind again. I heard Jarrod talking and all his teammates laughing. I shuddered. A piece of my ivory tower sheered off and tumbled to the ground.

Dad was gone again when I got home. Of course, Mum was nowhere to be seen. I dropped my bag in my room and took my lunch box to the kitchen. A note was on the sink from Mum:

> *Will be busy all evening in my studio. Please care*
> *for yourselves for dinner. There is some lentil*
> *soup in the fridge and some rolls in the pantry.*
> *xx*

Lentil soup! For some reason, I didn't much fancy eating anything Mum had made for us. She could eat her own lentil soup. Katie and I would be having something much nicer. I went to the crisper to see what vegies we had—nothing much, as usual. I decided to head down to the fruit shop to see what took my fancy.

I heard Katie singing in her room as I passed. Knocking on the door, I went in. She was sitting on her bed with her laptop scrolling through the latest *Vanity Fair*. She pulled out her earpieces when she saw me. I could hear her music from across the room. She liked it loud.

"Hey Katie, anything in particular you want for dinner? Mum's painting and left us some lentil soup."

Katie wrinkled her nose, "Ewwwh, what do you have in mind?" She grinned.

"I was just heading down to the fruit shop. Do you wanna come? We can make something together."

Katie shifted her computer and grabbed her shoes. "As long as it's got sugar and butter, I'm in!" she suggested, tying her laces.

"Well, I don't know about all that but let's see what we can find. I'm in the mood to try some exotic fruits."

Katie's face fell.

"But I'm sure we can rustle up some chocolate pudding, as well," I added.

"Now that's more like it," she said, jumping to her feet. "I'm glad you asked me. There's something I wanted to tell you. You know Callum in Year 10. Not blonde Callum but Callum with the dark hair who plays football, Callum . . ."

I nodded.

"Well, he asked me out today!" she bounced. "He is so, so hot and I can't wait. I know Mum and Dad wouldn't let you date alone until you were 16 but he is so cute and I really want to go. If Mum says no, do you think we could come out with you and Jarrod?" She was so excited. She reminded me of Kelly when she and Gav had finally got together.

"Sure, but not tomorrow. It's Kelly's party and you can't possibly tell him tonight—you'd look too desperate!"

"Hey, can we go to the fruit shop in the mall? I just saw the perfect outfit for you," Katie said, holding up a picture she'd just printed out.

I took the picture. It did look nice. Katie had the best taste—but the shoes!

"I can't wear those shoes! They'll make me too tall!"

"Ohh!" snorted Katie. "You'll look hot. Now come on—before the shops shut!"

We had a nice evening together. We found the outfit and some shoes that were almost exactly the same as the ones in the picture. When I complained, Katie just dismissed it as the price we pay to look like supermodels. Then she explained that if she had my height she'd be one already. I also grabbed a new hair straightener. It had a steam option and special ceramic plates to give your hair a "shinier glow." I was dubious but I bought it anyway.

We bought a couple of pomegranates, dragon fruit and some feijoas, imported from New Zealand. The dragon fruit was not nearly as tasty as it looked but I loved the feijoas. A visit to New Zealand during feijoa season was definitely on the cards. Apparently most New Zealanders had trees in their backyards from which they would collect bucketfulls to make pies, crumbles or eat raw—that's what Wikipedia said, anyway. Katie had googled them over a bowl of chocolate pudding and ice cream.

"So," Katie asked between mouthfuls, "have you set a date to dump the big V?"

"What!?" I asked, choking on a slurp of juice.

"Oh, come on—we were just talking about this the other day. You must have been giving it some thought. What with Cathy hanging round like a bad smell . . . He's a boy—he has needs!" she said, rolling her eyes.

I smirked, "And what would you know of a boy's needs?"

"Probably as much as you do . . . unless something has happened since we last talked!?" she added, leaning in. I paused . . . too long.

"Oh my! Something has happened—ohhhh, details, details!" she squeaked, clapping her hands.

"Shhh, and no—I haven't done *that* yet!" I replied, turning scarlet. "But something has happened."

"What was it like? Tell me! I have to know! I have to be prepared . . ." she bounced.

"Look, it really wasn't that big . . ."

I stopped short as Mum walked in. Katie ceased bouncing in midair and dropped back to the couch in shock. I stared at my mother and wondered if she would even notice we were eating in the living room. She used to go nuts at us if we ate anywhere but the kitchen or the dining room.

But she looked different. Her eyes were kind of glazed and she almost seemed to float. She just smiled at us and continued on her way.

When she left the room, I leaned over and whispered, "What's with her? Is she on something? She looked like a space cadet!"

"Yeah, I think so! I was in her bathroom yesterday . . ."

"What, snooping?!" I asked in shock.

"Well, do you wanna know or not?" She glared, perching a hand on her hip. I shrugged and waited for her to continue.

"She's on Valium. I saw a bottle on her bathroom sink."

"That figures! I bet that's not all she's on. She's nuts! You should have heard what she was saying the other night!" I whispered.

Katie leaned in, wide-eyed, as I recounted the evening's events. Katie shook her head sourly.

"Yep, a nut alright! Don't let it bother you too much, Heaven. She's high as a kite. She probably doesn't know what she's saying!" Katie yawned, "Well, I'm off to get in some homework before sleep time. If I don't pass this test tomorrow, I'm gonna get a D in Science!"

Katie rinsed her plate and put it in the dishwasher.

"Love you, Heav!" she added kissing me on the top of my head. "I think you're a super sister—and you are going to look hot as, in that new outfit. Cathy will just die a thousand deaths when she sees you." She flounced from the room.

* * *

Kelly had told me to be at Tom's by midday. A dishevelled-looking middle-aged man in sunglasses, who had clearly only just gotten out of bed, greeted me at the door.

"Hi, Heaven," Tom whispered, his voice was almost gone. "Sorry I look like death. Was a big night last night . . . Our team had a win and we partied . . . for . . . well, a long time. Lucky we have to be done by 12 tonight, hey!" He smiled and his breath smelt like a brewery.

"Oh Heaven, there you are!" Kelly was carrying a twisted pile of fairy lights. "Dad, you clearly didn't put these away very well last year. It's going to take forever to untangle them and I wanna put them all around the living room. Do you think you could go and buy a few more strings, please?" she scolded.

Tom scratched his belly, belched loudly and stretched. "Yeah, alright kiddo. Just let me have a shower." He staggered back to his bedroom with a yawn.

"Don't worry about him. He'll be fine by tonight," Kelly beamed. "Gavin's coming around after work to help. But

I guess we'll have most of it done by then. The DJ will be here at around 7 to set up and hopefully the place will be packed by 8:30. Mum's bringing all the food. Everything's going to be great." She clapped her hands with excitement.

I took the tangled string of lights from her. "I'll sort this. You go and work out where you want them. I'm only going to be here until 5, then I'm going home to get ready. You can't expect me to party like this!" I pointed to my sweat pants.

Kelly was still euphoric. Nothing was going to dent her night. "I wonder what Gavin's bought me for my birthday. Can't wait to see!"

We spent the afternoon tangled in tinsel and fighting with fairy lights. Kelly was directing Tom about moving the furniture and setting up the drinks table when I glanced at my watch—4.50 pm.

"I've gotta go, Kelly. Is there anything else you need before I leave?"

Kelly looked up at the clock on the wall.

"My goodness! Is that the time? I'd better go start getting ready myself. Gavin's going to be here early with the ice for the drinks. Thanks for all your help, Heaven. It's going to be an awesome night!" she beamed.

* * *

When our house came into view, I was surprised to see Dad's car in the driveway. He usually came home for the weekend but I hadn't expected to see him with all that was going on. I was crossing the street when Dad marched out the front door carrying his all-too-familiar suitcase. Mum was hot on his heels, yelling something—until they noticed me watching.

Dad didn't even acknowledge me. He jumped in his car, slammed it into reverse, and was gone in a snarl of gravel and gasoline. I looked up at Mum for some confirmation of the situation, but she just stared through me as if I wasn't there. Then she hurried back inside the house.

Wow, so pleasant to be nonexistent! As I dropped my keys on the hall table, I wondered how parents could fight in front of their kids yet be so oblivious to the impact. My stomach was churning and the pleasant afternoon with Kelly had all but evaporated, leaving me only with the stink of my family.

I wanted to get out of here, to somehow deaden the pain. I thought of the alcohol I'd seen Tom cart in by the caseload. Maybe tonight would be a good night to try some self-medication.

Jarrod picked me up just after 7 pm. I heard his car in the driveway and glanced at myself one last time in the mirror. My new straightener had worked wonders on my hair. It looked sleek and glossy, and the outfit and shoes looked sensational—even if I did say so myself. I smiled. *Not bad for an hour or two's effort.* I was pretty sure Jarrod would be impressed. I wasn't disappointed, his eyes almost popped out of his head.

Katie poked her head out the door just as I was leaving. "Hot stuff, sis!" she said with a whistle. I beamed. It felt good.

"Yeah, she certainly is!" Jarrod replied, tucking his arm around my waist. Tonight he didn't seem to mind I now stood several centimetres taller than him.

Quite a few kids were already there when we arrived. Cathy Davis was quick to make herself known to Jarrod. She got quite a shock to see me in heels. The DJ was cranking up and Jarrod went off to find me a drink. Tom went jiving past but did a double take when he saw me.

"Heaven, is that you?" he gushed. "Wow, I thought Kelly had invited Miranda Kerr to her party."

I sighed. He had obviously been drinking already,

"Miranda Kerr has lighter hair, Tom . . ." I began.

"Nah true, you look more like that girl from . . . What was that film? Ummm you know, *The Lord of the Rings*. That dark-headed Elvin princess."

"Liv Tyler?!" I smiled.

"Yeah, that's the one! Here, let me get you a drink. I promised you one of these," he said, holding up a bottle.

SEVEN

Should I? I wondered. I glanced across. Jarrod was on his way with the punch. It was now or never. I reached out and took the colourful bottle. He'd already unscrewed the cap for me. I put the bottle to my lips and took a sip. It was sweet like strawberries only with a bite after I swallowed. Jarrod pulled up short when he saw the bottle in my hand. He sent Tom a dark look.

"Heaven, do you know what you're drinking?" Jarrod queried.

"Yes, thanks, Jarrod, I do . . . and it tastes pretty good, too, I might add." I said, giving Tom a wink. Tom burst out in raucous laughter, then walked away to ply other unsuspecting girls with alcohol.

Jarrod shrugged and put the punch down on the hall table. "OK, well let's get inside then. There's no need to stand in the doorway." Then he stopped and ran his finger down my chin. "Unless you wanna pick up where we left off the other day." His eyes smouldered and my heart did a double take.

I felt my cheeks flush. I wondered if he would mention that. Lucky the room was dark, suddenly I felt embarrassed. I took another swig from the sweetness of the bottle. *What did they call it? Dutch courage, I think*. I forced a smile. "Come on, Jarrod, let's dance!"

The DJ was good. He kept the music pumping and I barely left the dance floor most of the night. Tom seemed to find me every time my hand was empty and supplied me with several more drinks. I didn't notice at first but after a while the room began swimming. I almost tripped over my shoes. Jarrod caught me and led me over to the couch.

He went to take the bottle from my hand. "I think you've had enough of those now, Heaven," he began.

But I wouldn't let him. "Hey, that's my drink—get your own!" I said, taking another swig.

I looked at Jarrod. He was a little fuzzy round the edges but—boy!—he truly was hot. He smiled at me and I felt my heart begin to race. I climbed up on my knees and winked at him, then seductively dropped myself in his lap. He looked surprised, as I was usually not up for public displays of affection. Before he could say anything, I grabbed his face and kissed him passionately. It only lasted a few moments before the nausea kicked in.

I ripped off my shoes and ran to the bathroom, with Jarrod hot on my heels. I only just made it before the fountain of vomit erupted. I dropped on the floor in front of the toilet bowl, suddenly feeling terrible. I couldn't believe the transformation. Just moments ago, I had been feeling on top of the world. Now I stank like a brewery and the whole room was spinning.

Jarrod and his twin looked down at me in concern. They spoke in unison. "Are you OK, Heaven? Let me get you a glass of water."

He went to leave. I stood up on shaky legs. I felt dreadful but he still looked extremely appealing. I tried to kiss him again.

"How about we wait until after I get you a glass of water,

OK?" He laughed. I staggered out of the bathroom, while he went to get my water. I found the door to the spare room and dropped onto the sofa inside. I heard someone enter the bathroom,

"Phew, who didn't flush—it stinks like vomit in here." The door closed. It was funny. Usually I would have been horrified but, tonight, I didn't care.

Jarrod found me in the spare room and offered me the glass of water. I took a sip to get the taste out of my mouth, then put it aside.

"Do you think maybe you should have something to eat?" he asked. "You do realise you are now officially drunk." He smirked at my predicament.

"First time for everything!" I said, grabbing him by the shirt and pulling him onto the couch with me. He laughed and I kissed him again. He pushed me away.

"Come on, Heaven. It's almost midnight and you haven't eaten all night . . ." He tried to protest but I just kissed him again. In hindsight, how much more could I reasonably have expected him to protest?

I tiptoed my fingers up his chest. "I think you and I should leave now!" I whispered.

"What?! What are you saying, Heaven?" He became suddenly serious. A look of hope glimmered in his eyes.

I didn't answer, just looked at him wickedly. He only paused for a moment before his face broke into a smile.

"I'll call Jeff!" he said and suddenly he was gone.

The room had gone from a shimmering pool to a full-strength ocean by the time he returned. Jarrod found my bag and shoes and helped me to the car.

I forgot to say goodnight to Kelly and I didn't even remember walking out the door. I think Jarrod may have carried me.

One of the last things I remembered was Jeff saying—from a long way off—"Don't you let that girl chuck up on my upholstery, OK?"

I kind of remember Jarrod carrying me to his room. I was so tired—all I wanted to do was go to sleep. I remember him whispering to me that he loved me and I felt him fiddling with my buttons. He was heavy. I tried to push him off so I could go to sleep but I had neither the strength nor the words. My voice was lost to me, so I just surrendered myself to the abyss and drifted into oblivion.

* * *

I woke with a thundering headache. My mouth felt like the Sahara Desert and my stomach like I'd been eating plates of raw chillies. I belched and felt bile run into my mouth.

I rolled over and was surprised to see Jarrod in bed next to me. I shook my head to relieve the fog. *Where was I?* I looked around. We were in Jarrod's bedroom. I knew that! As I rolled over I felt a rush of cold air. Something was wrong! Something was incredibly wrong! I lifted the sheets and looked down. I was completely naked. I glanced across at Jarrod again, not wanting to move too much in case I woke him. I couldn't tell what he was wearing. He didn't have a shirt on and I certainly wasn't going to check any lower. A section of my dress was sticking out from the end of the bed.

Pieces of the evening before came flooding back. The dancing, the drinking, the vomiting, the flirting, the . . . I couldn't bring myself even to say it aloud in my head! I knew I had done some dumb stuff before leaving Ted's—but I could remember none of it.

I burned with embarrassment as I thought of how I'd behaved. I slithered out of bed and silently slipped my clothes back on. I found my shoes and bag in the corner of the room, then opened the door. Jarrod snorted loudly and rolled over. I froze. I had to get out before he woke up. I backed out the door and pulled it quietly behind me.

On tiptoes, I slid out the front door of Jarrod's house and walked home barefoot. Smatterings of memories were coming back. Some from before the party, some from after we left.

I felt disappointed and strangely empty. I knew it was gone. I wondered why I felt so bothered. In the cold light of the morning, it wasn't even the thought of my locker-room nightmare that concerned me. It was something else. Something I didn't understand. I'd given it up during a night of drinking while in an alcoholic stupor. I would never truly remember my first time. I felt I had lost something I could never get back . . . I guess that is why they called it "losing" your virginity.

I glanced down at my stomach. Absently, I had wrapped my arms around myself. It was almost like I was trying to hold my soul in—like if I let go, it would drift away. I just couldn't understand it. I hadn't expected to feel this way.

* * *

I crept into the house unnoticed and made a beeline for the bathroom. I badly wanted a shower. I stared with disgust at myself in the mirror. I couldn't possibly be the same person who had left from here just the night before. My hair was dishevelled and matted, my make-up smudged and sleep-worn. I looked like a raccoon. My dress was splattered and vomit-stained—and I stank!

I turned the shower on and dropped my dress on the bathroom floor. I looked at it lying there and felt disappointed. I didn't know if the dry cleaners would be able to salvage it and somehow I wasn't sure I would wear it again, even if they could.

Turning the shower up as fast as it would go, I plunged my head beneath it. The sound of the water drowned out my internal voice for a moment. It took several washes but I finally managed to rid my hair of the vomit smell. I combed through conditioner and lathered my face with cleanser. I'd never left my make-up on all night before. I'd read it made your skin prone to pimples. On top of everything else, all I needed now would be to turn up on Monday with an enormous zit on the end of my nose.

By the time I'd showered, moisturised and dressed again, I'd been in the bathroom for almost two hours. I was just hanging up my towel when I heard Katie trying the handle.

"Hurry up, Heaven. You've been in their for hours and I'm busting!" she cried through the door.

I reached over and turned the lock. "This is not the only toilet in the house, you know."

Katie ran round the corner and disappeared behind the partial wall that had been built to provide privacy. I could never understand why the architect hadn't just put it in a separate room. I heard the toilet flush and Katie appeared back around the corner, adjusting her pyjama pants. She sniffed and looked at the pile of dress in the centre of the floor.

"Wow, Heaven, that reeks! What did you do? Fall in a distillery vat then roll in a pig pen?" She held her nose.

I smiled. Katie could always lighten the moment. "Something like that!"

She followed me to the laundry and watched me dump the dress unceremoniously in the washing machine with a liberal dose of washing liquid.

"You know that dress was dry-clean only, don't you?" she said, jamming her hands on her hips.

I shrugged and hit the start button after turning the dial to delicate. I really didn't care!

Katie followed me back to my room and watched me throw my shoes in the cupboard. I dropped down onto my neatly made bed. A wicked grin broke out on her face.

"You didn't come home last night, did you?" She knew me well.

"What makes you say that?" I asked dismissively.

She poked a finger toward my bed. "Now, don't you try and fib to me, Heaven! I want details . . . lots—or I'm telling Mum," she demanded with a grin.

I looked at my little sister. She was busting with excitement. I wished I had something exciting to tell her.

I sighed. "Well, if you must know I drank too much. Chucked up all over the bathroom floor and made a complete fool of myself. Jarrod took me home and I passed out on his bed. I was so embarrassed when I woke up, I sneaked out and came home. Truly, I'd rather not go over it in any further detail as I would really just like to forget the whole thing happened," I said as I edged her out the door.

Katie looked disappointed as I closed the door in her face. But I knew she wouldn't make good on her promise. Dobbing was not an option.

I wasn't in the mood to tell her about my recently adjusted virginity status. Besides, there was really nothing to tell—I didn't remember anything worth sharing.

* * *

The text messages started at about 9.30 am.

> *Heaven, where are you? I woke up and you were gone. Can I come round?*
> *Are you ok? Are you still sick?*
> *Are you up yet? Do you remember what happened last night? :)*

The last one did it. I was feeling pretty disappointed he'd do that when I was so obviously out of it. I felt like he'd taken advantage of me.

I replied:

> *I remember SOME of what happened last night.*
> *Don't come round. I have a headache.*

Then I switched my phone off.

* * *

I spent the morning "studying" in my room. When Katie finally managed to barge her way in again, I'd spread books all over my bed for cover and stuffed my novel under my pillow. Eventually she left disappointed and I threw myself back into my fantasy world.

I broke for lunch just after 1 pm. I hadn't eaten any breakfast. I'd felt too sick but, by noon, I was famished and, by 1 pm, I could ignore it no longer. I whipped up an omelette for myself—and one for Katie as a peace offering. We were just cleaning up when I heard the familiar knock at the door. I suddenly felt pale. Katie grinned wickedly and gave me a wink.

Jarrod greeted me with an almost sheepish smile when I answered the door—*or did I just imagine it?* The wall between us had returned. I didn't feel comfortable with him anymore. I couldn't trust him. He'd betrayed me, taken advantage of me instead of protecting me. W*ell, shouldn't he have? I'd already told him enough times, while sober, that I wasn't ready. Shouldn't that have counted more than the words of a drunken girl?*

"Can I come in?" he finally asked, stepping closer to me. I stepped back and allowed him to enter without saying a word. Out of habit, I led him to my bedroom and closed the door.

Jarrod dropped on the bed beside me but before he could touch me, I crossed to the spare bed on the other side of the room. He looked at me in surprise. *Was it possible? Could he really not realise what he'd done?* I continued to stare at him icily, while his face rolled through various emotions ending in confusion. Finally, he spoke.

"What's going on, Heaven? Why are you being like this?" His voice was edged with annoyance.

I wasn't sure what to say. I didn't really know how to verbalise my feelings. Everything felt too tumultuous. I had to say something.

"Well, what do you want me to say? You must be happy. You've gotten what you wanted all along so . . . so, go you!! I'm sure all the team will be happy for you on Monday," I said sourly, giving him a mock cheer. I wasn't going to let him know how hurt I felt.

"But you said . . ." he began.

"I was drunk!" I whispered.

"But . . ." He leapt to his feet.

"And . . . still drunk!" I cut in more loudly.

He began pacing the room. This was clearly not how he thought it would play out.

"So tell me, Jarrod," I whispered menacingly, "what were you expecting from me today?"

He said nothing. He just stared at me. Obviously, anger had not been on his emotional menu.

"Did you think maybe I'd be up for round two or something? Did you think maybe if you just got over the first-time hurdle, it would be all smooth sailing from this point on? I told you how I felt before . . ."

"But you . . ." he began again.

But it was too late. The anger had surfaced. Anger, which had been building for a long time. Anger, which was not only meant for him but also for my mum, my dad and maybe myself, too.

"So tell me Jarrod, was it fun?" I hissed getting to my feet. "Was it fun screwing your paralytic girlfriend? Was it all you'd imagined it would be? Did I scream your name at the appropriate moment? Tell me, Jarrod, 'cause I don't remember. I remember nothing of it—nothing! My first time will forever be lost in a haze of alcoholic stupor taken by a boy who just couldn't wait . . . wouldn't wait. Didn't care enough about me to wait. Too busy thinking about himself and the opinion of his teammates to wait."

"But that's . . . that's not what . . ." He looked horrified. He ran his hands through his hair, glancing around the room for support. I continued to glare at him. A deep-seated hate was beginning to emerge. Hate mixed with disgust. *Would all men be this much of a let-down?*

Suddenly, he looked angry. "So when, Heaven? When would you have given it up? Didn't I deserve it or something? You were never really going to give it to me, were you?" he spat.

"I guess we'll never know now, will we?" I replied as he spun on his heels and headed for the door. He reached for the handle.

"Just tell me one thing, Jarrod, before you go? Please tell me you used something?" I asked, still angry but anxious.

He paused, thinking. "Ummm, yeah."

"'Ummm, yeah'? What does 'Umm, yeah' mean? Either you did or you didn't!" I growled in disgust. *What had he exposed me to?*

"It means exactly that," he replied, grim faced. "I used one when it counted. Don't worry, Heaven, I'm not stupid!" he added, before disappearing out the door and slamming it behind him.

"No—but I am!" I whispered dejectedly, as I fell back on the bed. "I am!"

It was clear to me now. He never really loved me at all. He just loved what he could get from me. I felt the tears bubble over and run down my cheeks. Angrily, I tore the locket from my neck and threw it in the top draw. Then I fell on my bed, sobbing with empty disappointment.

* * *

About half an hour later, Katie knocked quietly on my door. I'd cried myself out some time before but was still lying lifelessly on my bed. I hadn't even reached for my iPod to try to drown out my sorrow. She tiptoed over and stroked my hair for a while. Clearly she knew what had been said between Jarrod and me. Usually I would have been mad at her for eavesdropping, but at the moment I was too exhausted to care and it saved her quizzing me later.

She lay down on the bed next to me. I rolled over when she picked up my iPod and handed me an earpiece. Scrolling through, Katie selected one of my angry playlists but it could have been anything for all the attention I paid it.

EIGHT

About an hour later, I was vaguely aware Katie was speaking. "Sorry, Katie, what was that?" I mumbled, picking at imaginary lint on my doona.

"I was just wondering what you plan to do now?" she whispered.

"Ummm, I don't know. I guess I'm still too hung over to really care," I lied.

"So have you guys broken up now?" she asked.

"I don't know . . . maybe. I can't see him coming back from that and I really don't think I care if he does," I replied glumly.

"Does that mean you don't care if Cathy Davis dates him now?" Katie questioned.

I prickled. "What is this—are you on some kind of reconnaissance mission for your friend Trinny? Since when did you care who Cathy dated?" I began.

"No, no, I just wanted to know . . . you know . . . in case Trinny asks if Jarrod's available . . . Oh, this is coming out wrong," she sighed.

I was too tired to be angry any more. I didn't want to think about the future—it was too painful. I thought back to that fateful day when Jarrod had first kissed me. His words echoed in my ears. "Now you're mine!" he'd said. At the time, it sounded romantic. Now it just sounded like ownership. Like I was his to do with as he pleased. I wished I could undo that day. If we'd never been together, seeing him with Cathy would never have hurt. The truth was I'd be devastated if I arrived at school on Monday and they were together.

"I guess Jarrod will do whatever he wants. He's already proven himself quite capable of that!" I replied.

The silence was heavy. Surprisingly Katie seemed to understand my sentiment. She restarted the playlist and took my hand. Eventually I dozed off.

* * *

It was really late when I woke up. I was hungry and a little angry that Kelly hadn't called. Then I remembered I'd turned my phone off. I decided to make a sandwich before turning it back on. I wasn't ready for Kelly's excitement on an empty stomach. I hoped her first-time story would be better than mine. There was a good chance she'd not even ask about me. It's not like she'd bothered with me the whole evening once Gavin had arrived. When Jarrod and I had just got together I'd never neglected my friendship with her but when I was at my most vulnerable, she hadn't even noticed. Truth be told, I wasn't feeling happy with her either.

I made myself a sandwich and flicked through my text messages. There were several more from Jarrod from before he came around. I didn't bother reading them. I just deleted.

Finally I found a message from Kelly, sent only 20 minutes earlier. All it said was,

Call me when you get home. I want details!

She must have thought I would be happy, too. *How could she be my best friend and still not understand me?* I finished my sandwich and went back to bed. She could wait until morning.

I slept fitfully and was exhausted when I woke up. I ate breakfast and packed my bag for school.

Only when I was about to run out the door did I realise it was the big race today. With everything that was going on, I'd forgotten. Pulling out was an option but by going, at least I'd miss having to face Jarrod at lunchtime. I contemplated not waiting for Kelly but figured I'd have to talk to her sooner or later. I couldn't cut everyone off, then I'd be single *and* lonely.

Kelly walked out of the house beaming—until she saw my face. "Heaven, what's wrong?" she asked, placing a hand on my shoulder.

"Can we not please, Kelly?" I said, shrugging her off.

Kelly stepped back looking wounded. I felt bad—*but why should I have to feel bad about her feelings when I was the one who'd been damaged?* I looked away.

"Why, what did he do to you? Was he rough?" she asked.

I spun around. Her expression had completely changed. She looked angry.

"No, it wasn't that. It's just . . . look, I was so drunk I don't remember. I feel ripped off, that's all." I tried to make light of it so we could get off the topic quickly.

"What about you? Did you and Gavin?" I questioned.

"Ummm, no." She looked awkward. I knew she expected me to ask.

"Why?"

"Ummm, well, I feel almost bad saying this now after . . ."

"It's OK—just tell me, OK?" I sighed silently.

"Well," she looked excited. "We've decided to go away for the weekend . . . You know, make something special of it."

I didn't want to hear any more. *Special! Now she was opting for special! After what she'd said the other week about just getting on with doing it. Hadn't I been the one who'd wanted special? But, no, I got a drunken stupor and an opportunistic boyfriend. Where was my "special"?*

Suddenly I realised Kelly had finished telling me her story. I wanted to scream, but all I said was "Hey, that's super, Kelly. Hope it goes well for you."

"Maybe you and Jarrod can come?" she suggested.

"No, I don't think so. I'm pretty sure that's all over now," I whispered. "After all, when the trust is gone . . . what is there, right?"

* * *

Kelly and I didn't speak again. Probably she didn't know what to say. I saw Jarrod from a distance when we got to school, so we walked the other way. I was sure he saw me and I hoped it would be enough to give him the message.

Cathy was thrilled when we sat apart in class. She tried to strike up a conversation with him but he ignored her. He sat up the back and left as soon as the bell went. Fortunately, it was the last I had to see him that day. The bus would be leaving from the gym in 10 minutes. All was looking good, but as I stepped out the classroom door, he was waiting for me behind a locker bay.

Jarrod wouldn't make eye contact with me. He just kept staring at the floor, then the classroom door, then the passing people who were staring and whispering. I felt incredibly uncomfortable.

"Ummm," he cleared his throat. "I . . . just wanted to wish you all the best with the race . . . that's all," he finally said lamely.

"Yeah, thanks. I'd better go . . . I'm going to be late," I replied, stepping round him. I didn't look back. I just put my head down and raced off to the bus.

I could feel his eyes on me all the way and wondered what he had really wanted to say. Part of me hoped it was "I'm sorry—and can you give me another chance?"

Mr Higgins was pleased to see me. At least, he was until he saw my face.

"Hey, champ, what's wrong?" he asked.

Arrghh! I didn't want to go into this with a teacher. What was I going to say anyway? Your super football legend banged me when my guard was down?

"Nah, I'm fine thanks, Mr Higgins. It's just . . . Jarrod and I broke up over the weekend." I thought I'd whispered it but suddenly everyone around us was silent.

Mr Higgins whistled through his teeth. He obviously didn't know what to say.

"Oh, ummm, wow, that's ummm, bad news . . . ummm, hope it doesn't mess with your time, hey!" he tentatively patted my shoulder. *What else could you expect from a coach?*

I climbed onto the bus. Some opportunistic Year 11 boy with an attractive face dropped into the seat next to me. The look on his face said it all.

"Look, can we like pretend you've tried your best line on me and I've already said no? You know, just to save time?" I said sarcastically.

His friends hooted with laughter from the back seat. It

had been a long time since I'd had to worry about this kind of rubbish. He flushed bright red and backed away from my spare seat, shot down in a blaze of glory. Before anyone else could do likewise, I hurled my bag on the seat, shoved my earpieces in and shut my eyes.

* * *

I had to endure five other races before mine came up. I wandered over to the canteen and bought a drink and a muesli bar. There was a calendar on the wall behind the boy serving. I'd been so consumed by Jarrod and what was going on with my parents I'd forgotten there was only one week of school left. On the upside, that meant there was only four more days to face Jarrod before school holidays. On the downside, we'd be going to Queensland for our mid-year family holiday with my dad's family.

Every year we'd go up to some resort in Queensland for two weeks and pretend we all got on. Dad's younger brother would come up from Melbourne and his sister would fly home with her family from the US and we'd all get stuck together.

Dad's sister had married late after a huge career working for some women's magazine. Katie was always pleased to see her but I didn't care. She'd go on about how she could get me a modelling job. I would say "No, thanks" and she'd spend the rest of the holiday telling me how like my mother I was! She was well over 40 and had IVF twins—I forget their names, but they were something stupid! Just like her fake American accent. No doubt I'd end up baby sitting them when the nanny had her afternoon off.

I liked Dad's brother, Ed. He and his wife had one daughter. Something had gone wrong after that and they couldn't have any more. They often fostered kids, so who knew how many others would be turning up. He sold real estate in Melbourne and Sally was a hairdresser. They had met on a package tour around Europe. Ed joked that they remembered nothing of the trip because they drank so much. The only reason they remembered each other is they were creatures of habit and kept sitting in the same seat everyday. Romance blossomed in the few hours they'd been sober. I thought it all pretty pointless. Why would you spend all that money to go on a trip round Europe only to drink yourself into oblivion? Couldn't you just do that at home for free? Ed had laughed himself silly when I'd told him that.

"Oh, Heaven," he'd said, wiping his eye, "You're 15 going on 45. If only more of us were as logical as you!"

* * *

Suddenly the loudspeaker was calling for my race. I shook myself back to reality. *What had I been doing?* I wasn't ready. I hadn't been stretching. Coach Higgins would be frantic.

I ran across to the starting line. The coach was almost in a coronary when I arrived but it was too late for him to berate me. We had to get to the starting blocks.

I glanced around at my competition. There didn't seem to be anyone new. Tina was the girl who won last year. She looked at me with surprise. Maybe she thought my late arrival was some kind of tactic to put her off. I just winked, pulled off my jacket and got into position.

I shook my head and focused. I was angry, bitter and hurt. I needed a win for no other reason than just to have something to be happy about!

The starter's gun went off and I shot from the blocks. I didn't look back. I knew I'd been quick. I had so much pent up energy. I was convinced I would be able to sprint the entire 400 metres.

I rounded the second bend and caught a glimpse of the last girl a long way back. I put on another burst of speed to make use of the straight before the third bend slowed me down. I could hear the crowd shrieking and Coach Higgins was jumping up and down. I didn't know if it was because I was well in the lead or if Tina was about to catch me.

As I came round the third corner, I thought I heard breathing. Picking up the pace, I risked a quick glance over my shoulder as I cut round the fourth. She was right on my tail, getting ready to make her move.

I set my jaw and put on my last burst of speed, which was usually meant for the last few metres. I shot forward, my arms burning and legs pounding. I had to win this. I needed it more than she did.

I visualised myself clearing the tape first and pushed myself harder. She was gathering momentum and coming fast. I had to squeeze more speed from my legs if I was going to win.

With every ounce of my being I forced myself forward. I was almost at the tape. I lunged forward with my shoulders and felt the light material brush my skin. I'd done it. I'd made it through first.

I collapsed on the ground just behind the finish line, gasping for breath. Tina came over and shook my hand in congratulations. Her words sounded good but the sentiment never reached her eyes—but I didn't care.

Mr Higgins was still jumping up and down when he arrived at my side. "Wow, Heaven, that was your fastest time ever. You cut a whole second and a half off your PB. Well done . . ."

He carried on about it at length but I pushed his words into the background. I took the bottle of water he offered and just enjoyed feeling happy, even if it was for just a moment.

* * *

My win was splashed over the common-room noticeboards the next day. I figured Kelly had something to do with it. I'd gone there for lunch to avoid Jarrod.

Cathy was nowhere in sight. She was probably tailing Jarrod and his friends around the school grounds. They were gearing up for a big game on the weekend. Fortunately, I would be flying to the Gold Coast on Saturday morning, so I could avoid that whole sorry situation.

I'd just sat down to eat my sandwich when Jarrod walked in. The room went quiet. His eyes locked with mine—and he was clearly angry. A confrontation was unavoidable.

He marched over to where I sat on the couch, sandwich still wrapped in my lap.

"Can we talk somewhere?" he asked. No point whispering—everyone was listening.

I nodded and dropped my sandwich back in my bag. Suddenly I wasn't feeling hungry. I wondered what could possibly have made him so angry that he'd come to talk to me.

He led me into the library and behind the reference shelves. He came to a halt and spun around so quickly we almost collided. Then he folded his arms and glared at me.

"You know, I've heard of some pretty wimpy ways to break up with people but dumping-by-coach . . . Wow Heaven, that's gotta be a first!!"

He stood silently waiting for my reply.

I was confused. *What did he mean?* I shook my head blankly.

Jarrod angrily pushed a pile of aged reference books off the edge of a shelf. They tumbled to the floor in a clatter of dust.

"Heaven, can you imagine how embarrassing it was to have Coach Higgins tell me how sorry he was that we'd broken up? You know . . . since how *I* didn't even know. He said you'd told him at the track meet yesterday. I knew you were mad but . . . wow!! That's really cold even for you!" He turned to face the wall and braced his hands on the shelving.

A damaged ego or a hurt heart? I wondered which was bothering him most— but he did have a point.

"I . . . I guess I just assumed you felt the same way," I began quietly.

He spun around. His face was contorted with rage. "You guessed! Well, it's a pity you didn't talk it over with me before making it public knowledge! Of all the selfish . . ." he began.

But it was too late. He'd said the word that summed up the whole sorry situation.

NINE

S elfish! *Selfish?* You wanna call me *selfish*?" I shrieked. I lunged forward and jammed my forefinger into his chest.

"*Selfish* is when you pester and pester someone for sex, even when they've told you time and time again they are not ready. *Selfish* is when you administer the guilt treatment when they put the brakes on and you still think you are entitled. *Selfish* is when you wait for your girlfriend—who you are supposed to love and care about—to be too drunk to think clearly.

"Jarrod, don't you see! My virginity was my gift to give—not your right to take! Of course, I don't want to be your girlfriend anymore. You betrayed me in a way I never thought possible! I trusted you, Jarrod, like I have never trusted anyone before! You see my family! It is a mess! I let you know me, which is more than I've ever done before. The damage you did to me on Saturday night by betraying me—that was and is irreparable. There is no way back from here, Jarrod!"

His eyes were filled with stunned surprise. I don't think he thought I had it in me to feel so much. His anger was gone and replaced by pools of sadness and resignation. I turned away. I couldn't face watching him as the last shreds of our relationship dissolved.

"You've hurt *me*, Jarrod, not the other way around. You've hurt me beyond what I thought was humanly possible. Now please just go. I want to be alone."

He stood there for a few moments longer. Part of me begged to be released from my words and fall into his arms. Without doubt, this was our last chance.

"Fine, Heaven," he sighed. "Have it your way!" He stepped around me. His arm brushed mine as he swept past, then he was gone.

Jarrod skipped school for the next three days. I hoped it was because he felt guilty for what he'd done to me. But more likely it was because the way our six-month relationship had ended was now sweeping the school like wild fire. The gossip was everywhere. I'd even heard teachers asking Mr Higgins if he needed to change his name to "Gossip King of Eastside High".

Even the teachers went quiet when I walked by. I'd earned a new reputation of being heartless, as well as cold. I'd even heard a rumour that I was gay and only dated guys to torment them.

Apart from being totally miserable, the only real down side was now Alex—the local self-proclaimed football legend—was totally unbearable. His jibes were getting more filthy.

The worst was when he pinned me against a locker and offered to show me what a real man looked like. I don't know what I would have done if Ms Renolds hadn't walked past when she did. I ran to the bathroom and threw up as soon as she got Alex off me.

I felt alone and lost. *Where was Kelly when I needed her?* Unfortunately I knew exactly where she was—with Gavin!

* * *

I closed my eyes and gripped the armrests as the plane's engines forced me back in my seat on take off. The weight of the previous week disappeared as gravity relinquished its hold on Dad's small plane. It wouldn't be long until we were on the Gold Coast and I hoped my misery could remain grounded in Sydney.

I smiled over at Katie as she scrolled through the latest magazine on her new toy. She'd left her laptop behind in favour of a newly purchased iPad. I'd tried to explain that with an iPhone and laptop, the iPad was really not necessary but she wasn't having it for a moment.

"It's so much more convenient and it's smaller for travelling," she'd said, as she handed over Dad's platinum credit card. I shrugged and left her to it.

Thankfully, Mum had decided to stay home. Facing the two of them together for the entire holiday would have been awful. She'd faked some exhibition and Dad hadn't tried to dissuade her. Once the plane levelled out, I closed my eyes again. I was so tired and hadn't been sleeping well. My night-time mind was a constant blur of memories. I guess my subconscious was trying to make sense of what I'd done.

"So . . . two single girls on the loose on the Gold Coast, hey?" Katie bubbled. I didn't even open my eyes.

"Katie, I'm done with boys! I'm sorry but you'll have to take them all on for the both of us. The only support you'll be getting from me are my best wishes!" I replied.

Katie giggled. "But don't you know the best way to get over the old man is to find a new one?"

"Did you just read that in that magazine?" I asked, opening one eye.

"Something like that!" she quipped. "But if you don't move on, you're going to get back and be bothered when Jarrod has . . ."

I sat up at that comment. "What do you mean Jarrod has? What do you know?"

"Nothing really . . . but Cathy was overjoyed when she found out you'd left Jarrod's ego in tatters. You can be sure she will be doing whatever she can to massage it back together."

Katie was probably right. *What more could I expect?* Hurting Jarrod's pride was sure to mean he would have no consideration for my feelings now. Maybe finding some new mystery man on holiday was exactly what I needed to rebound from this. After all, wasn't that why they called it a rebound?

"Well, Katie, let's just wait and see what we find lying about by the pool," I said with a laugh.

"Ohhhhooww, this is going to be soooo much fun!!" she enthused.

* * *

We hit the shops at Pacific Fair as soon as we got settled. I bought four new swimsuits and matching sarongs, some nice beachwear and a couple of cute date outfits, just in case.

Katie was thrilled. It was more shopping than I'd done all year. We jammed all the bags into a taxi and headed back to the hotel. If we hurried, we could hit the pool before it got too late. Once the rest of the family arrived, we'd be tied up with them for the rest of the day.

Dad had booked Katie and me a room to ourselves this year. Usually we booked an apartment suite for the whole family but I think Dad knew we didn't want to share with him because of the affair debacle.

With our own keys and freedom to come and go as we pleased, we felt grown up. We were already well aware of the unwritten rule: "Don't shame the family." But with Dad's current situation, he was in no position to judge!

I tore the price tag off my favourite new swimsuit and sarong, and analysed myself in the mirror. I really needed a spray tan if I was going to be spending time by the pool.

"OK, ready!" Katie beamed as she burst out of the bathroom. Her new hot-pink bikini was really something.

"Wow, Katie," I said, shading my eyes. "I don't know what burns my eyes more—your white skin or that fluoro swimwear!" I grinned.

She laughed, "Race you down. First there gets first pick of the hotties!"

"Katie, that's terrible!! You're too young to talk like that about guys. Where do you learn these phrases anyway?" I scolded as I chased her out the door. I could hear the ding of the elevator and the doors rumbling open. Rounding the corner, I dived in just before they closed.

"Don't be silly, sis. You know exactly where!" she giggled.

"Those magazines!" I said with feigned haughtiness, as we fell against the glassed walls laughing.

The pool was huge—not that we would be swimming in it! According to Katie, we would spend our time surveying the talent surrounding it. I was happy to humour Katie but what I really wanted to do was read a book and maybe spend a bit of time studying for our finals next term.

After all, Kelly and I had always planned to come back to the Gold Coast for a week of partying when our exams were done. We'd talked about it for years. I couldn't believe it would finally be our turn in only a few months.

"Look!" hissed Katie, flicking her head toward the two boys who had just climbed out of the water on the other side of the pool. I glanced over.

"Hey, don't look!" she whispered.

"But you just told me to look!" I protested.

"Well don't look like that. They'll see you looking!" she huffed in reply.

I shook my head, settled in on one of the deck chairs and pulled out my novel.

"The dark-haired one's cute," Katie interrupted. I looked over at her. Now she was staring and twirling her hair.

I snorted. "I'm done with dark hair," I replied, searching for my place on the page.

"Well, you can have the blonde then," she beamed.

"They're not produce, you know," I added, peering over the top of my book.

Katie rolled her eyes. "I know!"

When did she get so boy crazy? I wondered, shaking my head and returning to my book.

* * *

About 20 minutes later, a shadow fell on my page. I looked up, expecting to see Dad telling us the relatives had arrived. Instead, I was greeted by the handsome smile and blue eyes of "my" blonde boy from the other side of the pool.

"Hi," he said, dropping down on the chair next to me.

"Ahh, hi?" I replied. This was followed by a few moments of awkward silence. I could feel Katie's excitement building.

"Look, ummm," he began, "I lost rock-paper-scissors so I'm supposed to come over and, you know . . . get your number or something. My mate over there, we are on holiday from New Zealand and . . . well, are you Aussies? Do you know what's fun around here?"

I felt immediately sorry for him. This was not going so well at all. I cut in to give him a break.

"Yeah, we've been here a few times before. My sister and I are from Sydney. We come here every year, though not always to this hotel. My name's Heaven, by the way . . ."

The smile was back. He gave a thumbs-up to his mate on the other side of the pool, who burst out laughing and started collecting their gear.

"Heaven, you say—that's an . . . interesting name," he began.

"My name's Katie," my sister cut in. She must have been holding her breath because her words gushed out all at once.

"Oh, hi Katie . . . Heaven . . . umm, sorry. My name's Byron and my bro over there—his name's Sol." He hesitantly offered me his hand.

We made space for Byron and Sol. They both seemed really nice Kiwi guys. Katie laughed at their accents, which probably wasn't very cool, and kept asking them to say "six" and "fish-and-chips." They were from South Auckland and had only arrived today. Apparently they had come over with a school rugby team and were staying on with their parents for the holidays. They were just giving us an explanation about the finer points of rugby union when Ed stepped out of the elevator.

"There are my favourite nieces. Look, you come out to the pool for half an hour and already you're hauling in all the boys," he grinned. Uncle Ed turned to Sol and Byron. "Thought I should mention that this one's taken." He pointed his thumb at me. "She's dating the school football star!"

I flushed bright red. "Umm, Ed, Jarrod and I broke up last week," I mumbled.

"Choice, bro!" Sol laughed and shoulder-barged Byron in the side. They tussled about for a moment but then realised we were getting up to leave.

"Hey girls, can we have your numbers before you go?"

"I haven't got a pen," I mumbled. I wished Ed hadn't brought up Jarrod. It had been nice just chatting. I'd almost forgotten about it.

"I've got a whiteboard marker in my pocket," Ed offered.

"Cheh, just write it here." Sol grinned, pointing to his chest. He wiped the area with a towel so the pen would stick. As far as chests go, it was rather impressive. Byron punched him in the arm and flicked his head toward Katie.

Katie didn't miss the moment. She whipped the pen from Ed's waiting fingers and scrawled her number and name across his chest in large letters finishing with a stylised heart. I stifled a giggle. "There, now you won't lose it," she winked.

They grabbed their towels and ran off laughing. "Later, girls!" they called.

I flicked Katie with my towel as I collected it off the seat. She was still staring after them. "You little minx!" Ed laughed. "If this is what you are like now, what are you going to be like in a few more years?"

"Better and badder, Uncle Ed—better and badder!" She grinned wickedly.

"Oh, Katie, get a grip on your hormones!" I rolled my eyes.

"But did you like Byron, Heaven? Remember I've got dibs on Sol. Did you see his chest . . . ?" she began as we headed for the elevator.

"Yeah, I saw his chest—and, yes, Byron seems fine. But you can have both for all I care!" I laughed and turned to Ed. "I was never this bad!"

"Nah, not in the least." He grinned, patting my shoulder.

"Well, I wasn't!" I added indignantly as the door opened.

* * *

The rest of the family had gathered in Aunt Victoria's suite. She'd booked the penthouse, which had 180-degree views of the beach. After the initial pleasantries, I sat on the balcony with Katie and Abbie—Ed and Sally's daughter—while the adults talked and Aunt Victoria topped everyone's stories.

"Like wow, do you think she even realises how bad she sounds?" Abbie asked, rolling her eyes.

Katie snorted, "Yup, every year it's the same. You made a mill? Well, I made two. You bought a boat? Well, I bought a yacht and went sailing with Barack Obama!"

I burst out laughing. "Wow, Katie, how do you know who Barack Obama is? Oh no, don't tell me!"

Katie rolled her eyes, "They did a story on his wife Michelle in . . ."

"That magazine!" Abbie and I both yelled and fell about laughing.

"Well, they did!" Katie sniffed.

We hushed when we heard Aunt Victoria's voice from inside. "So she's going to the Australia-wide finals you say? Where is that being held?"

Abbie raised an eyebrow at me.

I shrugged. "I won State. It isn't a big deal really. The competition wasn't that steep this year."

"Well, that's cool. I wonder how she's gonna top that. The twins are only four!" Abbie whispered. We leaned toward the door to listen.

"Yes, I've enrolled the girls in athletics. I've been told they have a flare for it. These things must run in the family. Imagine where Heaven would be if she'd started earlier . . ."

I bit a smile.

"Oh, wow!" Abbie uttered in wonder. "That woman is something else!"

We all laughed again.

"It's a pity you weren't here earlier, Abbie. We met these hot guys from New Zealand—Sol and Byron—maybe they might know someone else . . ."

"It's fine, Katie. She can have Byron." I winked. "I'm really not ready to be back on the market again anyway."

Katie laughed and began filling Abbie in on all their details. She listened with interest.

I gazed out at the deep blue expanse of water, which seemed to stretch endlessly to the horizon. I loved the ocean. I found it calming. It made me feel small, shrinking my problems in the process. I deeply wished it was a year from now and all my troubles with Jarrod were long forgotten. My thoughts were interrupted by Katie's phone beeping. She picked it up and glanced at the message.

"Ohhh, it's the guys. They wanna know if we are coming down for a swim later," she bounced. Then I could see her doing the calculations—one, two, three . . .

"Hey, why don't you two go? Maybe if they meet Abbie now, they will dig up another friend from somewhere before dating us becomes an issue," I offered.

Katie messaged them back and they got up to leave.

"I might go back to the room for a bit. This is all getting pretty old anyway," I added. I was feeling quite tired. If I could just get some decent sleep, everything wouldn't feel so bad.

Katie changed into a different swimsuit, "Are you sure you don't mind us going without you?" she asked, with a touch of concern.

"No, you guys go. My heart's not really in it anyway." I smiled weakly.

"OK," she gushed. "I'll tell you everything when I get back. I'm meeting Abbie down there. I better not be late. She doesn't know where we're meeting"—and she was gone.

I lay down on my bed with my novel. Escapism was the best plan I had for the present.

* * *

The first week went by pretty quick. I "third-wheeled" it a bit. The guys didn't seem to mind my replacement and Abbie was loving all the attention. My feelings were still a bit too raw to move on, even if I did think it might make me feel better in the short term.

I woke up late on Saturday morning feeling really tired, but I always did when I was due.

It had been a big night and we'd gone to see a late movie. I went to the bathroom expecting to see its arrival but was surprised to find nothing. I stared at the toilet paper. I'd been getting my period since the day after my 13th birthday and had been exactly 28 days almost to the hour since then. *Did I have the date wrong?*

I found my diary and counted back to the asterisked date from the month before. Yeah, I had calculated wrong. It was in fact 30 days since my last period. I was two days late!

TEN

Suddenly I felt dizzy. I dropped onto my bed. Jarrod's words played back in my head: "I used it when it counted . . ." he'd said. *What does that mean anyway, "When it counted"? Does that mean he didn't use anything when he thought it didn't count?*

I was confusing myself! I tried again to remember what had happened that night but there was nothing but a few hazy images. I certainly wasn't on any birth control, so if he hadn't used a condom . . . *What if I was pregnant?!*

At that moment, our front door squeaked open. Katie danced in. I had to get a grip on myself. Two days late wasn't that big a deal. It could still turn up. There was no point making her worry. I forced a smile.

"Hi, Katie, how's the pool? Hope you remembered your sunscreen." My voice sounded higher than usual, like I was panicking. I needed to calm down.

"I just popped back for a towel. We're going down to the beach. You wanna come?" she asked. I tried not to make eye contact.

"Nah, thanks, I think I'll just stay here. Still a bit tired," I replied, faking a yawn.

"OK." She leaned in a little closer, scrutinising my face. "Are you sure you're OK? . . . You look a bit pale."

"I'll be fine. You go and have fun," I said giving her a push.

"Alright then." She grinned. "I'll see you after lunch."

I heard the door thump behind her as she left. I felt alone.

Who could I tell? I'd broken up with Jarrod. My best friend was so consumed by her new relationship that I'd only had a couple of texts from her all week. I couldn't tell Katie, she was just my little sister and I certainly couldn't tell my mum. *How could everything have gone so terribly wrong? I'd only had sex once and Jarrod had said he'd been safe. He'd said everything would be fine!*

I leapt to my feet. I needed to do something active. I couldn't just lie here waiting or I'd go insane. But what? I started wearing a track across the hotel-room floor as I paced between the bed and the couch. I glanced out the window.

I'd seen a pharmacy down on the main street. The obvious thing to do now was go buy a pregnancy test. At least then I'd know one way or the other. They were 98 per cent accurate and I'd heard they worked within days of a missed period. I pulled a brush through my hair, grabbed my bag and ran out the door.

* * *

The bell tinkled as I walked through the door. Fortunately, there were no other customers in the store. I glanced around the aisle but had no idea where to start.

"Can I help you?" asked a smiling middle-aged woman in a white uniform. I leapt. I hadn't heard her coming.

"Ahh, ummm, no . . . just looking, thanks," I replied absently, grabbing something from the shelf in front of me. She continued to smile.

"Just let me know if there is anything you need," she said and turned away.

I looked down at what I'd picked up. *Urrggh, haemor-rhoid cream!* I put it back on the shelf. I really did want her help. I wanted to ask her where the stupid tests were and if she could just grab the best one for me and stick it in a bag so I could get out of here—but I didn't.

Eventually I found them and there were so many. I was reaching up toward one called Clear Blue, when I heard the tinkle of the doorbell again. I snatched my hand back and waited for the customer to leave.

"Hello, Mrs Hutton," I heard the shop assistant say. "Just the usual is it?" she asked. "The pharmacist will be with you in just a minute."

I paused for a moment and held my breath. I had to do this and get out of here before someone else came in. I reached for the box again.

"You might like to choose this one, dear. It has two tests, instead of just one."

I leapt again—this woman could move quietly. I turned to face her. I was expecting to see her staring at me, eyes filled with judgment, but instead she squeezed my arm.

"Did you need to talk with someone? There's a medical centre in the building. I could get you . . ."

"No, thanks," I cut in. "But I will have . . . one of those, please." I pointed to the box. I didn't want to touch it. It would make the possibility seem too real.

I followed her to the counter where she quickly slipped it into a bag. "That will be $24.95, please."

I handed over the cash and as I did she caught my hand.

"Please come back if there is anything else you need." She looked so sincere that I almost considered confiding in her.

"Thanks . . . ummm . . ." I glanced at her name badge. CATHY was spelt out in capital letters. I swallowed. *Cathy Davis, that was who Jarrod was probably with right now!* I pushed the picture of the two of them together from my mind. I needed to focus. This could all still be nothing.

"Thanks, Cathy"—the name caught in my throat— "you've been so helpful already." I forced a smile, turned and tinkled through the door, feeling her eyes on me the whole way.

* * *

Back in the room, I locked the bathroom door and tore open the box. Two packages fell out. I put one on the counter, ripped the other from its wrapper and read the instructions. It was fairly simple. I had to pee on the stick, then wait two minutes. One blue line and I was home free. Two blue lines meant . . . I gulped. *Well, let's just hope it's one blue line.*

I sat down and felt my urine drum on the stick for a moment. *That should do it,* I thought. I finished and put the test down on the basin.

I glanced at my watch and sat back on the toilet to wait. Two minutes felt like forever. I thought of all the things that had led to this point. If only I'd just avoided one of them I might not be sitting here right now. *If I'd never kissed Jarrod, if Mum and Dad hadn't been fighting, if I hadn't gone to the party, if I hadn't drunk, if I'd just gone home instead, if Jarrod had just kept his hands . . .*

Two minutes were up. I held my breath and picked up the pregnancy test. There were two blue lines!

* * *

Two sets of twin blue lines stared up at me. The shop assistant obviously knew if the test came back positive, I'd want to double-check the results—and she was correct.

Despairingly, I tossed the box and second confirming test into the bin, burying them under a toilet roll wrapper. Jamming the other test in my pocket, I headed out the door. I wasn't sure where I was going but I needed to think. My mind was blank. Suddenly all my plans, my future had vanished with the appearance of two blue lines.

I ambled down the street with my hands buried in my pockets. Suddenly baby strollers and swollen pregnant stomachs were everywhere. Before I knew it, I'd stumbled back into the pharmacy. The familiar bell tinkled as I re-entered the shop. Cathy looked up from the counter. Our eyes locked. My face must have said it all.

Her look of pity was enough to push me over the edge. I'd never seen that expression used on me before. I was always the beautiful, lucky, rich girl. The world was my oyster. I couldn't face it. The pity was more than I could bear. The dam broke, all the carefully concealed emotion burst in a flood of misery and I crumbled into her arms.

"There, there," Cathy cooed, offering me a cup of tea and a box of tissues in the back room of the shop. Fortunately, the pharmacist had been at lunch and hadn't witnessed my breakdown. I was already deeply regretting my outburst.

"I'm fine, Cathy, truly. It was all just a bit of a shock, that's all," I began.

"Does the father know?" she asked. "Is he here with you?"

"Ummm, no—we broke up," I whispered.

"Oh!" she replied. There was that pity again.

"What do you think you'd like to do . . . about the pregnancy?"

There it was, the word spoken out loud. I shuddered with revulsion at myself. *How could I have sabotaged my life like this? Without question, this thing growing inside me had to go.*

"There's a doctor's surgery up in the mall behind us. It will be open for another hour. If you head up there now, they might be able to see you," Cathy suggested.

"What?! Can they do one that quickly?" I asked.

"One what?" she replied.

"You know, an abortion." I quaked at the word. I didn't like saying it aloud. It was right up there with *pregnancy* and *baby*. But if I could get it done that quickly, maybe I wouldn't have too long to think about my moral standing.

"No, dear, they can't do it today. They will have to refer you to a clinic."

"Right," I replied.

* * *

Cathy had wanted me to stay and chat. She was just trying to be supportive. I suppose it wasn't everyday someone broke down in the pharmacy. I filled out the paperwork at the doctor's office and sat down to wait my turn. Cathy had told me Doctor Green was a lovely woman, that she would be kind and sympathetic.

Unfortunately, it was a much older man who called my

name. He was balding and had dated gold-framed glasses, which he kept pushing off the end of his nose. I sat down in the chair on the other side of his desk, while he shuffled his squeaky chair into position under the desk.

I knew what he was about to ask so I hit him with a pre-emptive strike. "I'd like a referral for an abortion, please." As I spoke I forced myself to make eye contact. If I sounded reasonably confident, perhaps he'd just do what I asked and let me go.

Dr Gilbertson cleared his throat and stared at me as he pushed his glasses back up on his nose. "An abortion?"

He was going to drag this out. The moments ticked by. I could see him sizing me up, then he shrugged and looked back at his computer screen. He began pecking away at the keyboard with his index fingers.

"You'll be required to make an appointment. I would suggest you do this quickly as sometimes there can be a short wait. You'll be required to have a blood test to confirm your result." He glanced back at me again over his specks. "You have taken a pregnancy test, haven't you?"

I pulled the test from my pocket and tossed it across the desk for him to inspect. He peered at the twin blue lines and gave a satisfied nod.

"Right then—but you will still be required to do a blood test. I will include all the usual STIs on the list, that way we can be sure he hasn't left you with anything else that might require treatment."

I shuddered. I felt violated. *Could this get any more embarrassing?* Suddenly a picture of me with my legs in stirrups and several doctors peering down at me flooded into my mind. *Yes,* I gulped, *this could—and would—get a whole lot more embarrassing before it was finally over.*

Dr Gilbertson handed me the referral and necessary blood-test forms. I stood and turned to leave.

"Would you like a script for birth control . . . for afterwards . . ."

"No, thank you," I interrupted. "That won't be necessary."

"Heaven," he said, pushing up his glasses and his eyes softening, "is there something else you should be telling me? Was this . . . consensual?"

I didn't know where to look. *Of course it wasn't consensual. But I would never be able to prove it. After all, who would believe me? It would be my word against his and I had certainly left the party looking like I wanted to . . .*

Well, that's what everyone would attest to. Besides, I wouldn't want to do that to Jarrod anyway. On some level, I still felt strangely connected to him. It must have something to do with the fact that I had his kid growing inside me. *If I dragged him through the courts, I would inevitably lose and what would that achieve?*

"Heaven?"

I had forgotten Dr Gilbertson was still waiting for a reply. *What would I say?*

"Ummm, I had too much to drink."

I watched his sympathy evaporate and his eyes harden. He scrawled something on a page and handed it to me. I couldn't read it.

"You'd better take this then—just in case you change your mind."

"What is it?" I asked.

"A script for the contraceptive pill."

He squeaked his chair back into position in front of the computer and began finger pecking out my bill. It was his cue for me to leave. I skulked out the door feeling demoralised and exposed. Like instead of just writing me a script he'd branded me with a scarlet letter.

I quickly paid my bill and rushed out the door.

ELEVEN

"Wow, Heaven, that's serious!" Kelly offered after I finished. All she'd asked was how my holiday went—and this is what she got. She took another sip of her latte, trying to come up with something else to say. But she shook her head.

"Oh, Heaven, why didn't you go get the 'Morning-after Pill'?" She stroked my arm.

"He said he used something," I explained with a shrug.

"Well, don't you remember him putting it on?" She looked exasperated, like I was some kind of idiot.

"I don't remember anything," I whispered.

She paused for a moment, eyeballing me seriously. "What do you mean you don't remember anything?"

I broke eye contact. "Just that—I passed out."

"And he still . . ."

I nodded

"Heaven," she said, "that's . . ."

I leapt to my feet. "Look, can we not have this conversation. It's not going to get us anywhere. This is the situation—right now—and what I really want to know is, will you come with me when, you know, when I get the . . . termination?" My voice cracked on the word, but *termination* was still easier than *abortion*.

Kelly looked like she was going to cry. She squeezed my arm again. "Of course I'll come—but are . . . are you going to tell *him*?"

I turned my back. "What difference would it make?" I swallowed the lump growing in my throat. This conversation needed to be over before I lost control.

"Well, he should at least know what he's done to you." She grabbed my hand. "You know he's seeing Cathy now," she whispered.

Her words hit me like a freight train. I'd known he would but somehow imagining it and facing the reality were totally different things. I only had to get through one more term, then it would be study vacation and school holidays. It helped a little knowing once school was over I never had to see either of them ever again.

* * *

I went for a long run the following morning. Somehow I hoped it would make me more prepared for the first day back at school. I enjoyed forcing my body into submission and I pushed myself extra hard, perhaps stupidly hoping it might be able to jar out my unwanted guest. It didn't!

The bell that signalled the end of the class shook us from our silent study. I'd managed to keep Jarrod out of sight the whole morning but, according to the new timetable, we were about to share a class just before lunch.

Taking a deep breath, I walked into the room and tried to keep my eyes away from Cathy's usual seat. I failed dismally. He was slouching in the chair next to her with his arms folded across his chest. He glanced absently across as the door squeaked. Our eyes locked. I felt a searing pain burn through my chest.

He had such beautiful eyes and I was sure I saw them soften for a moment. But then they seemed to cloud over with anger—or maybe it was hurt. I shook my head. *Of course, it wasn't hurt—that was me!*

He leapt from his seat and slammed the chair under the desk, stomped to the rear of the classroom and dropped into a seat at the back of the room. I took a seat in the front row, as far from him as possible. I felt his eyes burning into the back of my head and didn't dare look over at Cathy. His reaction surprised me. I'd thought he would have enjoyed rubbing the new relationship in my face.

Kelly slipped quietly into the seat next to me. It was the first time we'd ever sat so close to the front—ever!

"Go sit with Gavin if you want, Kelly. I'll be fine," I whispered.

"Don't be ridiculous," she replied. "I'm not leaving you here on your own. Besides, he's gone to sit with Jarrod. He looks pretty . . ."

"Angry, annoyed, put out . . ." I said offering alternatives.

"No, I was going to say upset." Then she leaned in and whispered behind her hand, "And don't look now, but Cathy is glaring at you. Seems Jarrod is happy to be with her—so long as you aren't around."

I felt my heart unwillingly jump in my chest. After all he'd done to me, I still couldn't stop having feelings for him. I was a sucker for punishment!

The class was uneventful. As soon as the bell rang, Jarrod disappeared out the door. I looked around and noticed Cathy was still in her seat, staring angrily at her desk. Unfortunately, I wasn't quick enough to look away. Our eyes met, hers smouldering with rage. Kelly pulled me from my seat and out the door.

"I think we've done enough of the front row for one day. Did you notice Cathy's hair? She's dyed it darker. It's uncanny how much her new style looks like yours," Kelly winked. "And wow, Jarrod was outta here fast . . ."

I let her voice burble into the background as she dissected our first class together, giving a minute-by-minute account of what Jarrod did throughout the lesson.

"You know he didn't take his eyes off you, Heaven?" she finished.

"Who?" I asked absently.

"Jarrod, of course. Are you sure you wouldn't like to—you know—tell him? Maybe the gossip about him and Cathy isn't quite what she would like it to be. Maybe they aren't together at all. Maybe he's just . . ."

"What?! Using her for a booty call?" I grimaced.

Kelly opened her mouth to speak but then closed it again. Obviously she thought I was right but didn't want to verbalise it.

* * *

The rest of the week followed much the same pattern when Jarrod and I shared a class. I would always arrive at the last possible moment and he'd shift to the back of the room—away from me and away from Cathy. By Friday, it was starting to get a little easier.

But I was beginning to feel a little apprehensive. The "termination" was scheduled for 1 pm the next day. I watched

121

Jarrod fly out the door as soon as the bell rang. *Maybe I should tell him. Were Kelly and Pharmacy Cathy right? Did he have a right to know?*

"What time do you want me to pick you up tomorrow for the . . . ?" Kelly asked as we walked home. She let the rest of the sentence die on her lips. She'd gotten her driver's license over the holidays and was busting to take me for a ride. "Mum's already said I can borrow the car. How long do you think it will take? Did you wanna do something afterwards?" she asked.

Afterwards? I hadn't thought about afterwards? Would there even be an afterwards? I couldn't imagine one. Those dreadful "pro-life" films they showed in General Studies last year were playing through my mind. The one that showed the tiny foetus with its little beating heart and big black eyes, which stared lidlessly at you while they sucked on their minuscule thumb nubs.

I shuddered and tried to block the vision from my mind.

"Let's not get there early. I don't want to wait around too long. I hate doctors' rooms," I replied.

"So are you gonna tell him?" she asked.

Kelly thought I owed it to him to make him feel as rotten as possible about this—and maybe she was right. But I didn't need to see any more pity or pain.

"You catching up with Gavin over the weekend?" I asked, changing the subject.

Kelly took the hint and moved on.

* * *

Saturday dawned bright and clear. I woke up early. I tried to go back to sleep. I didn't want to lie awake and think about what I was doing today. But sleep evaded me. Finally I got up and went for a run.

It was a beautiful day, but unseasonably cold. I picked up the pace to keep warm. I wasn't paying attention to where I was going. I was listening to the new playlist Katie had put on my iPod. It was a New Zealand band that one of the guys we'd met in Queensland had given her. They weren't half bad either.

I was just rounding the corner to the play equipment when I saw him sitting on the swings. I ducked behind some bushes so he wouldn't see me. Jarrod was just sitting staring down at his hands.

Was he waiting for me to come past? He knew my running route well. I pulled out my earpieces and stood watching him. Kelly's voice echoed in my head prompting me to tell him. Then I imagined this ridiculous scenario of me telling him and him falling on the ground in front of me confessing his undying love and offering to marry me.

The thought warmed my heart but in my head I knew even if he did I could never agree to it. There was no way back. He'd betrayed me, it was only a matter of time before he would do it again and I'd rather not be saddled with his kid when it happened.

I gasped. That was the first time I'd referred to it as a kid—his kid. Jarrod looked around. He'd obviously heard me. I had to choose: *Would I tell him?* He was about to get off the swing. I saw him pull his weight off the seat. *Was I going to let him find me?*

I turned and ran as fast as I could go and didn't let up until I broke through the front door. Katie was heading for the bathroom but I streaked past her and locked the door as best the broken lock would let me.

"Heaven!?" she whined through the closed door.

"I'm sweaty. I'll be quick," I replied, as I pulled off my exercise-drenched sports top.

I buried my head under the hot water and tried to drive the thoughts of the day ahead from my mind. If I could just get through it, everything would return to normal—at least as normal as it could be without Jarrod.

Kelly pulled up outside my house at 12.30.

"I'm going now. I'll be back tomorrow sometime," I called out to no-one in particular. Mum and Dad were used to me staying over at Kelly's, so they wouldn't ask any questions. Well, that is if they even cared about what was going on in my life. Dad was hardly around anymore and Mum was always painting in her studio.

* * *

We arrived at five minutes to 1. It wasn't a dirty sinister-looking place like I'd imagined. It was just like any other doctor's office. The woman behind the desk handed me the forms to complete and I sat down to fill the boxes with my name, address and Medicare card number along with emergency contacts and next of kin. Even though by the looks of it they did hundreds of these procedures everyday, I guess things could still go wrong.

I paused for a moment before signing the consent and

forcing the picture of a dying foetus from my mind. I scribbled my signature across the bottom of the page, handed the forms back to the woman behind the desk and took my seat beside Kelly again.

"You nervous?" Kelly asked.

Of course, I was nervous. The whole thing was making me want to throw up—or maybe that was just the morning sickness kicking in. I didn't reply. I'd say something I'd regret. She was just trying to make conversation.

I looked around at the other patients. There was another girl my age sitting across the other side of the room. She had yellowing bruises on her face and was sitting all alone. Surely her story was worse than mine. At least I had Kelly. Sitting a few seats down was an older woman and her partner. They were probably in their mid-30s or perhaps older. She was sobbing quietly in his arms, holding her stomach. I listened as he whispered quietly to her. "It's OK, honey. This is the best thing. We can try again . . ."

She was still crying when they called her name. Her sobs became more pronounced as he led her into the room and closed the door.

Another girl sat in an easy chair. It was obvious she'd recently had her . . . procedure. She looked groggy and winced a little as she moved. I looked at my watch: it was 1.15. They were running late—but weren't doctors always running late?

Kelly had obviously been watching them, too. She grabbed my hand and squeezed it. I looked around at the rest of the women in the room. Many were older than me and some were younger but all of us wore the same expression of grim determination accented with varying degrees of sadness. All of us wishing the whole sorry situation was already over. Or better still had never happened in the first place!

"Heaven, Heaven Symons."

I looked around. A woman wearing a plaid skirt with bobbed jet-black hair was calling my name. I felt rooted to the spot. I needed to stand but couldn't pull myself out of the chair.

"Come on, Heaven, it's your turn. Let's go," whispered Kelly. She pulled me to my feet but I couldn't move.

"Heaven, let's go!" she tugged.

And that was enough. She said "go"—so I turned and ran.

TWELVE

Kelly called after me as I ran down the stairs and out of the centre. "Heaven, Heaven, where are you going? If you don't come back, you'll miss your turn. Come on, it's just the counsellor. She only wants to talk to you."

Her words faded behind me as I disappeared up the street. *I couldn't do it. I'd grown up thinking meat was murder. I would have to have this baby, even though I didn't want to.* I didn't know what else to do. I'd just have to wing it and see. At least I still had plenty of time to decide.

I messaged Kelly from the bus station and she picked me up. It was a quiet drive back to her house. She started to say something a few times—but stopped. In the end, she would know all the answers to the questions she was trying to ask and I knew all the questions she wanted to verbalise. The bottom line was I was pregnant and wouldn't have an abortion. It left only one other option really: to hope that maybe it might fall out of it's own accord over the next five or six weeks. After that, it would be extremely unlikely.

"You know, one in four pregnancies ends in miscarriage in the first trimester," I finally said.

"What's a trimester?" Kelly asked, not taking her eyes off the road.

"They break the 40 weeks up into three. The three parts are called trimesters," I shrugged.

"40 weeks?! I thought it was nine months…you've obviously been reading up on this." Kelly frowned. "You know you've got no choice but to tell Jarrod now," she added.

"Let's just wait and see. It might go away by itself." I forced a smile I didn't feel.

"That's not the Heaven I know," Kelly replied, shaking her head. "She left nothing to chance. You're burying your head in the sand if you think this will all just go away . . ."

"Yeah, I know . . . but I just can't be there and do that." I gestured back toward the clinic. "Besides, it will be ages before I show. I can get through the rest of the term and no-one will even know."

"Somehow, I don't think it will be as simple as that. From what I've seen, pregnancies are never simple!" Kelly added.

* * *

The next couple of weeks went by with little hassle. I'd been waiting for the morning sickness to kick in but, fortunately for me, I seemed to be one of the few lucky women who didn't get it. The main problem I was facing was my breasts. They felt like they had doubled in size and I was hungry all the time. I kept up my usual running routine but my breasts were really beginning to hurt.

I pulled off my shirt and glared at them in the mirror. I was already bursting out of the new bra I'd bought. If they didn't stop growing, kids would start asking questions. Suddenly the bathroom door flew open. I should have got someone to fix that broken lock myself instead of just telling Dad. It hadn't been working properly for months.

Katie stared in the mirror at my chest. "Holy ballooning boobies, Batman! What's going on with you, Heaven?"

"Guess I'm filling out," I shrugged.

"More like blowing out!" Katie exclaimed. "What have you been eating? Obviously you're one of those lucky girls whose excess weight goes straight to her breasts. Wish that's where mine went!" Katie ducked behind the partition to the toilet and continued, "Mine always lands on my butt."

I snorted. "What weight? You're as skinny as a rake," I replied as I got into the shower. I tried to look down at my feet, but they were well hidden by my chest. I shook my head, they would be stretched beyond recognition. *Who knew what they would look like after this was all over! Most probably never the same again!* I'd been wearing so much baggy stuff lately to try to conceal them but what would I do when summer arrived? I did a quick calculation. I'd be half way by exam time.

Suddenly the shower door burst open. A flood of cold air washed in. "Katie! What are you doing? You're gonna get water all over the floor. Get out!" I shrieked, pushing her away.

"Nah, I had to have another look . . . What's wrong with them, Heaven? They look all veiny, like someone's attacked you with a marker pen. Are they real? Did you get a boob job without telling me?" She reached into the shower and gave me a squeeze.

"Ouch, Katie, get out!" I screamed, pushing her again.

Katie shrugged, "They feel real enough but—wow—they look like blue vein cheese. Maybe you should see a doctor or something. They look creepy!"

Katie backed out of the cubical, "Oh Heaven, you wet me!" she said, looking down at her night shirt.

"Well, dahh, you climbed in the shower with me, you perve. Now get out of the bathroom!" I hollered, throwing a sponge over the side of the glass wall.

Katie ducked and laughed as she left, closing the door behind her. But she was right—they did look weird!

* * *

The term flew by in a storm of study and extreme tiredness. I'd go to bed early and wake up just as sleepy the next morning. I felt like I was stumbling around school in a daze.

I barely even noticed Cathy any more. She seemed to have gotten used to the reaction Jarrod had when I walked into a room where they were. I hadn't seen him on my morning runs either. Not that I was going often—I was too tired and it made my breasts even sorer.

The holidays were just around the corner again. The 10 weeks had flown. I'd gotten out of the Nationals—much to Mr Higgins' dismay. I couldn't compete in my second trimester. In fact, I'd been to the doctor and gotten an excuse letter to get me out of sport and training completely for the rest of the term. I faked chronic fatigue and that covered most of the bases including my weight gain, which I'd passed off as water retention.

The hardest part was seeing the 14-week mark arrive. I'd circled it in my diary just a few weeks earlier. It forced me to face reality. Sooner or later I would have to tell my parents but I'd decided to wait until after exams. At least I could deliver good exam results for them before I delivered their grandchild. I shuddered.

Kelly had been making plans for the end-of-school "school-ies" week. "Dad's booked us a place right on the water. He's got some contact up there. It's cost a bomb but it's going to be great!" she enthused.

I hadn't told her I wouldn't be going. What was the point? I'd be past halfway by then and probably well and truly showing. I wouldn't be up to partying all night and certainly didn't feel like watching her and Gavin ogle one another for an entire week.

I was about to reply when I felt a tap on my shoulder. I grabbed my books from my locker and turned around. Jarrod had his hands jammed in his pockets and was looking around nervously.

"Jarrod," I squeaked in surprise and dropped my books on the floor.

We both bent to pick them up and crashed heads on the way. I fell back against the lockers and rubbed my forehead. I didn't need this extra stress. I was already right on the edge.

"Ouch, Jarrod, what do you want?" I sighed, leaning against the lockers.

He stood up, pulled me to my feet and handed me my books. "I know you've got a free next. Can we talk?" he asked.

I glanced over at Kelly, my eyes narrowed. She shook her head innocently. I looked back at Jarrod. No, this wasn't the expression of a young man who'd recently found out he was going to be a dad.

"Ummm, OK, I'm going to the library. Suit yourself!" I said, heading off and subconsciously sucking in my stomach. Not that it was easy these days. I'd noticed a slight rounding down there—and it was only going to get rounder.

We found an empty study room and closed the door. Quite a few kids had given us surprised looks as we passed. The gossip mongers were probably already at work.

I sat down and opened an English text. It was the first exam. This was his "talk" so I was going to leave it up to him.

Jarrod didn't say anything for some time. I was beginning to feel uncomfortable.

"Did you want me to quiz you?" he finally asked.

I paused. *What did he want?* "Look—no, not really. What's all this about anyway?" I sighed impatiently.

Jarrod rubbed the back of his neck and turned to stare through the glass wall. "Cathy wants me to take her to the school formal," he whispered.

I felt my stomach lurch, but guessed it didn't matter. It wasn't like I was going to go.

"So take her then," I replied, not looking up from the page.

Jarrod spun around. "Is that it? Is that all you're gonna say? Take her? Look, we were together for six months. Clearly I made a mistake and . . . and I'm sorry, OK? But can't we just move on? Can't we forget what happened? I want to take you to the formal, Heaven!"

He dropped onto the seat opposite me and tried to take my hand. I flicked it away.

"I know I was stupid trying to make you jealous with Cathy but I didn't know what else to do."

I buried my face in my hands. I didn't need this. "So did you sleep with her, too?"

"What's that got to do with it?" he asked defensively.

"A lot, actually. Have you slept with Cathy?" I asked glaring at him.

"Well, you made it clear we weren't together anymore, so I don't think that matters," he replied, grabbing my hand.

This time I didn't have the energy to flick him away. I was getting close to tears. *He'd slept with her, too. I just knew it!*

"I was only trying to make you jealous, so you would come back to me," he whispered.

"You wanted me back so you slept with someone else! Well, that makes sense!"

I tried to pull my hand away but he wouldn't let it go. "Forgive me. Please give me another chance. Let me take you to the formal. Let's try again. I promise I'll do it right this time," he said, brushing his lips over my fingers.

The pregnancy hormones were making it much harder to control myself. I felt the tears pooling in my eyes. "Jarrod," I whispered back, "we can't just go back to how things were. Things are all messed up now. Jarrod . . . I'm . . . I'm pregnant!"

The room went silent. I couldn't even hear him breathing. I wiped my eyes on the back of my sleeve and looked up. Jarrod's face was frozen in shock.

"Is it mine?" he finally asked.

"What?!" I was stunned. *What kind of question was that?*

"Of course it's yours, Jarrod. You're the only person I've ever been with!" I gasped.

"OK, OK—you just caught me by surprise. I couldn't see how . . . I did use something . . ."

"Yes, I remember what you said. You said you did when it counted! Well, clearly you didn't or I wouldn't be in this mess now, would I?"

I'd given up on keeping my tears in check. They were

running down my cheeks. Now that it was all out in the open, I wanted him to see how badly he'd hurt me and how angry I was.

Jarrod dropped down next to my chair, put his arm around my shoulders and whispered, "Shhh, shhh, it will be OK. We can get through this." He rubbed my arm.

Despite the fact that he'd caused all this, it did make me feel better having him with me.

"I'll come with you when you go . . ." he continued.

"When I go? What do you mean, 'When I go?' When I go where?" I asked, wiping my eyes.

"You know, when you go for the abortion," he said matter-of-factly.

I blinked. "Sorry, Jarrod, you're too late for that one. I tried but I couldn't go through with it."

Jarrod leapt to his feet. "You're keeping it?" He looked horrified.

"I never said . . ."

"You can't have it, Heaven. You'll be ruining both our lives. I can't be a dad. I've had a meeting with football scouts today and they . . ."

"It's a pity you didn't think about that when you slept with me then, isn't it?" I spat. "At least you knew what you were doing, I had no idea what was going on!"

Jarrod snapped his mouth shut.

"Please, please, Heaven . . . don't do this. Let's go back again. I'll be with you this time. You don't have to go on your own," he begged.

"I wasn't on my own, Kelly came with me!" I replied, folding my arms angrily.

"I should have guessed you already told her!" He shook his head. Then he was down at my side again, his eyes level with mine. "But what about all your plans? What about medical school? Have you told your parents?"

"No, I haven't told my parents yet. I was waiting until after the exams to tell them. I don't know how they will react . . ."

"Well, that's easy. You're Dad's going to go nuts. He'll kick you out!" Jarrod said, still in disbelief. "You can't do this, Heaven!" He ran his hands through his hair.

"No-one said you had to come along for the ride . . . Ooopps, no pun intended," I hissed sarcastically.

"Look, if you hadn't asked to talk to me, you still wouldn't know, so . . . why . . . why don't you just leave and pretend this conversation never happened?" I said, pushing him toward the door. "This is my body and my child. I will deal with it the way I choose."

"But it's mine, too. You need to consider both of us before you go ahead and make a decision . . ." he began.

"What, like the consideration you gave me when you put it there? I *will* handle this *my* way. Just get out, Jarrod—and keep your mouth shut. I think that's the least you can do, considering!" I whispered forcefully.

"If you keep it, you won't be able to keep it secret for long. You're already getting fat!" he spat, his hand resting on the door handle.

That stung! I couldn't believe he would say something so mean. I threw my pencil case at him. "Get out Jarrod. Just get out!"

"Fine! But if you keep it, don't expect anything from me!" he added menacingly, before slamming the door behind him.

THIRTEEN

I put my pen down from my last exam and stretched the cramp out of my back. I should have been feeling exhilarated, but Jarrod was right—I couldn't keep it a secret any longer. Most of the kids were high-fiving each other and dancing in the parking lot. But today meant I had to face another challenge. I'd reached 20 weeks. The possibility of miscarriage was a distant memory. It was time to tell my parents.

Most girls at least had their boyfriends at a time like this, but Jarrod had barely looked at me since our conversation in the library. Cathy was thrilled he'd finally agreed to take her to the formal. Katie was keeping me informed via her friend Trinny. I couldn't help wondering how Cathy felt about being second-in-line. Though I guess it didn't matter now. There was definitely no going back from this.

Kelly had agreed to be there when I told my parents. I really appreciated our friendship. I don't know where I'd have been without her. I knew how it would play out. There would be screaming, crying, yelling and insults. I thought back to Kelly's party and shook my head. What a bitter pill I had to swallow for drinking too much.

It was uncomfortable. Mum and Dad had spent hardly any time in the same room since Dad's "indiscretion" had broken. You could have sliced the tension in the air with a knife. Dad was probably only putting up with the whole family meeting thing because he would be expecting to hear

I was dux of the school or something. I looked down at the three pairs of expectant eyes. This would be the last thing they would have thought of and possibly not even then. I took a deep breath.

"Thanks for coming, everyone." *What was this? I sounded like I'd called them to a snap student council meeting.* "I wanted you all here so I only had to say this once." I paused. As soon as I said what I had to say, everything would change. I took another deep breath. Everyone leaned in a little closer. Kelly held her breath.

"Ummm, I just wanted to tell you that . . ." My throat was so dry. The room had started to spin.

"Ummm . . . I'm pregnant," I whispered.

It was out. There was another great pause as everyone before me was blown back in their seats. There was a unanimous gasp. The next part rolled through in slow motion.

I watched my mum sink into the couch in horror. Her hand flew to her mouth in shock, as Dad simultaneously leapt to his feet. I felt a sting across my right cheek and instinctively raised my hand in defence as the blood pulsated to the surface. Dad's face was purple with rage. His jugular and eyes bulged as he spun off a string of expletives that would have made a sailor blush.

"How could you have done this, Heaven? I thought you had more sense. You had such a promising future and you've just thrown it all away. Clearly there's more of your mother than me running through your veins . . ."

"How far along are you, Heaven?" my mother interrupted.

"Twenty weeks."

"Is it too late to get rid of it?" Dad asked my mother.

She just shook her head. I didn't know whether she was responding to his question or still in a daze.

"I'm not having an abortion, Dad . . ."

"When I get my hands on that Jarrod, I'll . . ." His hands clutched at empty air as he paced the floor. Mum was crying again. But that was to be expected. She wasn't really capable of anything else.

Katie came over and squeezed my arm. "I'm so sorry, Heaven. Come see me after . . . It's tough to be you right now"—and she left the room.

My dad exploded with more obscenities and Mum leapt to her feet to try to calm him down.

"If you must keep this . . . this thing, you can't stay here. We'll not be going through all this again . . . I just can't believe it . . . You—of all people. I wouldn't have expected this from you!" He stormed from the room, slamming the door behind him.

Now there were just Kelly and Mum left. With tears still in her eyes, Mum stood staring at me. I expected to see condemnation but there was only pity—and perhaps a touch of something else. She stepped forward and wrapped her arms around me and patted my back, like she'd done when I was a child.

"It will be OK, Heaven. We'll sort this out."

"I'm not killing it, Mum . . ."

"Shhhh, I know . . . I know," she cooed. "But you watch, everything will turn out OK. Everything's going to be OK."

Mum pulled me down onto her lap on the sofa and stroked my hair. It was strangely comforting. Mum and I had been at odds for so long. What was even weirder is I believed her.

Somehow I felt it would be OK . . . somehow—or maybe it was just vain hope!

* * *

Exhausted, I went to bed early after another long shower. Dad had left again. No-one knew when he'd be back. I was drifting off to sleep when Mum opened the door a crack and peeped in.

"It's OK. I'm not asleep," I yawned.

Mum tiptoed in and sat down on the bed beside me. She patted my hair again. I was almost asleep again when she spoke.

"Don't be too mad at your father, Heaven. There is more to this than just your pregnancy," she whispered.

Suddenly I was wide awake. *What did she mean? That didn't make any sense!*

"You see, it's my fault really," Mum continued. "I know you girls have wondered how we ended up together. I knew a good thing when I saw it. Your dad wasn't always as worldly wise as he is now and I wasn't always like . . . like this . . ." She laughed bitterly. "If I knew then, what I know now . . ." She paused then sighed. "But then . . . I guess . . . I wouldn't have you or Katie."

I turned to face her. I could see the intensity in her eyes, even in the half-light.

"You didn't do this on purpose, did you, Heaven?" she asked hesitantly

My voice jumped an octave in reply. "What, Mum? No . . . why would I?"

Mum patted my hand. "Shhh . . . it's OK—I just needed to ask. You see, not all of us are as honourable . . ." She paused again.

Her riddles were becoming frustrating.

"What are you talking about, Mum?"

She sighed again. "Simple, really . . . I never admitted it, but he knew—I trapped him."

"Trapped who?" My eyebrows knitted together in confusion.

"He had it all, Heaven. Money—power—prestige . . . I used to say I did it for the cause. So I could raise the awareness of the plight of our . . ." She stopped and shook her head. "But really, I just did it for me. I was tired of my life and I wanted his. I knew he'd never have married me otherwise . . ." She trailed off again.

Suddenly the confusion cleared, I gasped at what she was saying. It explained everything! "Are you telling me you . . . you trapped Dad by getting pregnant with . . . me?"

She didn't answer the question—but continued, "It's lucky, really, that you were so like him. It almost made up for the betrayal. He always said you were the only decent thing I'd ever done." She reached out and tucked a strand of hair behind my ear and looked down at my shock-frozen features.

"And he was right—you and Katie are my real masterpieces. I guess that's why I understand why you are doing what you are doing. Maybe you weren't as devious as me and your reasons . . . well, they are yours, too. But I understand why you wouldn't want to . . ." She sat in silence again.

I tried to imagine her at my age, plotting for a place in

high society. I could kind of understand it. Not that our situations resembled each other's—but I wasn't about to explain *that* situation to her. She could think what she liked.

Then she was speaking again. "We have to make this easier for your father. I've got a cousin who lives in Auckland. I could make arrangements for you to stay with her. We could have it all sorted in a week. There is no reason why we can't keep this to ourselves . . ."

"What?!" I sat bolt upright. "You'd send me to New Zealand because you don't want me to embarrass Dad?"

"Come on, Heaven. You know there is more to it than that. Do you really want to be here when the media turn up? Do you want to see fat photos of yourself plastered through the magazines and over the trashy newspapers? They'll interview your friends and people who say they are your friends.

"Yes, it will be easier for your dad if you're not here—but it will be easier for you, too! Trust me, I know. Reading damning columns about yourself is hard enough. Imagine how it feels when you know their speculations are true."

It was my turn to sigh. The wisdom of it was clear—but to be all alone in another country a long way from my friends? It seemed like a high price to pay for anonymity!

"Did you want me to come with you?" she asked. "I can . . ."

"*If* I go, you'll need to stay here," I replied. "Who knows what Dad will do—and you can't leave Katie."

She nodded and sighed sadly.

As we sat in silence, I watched the last of the pink disappear behind the house-covered hills. The first of the evening stars was winking down through my window. I stared up at the brightest one and wished with all my might that all this would just go away. But I knew it wouldn't.

Then Mum was speaking again. "I really am sorry, Heaven. I'm sure there is a good deal more to this story than you are letting on . . . "

What could I say? I didn't want to tell her the truth.

She nodded as if I'd given her confirmation.

She leaned over and kissed my forehead. "I'll see you in the morning, Heaven."

The door closed with a muffled click. The room was darkening by the minute—like my future! I had no idea what was going to happen. Except I would probably be taking a lonely trip across the Tasman.

FOURTEEN

I closed my eyes as the plane pushed back from the gate and we began taxiing toward the runway. It had been a sad goodbye. Kelly, Katie and Mum had dropped me at the airport. Kelly burst into tears, saying how she didn't know if she could go away up the coast without me. I was missing my end-of-year formal and graduation, too. All the things she and I had dreamed about since we had been in primary school. I dragged myself away from her. It was too much.

Katie just wished me all the best. Mum had promised to send me all the university offers. I didn't have the heart to point out I could find them all online, so I just nodded.

Picking up my carry-on and grabbing my passport from my back pocket, I strode through automatic doors, turning back only for a quick wave. I noted the sadness reflected in the three sets of eyes. It nearly broke my heart. Then the doors closed and I was alone.

The flight was uneventful. The airline had forgotten my vegetarian meal so I was forced to pick my way around the chicken in the chicken parmigiana. But the hostess had been so pleased to be able to present it to me and seemed almost to have convinced herself chicken wasn't really meat.

I looked out over the green rolling hills below me. I'd never been to New Zealand before. It was beautiful from above, with its moon-shaped harbours, miniature houses and patchwork fields. The plane banked back toward the airport and the tightly clustered houses that hugged the western shores of the city of Auckland. I couldn't believe I had been looking at both the west and east coast of New Zealand at the same time. If the country were any narrower, it would disappear all together.

The pilot landed the plane with a gentle thud and the engines roared as he applied the brakes. It didn't take long to get to the gate. The hostess was busy announcing for people to remain in their seats until we docked, but almost everyone ignored her and was up and unlocking the overhead lockers to retrieve their belongings. I was content to wait. After all, it wasn't like I actually wanted to be here.

* * *

Auckland had a lovely airport. All the staff were friendly and a nice young guy helped me with my bags at the carousel. Clearly, I wasn't showing as much as I thought—he offered me his phone number but I politely declined. He didn't seem bothered and we chatted until we reached customs and quarantine. Since he was a local, he managed to get through without having his bags x-rayed.

After what felt like forever, I passed through to the arrivals area. The room was a sea of faces waiting expectantly for friends and family coming home for the holidays. I had no idea how I was going to find my mother's cousin and couldn't just stand there. I had to keep moving or I'd stop the flow of human traffic. I pushed my way to the end of the metal barriers and was approaching the exit when I felt a tap on the shoulder.

"Are you Heaven?" a girl asked in a thick New Zealand

accent. I sighed with relief and turned to face my rescuer. She was only a little shorter than me, with long black hair and tanned skin. I had my jacket on because it felt cold but she was standing there in a pair of flip-flops, faded ripped shorts and a short-sleeved tee.

"Oi, Mum, Dad—it's her, ay? I told yous," she called back, waving them over.

"Thanks, what's your name?" I asked politely.

"Aroha," she replied with a wide smile.

"Ah-row-ha," I tried.

It sounded nothing like her pronunciation but she laughed good-naturedly.

"Ah, don't worry. You Aussies can never get it right, ay?" She clapped me on the shoulder.

A man and woman appeared from out of the crowd. The man had a toddler draped across his broad shoulders. The woman was obviously my mum's cousin—the family resemblance was uncanny. Her partner, by contrast, was local. He and his daughter had the same dark hair, eyes and complexion.

"Pleased to meet you, Heaven," the man said, thrusting a large hand toward me while the toddler on his shoulders twisted knots in his hair. He had gentle eyes and a kind smile. I immediately relaxed. There was something calming about him. I could see why someone would jump countries for such a man. I returned his smile.

"Welcome to New Zealand," Jill said. A slight twang of her Australian accent remained. "You've met Aroha, and this is my husband Ricky and our son, William—but everyone calls him Billy."

Ricky picked my bags off the trolley like they weighed nothing and carried them to the car. I followed behind, while Jill gave me a short commentary about Auckland that washed past me. Ricky loaded my bags into the car, while Jill wrestled Billy into his car seat. I hadn't had much to do with little kids and was relieved when Aroha jumped into the middle, leaving me the other window seat.

* * *

Our drive was much shorter than mine had been to the Sydney airport. We turned right onto Great South Road then left onto Grand Vue Drive. As we reached residential suburbs, I noticed a kid's playground and a block of shops with a burger bar called "Gold Coast Take Away", which made me smile. We continued over the motorway and past the entrance to the Botanical Gardens.

"It's really nice in there, ay? I take the dog up there most days if you wanna come?" Aroha offered.

I smiled. She was being very kind and I wondered how much she knew about my visit.

We soon turned into a short cul-de-sac—signed as a Court—containing several large houses. They pulled up to the largest and I raised my eyebrows in surprise. These people didn't look like the type to own such a house. It was time for me to stop assuming things about our Kiwi cousins.

Ricky carried my bags up to my room while Billy weaved himself around his legs. Ricky seemed unfazed by the process. Jill followed behind, showing me where the bathroom was and describing the layout as we went.

"There's a chute in the bathroom to drop your dirty laundry into and extra toilet rolls under the basin. This will be your room," she indicated.

It was a large room overlooking the dead-end street. The road below dropped away quickly and the view reached over the undulating emerald hills to the distant harbour. If there had been no other houses, it would have been breathtaking. Pictures from those New Zealand ads flashed into my mind. This place was truly picturesque!

But Jill was still talking. ". . . will that be OK?" she asked.

My cheeks began to redden. "I'm sorry, Jill. I was distracted by the view. I didn't catch what you said."

She smiled sadly and stepped over to wrap her arm around my shoulders. "I'm sorry, Heaven. You must be missing your mum. You have a hard road ahead of you. Let me know if you need anyone to talk to, OK?"

She squeezed my shoulder.

"Tomorrow, we'll go see my midwife—she's a lovely woman. She delivered Billy."

"Midwife?!" I cut in. "What about a doctor?"

"Tell you what, you come and meet Bev, then you can decide for yourself. But you need to get some plans in place. You'll be amazed how quickly the next 18 weeks will fly by."

She ruffled my hair and headed for the door. "I'll leave you to get settled in. There are hangers in the closet and the drawers are empty. Just make yourself at home. I'm ordering fish-n-chips for dinner from Bunters. Gotta introduce you Aussies to decent Kiwi fare," she said with a grin.

"Oh, ummm, I'm vegetarian . . ." I began, feeling somewhat embarrassed about laying down my dietary requirements

147

to the woman who was looking after me for the next few months. But she only smiled.

"Don't worry, your mother already filled me in. I'll order you a vegie burger," she said, with a wink. I smiled and nodded my thanks and she closed the bedroom door quietly behind her.

* * *

It didn't take long to unpack. Mum had bought me a whole pile of maternity wear before I left. She and Katie had picked out some beautiful stuff but the wide stretchy waistbands and ballooning tops were too much to face right now. I only unpacked my "skinny" clothes. The rest could wait in the bags until they became a necessity, probably pretty soon.

I put my iPod on the bedside table, then changed my mind and began scrolling through my photographs. I paused on one pic of my mum and thought about how much my opinion had changed about her in the week leading up to my departure. She seemed like a different woman to the one I'd known all my life. Maybe she'd been this all along and I'd just not seen it.

Flicking through several more photos, I lingered on the only picture of Jarrod I hadn't deleted. A stabbing pain filled my heart and I slipped sadly onto the bed. My feelings were so confusing. One minute I hated him, then the next I was missing him. Burying my face in the pillow, I allowed the loneliness to overcome me for a moment. I wished he was here right now and hadn't said those hurtful things in the library. Suddenly I felt a strange bubbling sensation in my stomach. Absently I shifted my hand to the place. *Could it be?*

There was a knock and Jill poked her head around the door.

"Dinner's here." She glanced at my hand-enclosed stomach and frowned. "Are you OK, Heaven?"

"Ummm, I think . . . I think I just felt something," I replied shyly.

The smile returned. "The first movements. It takes longer to notice the first time around. It's a lovely feeling." She looked in two minds for a moment. I wondered if she might ask to feel but she pulled me to my feet instead. "Let's feed that little sucker," she suggested.

I tentatively touched my stomach as I walked down stairs with Jill. I didn't feel quite so alone anymore.

* * *

The food was great. New Zealanders really could make better chips than us. I tried one of their "chip buddies"—hot chips wrapped in buttered bread—but didn't really like it. The burger was great and I washed it down with a can of New Zealand's own soft drink, L&P.

"That was wonderful, thank you," I announced, as I got up to take my plate to the sink.

"Oh no, you don't," Jill said, hipping me aside. "It's Aroha's night on dishes. You enjoy the visitor status while it lasts. Ricky," she called into the lounge room, "give Heaven the remote."

"No, no, it's OK. I know you never get between a guy

and his remote. I'm feeling a bit tired. I might just head upstairs and have a chat to Mum before I go to bed . . . if that's OK?"

"Oh, OK, the phone's over there if you want it," Jill began

"No, Mum, she's gonna Skype her . . . it's OK, Heaven," Aroha said, rolling her eyes. "We've got wireless upstairs."

It was my turn to grin as Jill flicked a towel at Aroha and told her to get on with the dishes. Aroha growled in mock anger and stomped into the kitchen, while little Billy dropped greasy potato pieces on the floor. The TV burst into life in the other room and Ricky eased himself into the armchair and began scrolling through the channels. The house felt happy and contented, warm and friendly. *If only our house felt like this.*

I headed for the stairs. "Thanks, Jill," I called back.

"You're welcome, dear," she said warmly. "I'll see you in the morning."

I nodded back, then went to my room.

FIFTEEN

B ev, the midwife, was a kind, motherly woman and she made me feel relaxed. She checked my measurements and confirmed my expected due date.

"Now, why don't we have a listen to the heartbeat, shall we?" she asked, as she put a glob of clear lube on my stomach. She rotated the little ultrasound tool around my stomach and it made a variety of electronic sounds, until it settled on a rhythmic flutter.

"Ahh, there's our little one." She smiled in triumph.

I listened in amazement. "Is that my baby?" I asked, a little awestruck.

She giggled. "Yes, it is, dear."

There was a little person in my stomach. I imagined him or her lying there, comfortably unaware that his or her vital organs were undergoing an assessment. My forehead crinkled in concern, "Is he—or she, whatever . . . you know, is everything OK?"

"Yes, everything sounds shipshape but we'll have more idea when you have your first scan. Usually we offer an early one at around 12 weeks but you've missed that. Let's get you organised for one next week. They will be able to tell you the gender, if you're interested," she smiled.

"Wow, thanks, Bev," I replied.

"Let's see you again in two weeks, I'm free on the 16th at 2 pm," she said, glancing over her paper diary.

"Sounds fine, Bev," Jill replied. "I'll bring her in."

She turned to me. "That will make 24 weeks—almost into the last trimester!"

Suddenly Bev looked serious. "Heaven, I know we've only just met but I'm required to discuss your options with you. I'm not asking you to make a decision right now—there is still time enough—but here are some pamphlets you might like to read," she said, patting my arm.

I slipped the pamphlets into my bag. I knew what they'd be about. Since deciding to go ahead with the pregnancy, there were only two options left. She was right. I did need to start coming to terms with what I was going to do with Bubbles—that's what I'd been calling him or her. I needed to decide if Bubbles was going to live with me, or if I was going to give my baby to someone else to raise.

I looked down. Bev was squeezing my arm.

"Until next time then, Heaven?"

I nodded and rose from the chair. I couldn't put it off much longer. I knew I had to make a decision.

* * *

"I'm going into work for a bit. Did you wanna look at the shops? I won't be long. I can pick you up outside the supermarket in about an hour," Jill said as she backed out of the Rainbow Medical Centre.

I didn't feel like dropping into Jill's work. I was sure everyone probably knew why I was here and thought it better not to have to face the inquiring looks. I noticed a McDonald's in the car park. "Can you pick me up from over there?" I pointed to the golden arches.

"Sure, see you in about an hour," she smiled.

Slamming the door of her Civic, I waved her off before heading into Manukau Mall. It was a small shopping centre by Australian standards but it seemed to have everything necessary including a really cool art shop. Mum would have loved it.

I moseyed around for a bit, then headed to get a chai from the McCafé I'd spied in the parking lot. There were still about 30 minutes before Jill would pick me up.

"Skim chai latte, thanks," I said, digging through my wallet for the right money. I hadn't really paid attention to the person serving until I looked up with the five-dollar note. My eyes fell directly on his nameplate—"Brad". I was forced to keep looking up to reach his face—not something I was used to.

"Wow, how tall are you?" I muttered.

"A little over 2 metres actually. Mum thinks her milk must have been straight growth hormone. You'd be amazed the number of times basketball teams have tried to recruit me—until they discover I'm completely unco." He grinned, offering me my change.

I flushed. "Oh, you heard that, did you . . . ? Sorry—I'm not used to looking up quite that much."

I shoved the money in my pocket and went to take a seat.

I watched the kids in the playground. That would soon be my life. At least with Jarrod's and my genes, there would be little chance of un-coordination—although the thought didn't really make me feel any better.

A few minutes later, I heard the squeak of a chair. It was Brad, sucking on a Sprite and sitting down opposite me. This did not bode well. I was in no position to date. I felt a twinge of regret. There was something pleasant about this giant guy.

"You visiting from Aussie?" he asked casually.

"Yep, my father sent me over here so I could give birth to my illegitimate child in secret—what brings you here?" I replied dryly.

I heard a rush of breath and the coughing fit begin. I glanced over. It appeared Brad had breathed in his drink. I couldn't help but smile as he bashed his great club of a hand into his chest in an attempt to clear the blockage. I would have expected him to get up and leave at that point but instead he burst into peals of laughter.

"Oh, that's brilliant—that's the best brush-off line I've ever been given. . . . So who's your daddy?" he said between laughs and coughs, "get it—who's your daddy?"

I couldn't believe it—he'd just snorted. I had just told him I was pregnant and he was snorting with laughter.

"No, I really am pregnant—22 weeks to be exact. My dad is a former senator and my 'delicate state' was a little more than he—or his public image—could take."

Brad stopped laughing immediately. "Oh, sorry . . . I just thought . . ."

"Well, you thought wrong. I've been shipped off away from my friends and family 'cause my stupid, selfish boyfriend decided to take his opportunity while I was drunk. My life is in tatters, my plans are ruined and now I'm the joke of some oversized oaf who can only get a job in McDonald's!"

I sniffed. *Oh no, I was crying! What was it with me these days? First the pharmacy lady now the Maccas boy?* I buried my face in my hands so he couldn't see me cry. To top it all,

I'd just delivered him with the truth of my sorry situation. *What was I thinking!* This was too embarrassing for words.

I felt something being thrust into my hand. I wiped my eyes with the large wad of napkins.

"S-sorry," I said looking up at him through my tears. His face was twisted in concern, frown lines etched into his forehead. Maybe I was wrong but I was sure I could see his eyes glistening.

"Wow, that really . . ."

"Stinks—yeah I know. And believe it or not, you're only the third person I've told outside my family," I added, blowing my nose.

He just sat there, his big hands opening and closing. Then he reached up and scratched the back of his head, following through with a tentative pat on my back. *Poor guy, he was trying to be comforting.* I smiled and he seemed to relax a little.

"Shouldn't you be—you know—serving?" I flicked my eyes toward the counter.

"Nah, my shift just finished . . . and I saw this hot Aussie chick and I thought I might chat her up a bit but she burst into biscuits on me." He grinned and winked.

I couldn't help laughing. Then his face turned serious.

"Hey—but really, I'm sorry. If there's anything I can do, ay?"

He suddenly sounded just like Aroha. "Do all you Kiwis finish their statements with a question at the end?" I asked, shaking my head.

"What?" He scratched his head.

"Oh, never mind," I replied with a sigh.

I saw Jill's car pull up outside.

"Well," I said as I stood up, "it was nice meeting you."

"You may have met me but . . . I never got your name." He smirked and held out his hand.

"It's Heaven." He opened his mouth to interrupt but I held up one finger. "Yes, you heard right—like the place in the sky—and whatever smart retort you've got ready to go, I've heard them all, OK?"

"Did you just finish a statement with a question, Heaven?"

I grinned. He'd got me. I heard the door squeak and glanced up just in time to see Jill walk in.

"Hi, Mrs D," Brad greeted her.

"Brad"—Jill's eyes widened in surprise—"I see you've met my cousin Heaven." She beamed.

"Guess I won't have to ask for your number after all." He winked. This guy thought he was *really* funny!

* * *

I got into the passenger seat and slammed the door. *Why did all car doors require slamming?* Jill signalled to get out of the car park and moved off just as an old patch-painted Toyota pulled out in front of us. Jill slammed on the brakes and jumped on the horn. The car full of guys completely ignored her and sped off up the road. Jill muttered something about unlicensed drivers and being wet behind the ears. As we waited for the lights to change, Jill must have felt she needed to make conversation. I already knew what it would be about.

"So . . . Brad's a nice boy?"

I wondered if she meant that as "Brad's a nice boy, keep your trashy hands off him" or "Brad's a nice boy, you'll enjoy spending time with him." I checked her gaze in the rear-vision mirror but there didn't seem to be anything in her eyes that suggested I wasn't suitable company for her young friend.

"Yeah—he seems nice. Pity about his career prospects," I said with a shrug.

"What do you mean by that?" Jill asked in a puzzled tone.

"Only that he works at Macca's, which doesn't bode well for a strong earning capacity," I replied as I looked dejectedly out the window. Grey clouds had rolled in and were now drizzling over the suburbs.

Jill suppressed a smirk. "And did you happen to mention this to him?"

"Something along those lines—only after he tried to chat me up, that is," I added quickly.

Jill snorted and jammed on the brakes to avoid crashing into the car that had stopped for the orange light. "It's only a holiday job, Heaven. He's studying . . ." She stopped.

"What? What's he studying?" I inquired. Suddenly I found myself interested in what this large boy was planning to do with his life—other than flip burgers.

"How about we leave it to him to tell you that, ay?" Jill continued to smirk, her eyes dancing on the edge of a laugh.

* * *

Saturday morning dawned bright, blue and clear. I threw back my curtains and smiled. *This was more like it!* I dug through my drawers looking for my sweats. It looked like the perfect morning to go for a run in the Botanical Gardens up off the main road. I went to the kitchen to fill my water bottle.

157

Ricky was already downstairs in the lounge. I was curious to see what someone was doing up so early on the weekend. He was sitting in his armchair and in his hand was a thick, leather-bound book. It looked well thumbed. I backed out of the room, not wanting to intrude on his meditative moment.

As I closed the door and nudged in my earphones, I'd decided these relatives must be Christians. Living with a mother like mine, you got a fair exposure to various belief systems. She'd made us go to Sunday school for a few years when we were younger. She told us it was good to be open-minded and learn about all the different religions. But in the end we stopped going.

It didn't take long to make it to the gates of the park but it was tougher going than usual. I figured it must have had something to do with the extra person I was carrying. The thought made me smile.

I powered through the car park and started heading down the bitumen walk way to the ornamental lake below. It was quite beautiful with all the deep green bushy trees. I turned right and kept going until I reached the rose gardens. The scent was amazing with an array of pink, yellow and white flowers bursting from every bush.

There was a park bench in the middle of the lane, tucked up against a large tree. I dropped onto it to appreciate the view and have a swig on my water bottle. I pulled out my earphones to listen to the morning chorus of birds—and sighed. It truly was a beautiful place. *If only I was here under better circumstances.*

Frowning down at my sweat pants, I adjusted the

waistband over my belly. It was feeling tight and was only going to get worse. Pregnancy had a way of doing that.

* * *

When I got back, I was surprised to see everyone already up. The smell of pancakes wafted from the kitchen. "Don't New Zealanders sleep in on weekends?" I asked, refilling my water bottle at the kitchen sink.

Aroha turned a perfectly round golden pancake out of the fry pan and onto a plate. "You want it? There's real maple syrup in the fridge," she offered with a grin.

I'd never been one for pancakes but suddenly the smell became overwhelmingly attractive. My mouth watered. "You know, I will . . . but I think I'd better have a shower first. Bit sweaty," I said, returning her smile.

As I showered, I wondered what was going on. There seemed to be a buzz of activity in the house, like they were in a hurry or something. I finished in the shower, dressed and bounded back down the stairs.

Ricky was still at the table, waiting for Billy, who was thumping his chubby hand on the remaining pancake on his plate, his face covered in maple syrup.

"You wanna eat that one or have you had enough?" Ricky was asking as he reached for the wet wipes on the bench.

Billy seemed very considered as he looked sadly down at the pancake. He patted his stomach then nodded. "'Nuff."

Ricky laughed and finished wet wiping his sticky son. "OK, I don't think there's enough wipes in here to get you clean. Let's go have a shower before Sabbath school."

SIXTEEN

"S abbath school? What's Sabbath school?" I asked sitting down at the table.

Ricky jumped. "Hey, I didn't see you come down. How was the run?" he asked, unclipping Billy from his high chair.

"Great, thanks. The gardens are beautiful," I replied, reaching for a pancake. "Are you guys all going out?"

"Yeah," Ricky said, carrying some plates to the sink. "Church."

"Church—but it's Saturday?" I asked, a little puzzled.

"Yeah, we go on Saturday. You can come, if you like."

I had no desire to go to church. I knew about Christians— and me an unwed mother. They'd have a big red letter "A" tattooed on my forehead before I could turn around. I didn't need that kind of Christian "love" right now. The whole "I love you but I want to kill you"-thing God had going on was rather unappealing.

"I think I'll pass," I replied.

Ricky shrugged. "OK. Well, we'll see you about 1. Have a nice morning." Then he jogged a giggling Billy up the stairs.

The pancakes were delicious. I ate four, each with a good dousing of maple syrup. Usually I would have stopped at two—but now I was eating for two. I carried my plate to the kitchen and sighed at the mess. Probably everyone was in a hurry. I started loading the dishwasher but stopped as I heard voices on the landing. Maybe I'd make myself scarce until they were gone. They had been so nice to me but I really didn't want them to ask me to come along again. I didn't want to hurt anyone's feelings.

Rushing into the lounge room, I grabbed a magazine and feigned deep interest. Moments later, Jill tucked her head around the corner.

"We're off to church now, will you be right?" she asked. "Just leave the dishes, I'll get to them when I get home. Sabbath morning's always a bit of a rush."

Sabbath? What are they—Jewish? The whole Christian theory was out the window. There were quite a few Jews in my grandparents' neighbourhood. Suddenly, I realised she was waiting on an answer.

"Oh ummm, sure . . . have a great time." I smiled widely.

She nodded and backed out of the room. "Aroha?" she hollered up the stairs. "Come on, you look beautiful—now get down here, we are going to be late!"

I heard feet running down the stairs and heels tapping on the tiles. They paused outside the lounge entrance. I held my breath, "Just go—please don't invite me!" I said under my breath.

"Bye, Heaven," she called.

"Bye, Aroha," I called back. "See you later," I added as an extra incentive for her to leave.

Ricky already had the car running in the driveway. Finally the front door slammed, the car backed out and I heaved a sigh of relief.

I glanced at my watch: 9 am. Clearly I would have to make my runs last longer on Saturdays to avoid this unpleasantness again. *But then I might not get any pancakes,* I frowned to myself. Putting the magazine back on the stack I smirked as I realised I'd been "reading" a car magazine. I'd never even driven a car let alone had any interest in one. I went to the kitchen and began loading the dishwasher. It wouldn't take long and these people had been so nice to me, it was the least I could do.

* * *

The door clicked open on the dot of 1 pm. I heard little Billy's feet racing around on the tiles. The rest of the family blew in the door with much laughter. I was in my room and quietly got up to shut the door. I didn't fancy a run-down of the morning's events. I could still hear their voices through the closed door but more than that I could feel their closeness. Our family had never been one to joke together. But these people seemed to enjoy one another's company. It made me feel sad—not because I was homesick, more because I wasn't.

"Lunchtime!" Aroha called. I'd smelled the aroma wafting up the stairs for the past half-hour. It smelled delicious. Once I was satisfied everyone had started, I tramped downstairs to join them.

"How was your morning?" Jill asked as she passed me the bread rolls.

"Great, thanks. What about yours?" I asked it without thinking, then cringed, realising what I had asked. I held my breath.

"Fine, thanks," she smiled.

I released my breath. You could never be too sure. I remembered the time Mum had opened the door to a pair of "missionaries" and they'd stayed for hours.

"We're going to '3D' this arvo if you want to come," Jill offered.

I swallowed. *What was that?*

"It's just some friends of Mum's. They always get together on Sabbath afternoon—it's short for 'Drinks, Dessert and Discussion'. It's just quicker to say 3D," Aroha added.

"Ummm, I think I might just stay home if that's OK. Still feeling a bit tired." I scooped up another mouthful of pasta to avoid saying anything else.

Jill shrugged and smiled, and I heaved an internal sigh of relief. Clearly there was no pressure, she was just being polite.

It was quite late by the time they got home. I was relieved to see them. It had been a boring afternoon. I'd Skyped Kelly but all she did was rave on about Gavin and what everyone had been up to without me. Katie was out, so I'd sent her a text or two. Things were pretty much the same as always at home. Dad was still away. I felt so disconnected and alone—apart from the baby. Now that I had noticed it move, I felt its little butterfly bubbles often. It was such a heart-warming sensation in an otherwise depressingly colourless time in my existence.

I was just coming down the stairs when I heard Ricky say, "Well, shall we close Sabbath?"

I froze. If I went in now, they might make me join in. I had no idea what "closing Sabbath" might entail. I heard someone go over to the entertainment system and put in a DVD. I crept closer so I could see around the door.

The screen filled up with a man telling a story about a time when he'd taken a walk with his son and been caught in a rainstorm. I watched as the little boy in the backpack was soaked by the rain and frightened by the noise and lightening. My hands absently crept to my stomach.

The guy explained how the little boy was like us. Each of us had to weather storms in our lives and many of us feel alone—but we are not. Like a father, God takes us in his arms, holds us close and stays with us. I thought of my father—clearly he wasn't anything like God! Anyway, the guy talking said God says he doesn't expect us to be perfect and he is close to the broken hearted. That he will be with us and show us the way home.

It was beautiful—if only it were true. The family discussed it for a few minutes, while I swallowed hard past the lump in my throat. But I shrugged it off—it was probably just the hormones again.

But if their God was truly like that . . . I pushed the thought aside and squared my shoulders. It was definitely pregnancy hormones. I waited until they had finished praying, then went in.

SEVENTEEN

I fidgeted in the waiting room. Jill had come with me but I was nervous about meeting my baby for the first time. I'd heard they had these three-dimensional scans where you could actually see the baby's face.

Finally the sonographer called my name and I followed her into the little room. She signalled for me to get up on the bed and Jill helped me up. She was a busy-looking woman. I didn't feel comfortable asking her any questions and she didn't seem like the kind who would offer anything either.

"Pull up your shirt, please" was all she said as she dumped a warm jelly-like substance on my stomach. She figure-eighted around in the clear goop until she found what she was looking for.

She pushed down harder and said, "Ahhh, here we are."

I gasped. The pressure seemed to land directly on my bladder. I feared I was going to wet myself.

"Look," Jill said pointing at the screen, "you can see him!"

"Can you tell?" I asked, squinting at the black-and-white speckles that made up the shape of the disproportional baby on the screen.

"I'm measuring the heart at present. Would you like to know the sex?" the sonographer snapped. She seemed to lean too heavily on the word *sex*. It felt like she was having a go at me, as an obviously unwed mother.

I swallowed. "No, thanks. I think I'll wait."

The woman nodded curtly.

"Are you sure you don't want to find out? This is your only chance," Jill pressed excitedly. It was clear she wanted to know. I guess I didn't really mind.

"OK, yeah, can you tell me . . . please?" I asked.

She glanced over at me again, eyebrows raised. She was certainly a minimalist with words. I nodded. She turned back to the screen.

"I can't guarantee this 100 per cent but it is most likely you are having a girl."

Jill clapped with excitement. "Great, now we can start getting things together for you."

I was vaguely aware of Jill as she began listing off all the things I would need. But all I could focus on was the screen showing my wiggly pre-baby. She seemed to stare back at me with her empty black eye sockets.

"3D?" the sonographer asked in a disappointed tone, as if already knowing the answer.

I nodded. She flicked another switch. The black dots disappeared, replaced by golden skin tones. I gasped. I could see everything. My baby girl had just reached up a minuscule fist and slipped a teeny thumb into her tiny mouth.

"Look, Jill, look. She's sucking her thumb!" I screeched. Jill clutched my hand.

"Not a bad angle, actually. I'll print it off," the sonographer added flatly.

The baby continued to wriggle and shift. It was amazing to think all this was taking place inside me. I looked down as the woman continued to move the device over my belly. She might be a grumpy old crow, but what she was showing me was . . . a miracle!

I stared at the picture as we got back into the car.

"Amazing," I kept saying, "simply amazing!"

"I've got to drop into the office. Did you want to wait at McDonald's again? I'm pretty sure Brad will be there." Jill said, turning into the shopping mall.

It would be good to talk to someone my age for a change. I'd been hermitting for too long and the thought of chatting with Brad was surprisingly appealing.

"Yeah, OK."

Jill veered left and dropped me off in the McDonald's car park.

"I'll be back in about an hour."

I nodded and waved as she drove off.

The dining area was quiet. The lunchtime rush had finished and the after-school crowd was yet to arrive. Brad looked up from cleaning the coffee machine when he heard the door squeak open. He smiled as I walked over.

"Here to kill time again?" he asked.

I shrugged.

"Another . . . skim chai latte?" he asked.

"Yeah, thanks," I replied, dropping the coins on the counter. "Good memory."

"Well, it's not every day I get accused of hitting on pregnant women," he said with a wink. I felt the beginnings of a flush. Maybe this wasn't such a good idea after all. Then I remembered the picture.

"I've got a photo of your potential step-daughter here," I said, flicking it across the counter. He handed me my drink while reaching for the photo, then walked around the counter to join me at a table.

"Wow, that's something else! And she's got your skin colouring," he added with a grin.

"Ha ha." I snatched the picture back and slipped it into my wallet.

Brad's face sobered and he shook his head. "Big responsibility, Heaven. Have you decided what you're going to do?"

His voice echoed the question I'd been putting off for some time, but now I'd heard it asked audibly for the second time I knew I needed to think about an answer.

"To be honest, Brad, I have no idea. In the beginning, I just hoped it would go away. I was going to have an abortion . . ."

I began telling Brad about the day Kelly and I had gone to the abortion clinic and finished with what happened when I told my parents. He never interrupted me once. I couldn't believe I was telling so much personal stuff to someone I barely knew.

". . . Dad couldn't understand why I couldn't just have an abortion and—to be honest with you—I don't know why either. The idea just felt suddenly . . . repulsive. There have been plenty of times since that I wished I had, but now . . ." I trailed off.

I couldn't bring myself to say it was too late. But even if it wasn't, I'd seen her face. I'd felt her move inside me. There was no way now. She was my own little miracle. Unwanted—no, unexpected, but still a very special miracle.

"What about the father?" Brad asked. "How does he fit into this?"

I'd purposely left Jarrod out of the conversation. Brad was

168

sharp. He could sense there was more to this than just an unprepared encounter. I could feel it in his voice, though he wasn't actually saying it. The door squeaked open again. A couple headed toward the McCafé counter. I sighed, saved by the bell—or in this case, the door.

I watched him chat easily with the young couple. They laughed at his jokes and took their coffees to go. He dropped back down next to me.

"You know what, Heaven? You've got a lot of stuff to consider but it sounds to me like you could use a break. A few of us are going to catch a movie tonight. I'm happy to pick you up, if you'd like to come. Some mind-numbing unreality is probably just what you need," he suggested with a grin.

I nodded. Though Jill's family had been lovely to me, it would be nice to spend some time with people my own age.

"Thanks, Brad. That would be really nice." I smiled.

"Then, Heaven," he said, thumping the table, "it's a date." He winked. "I'll pick you up about 7.30."

He rose from the table and I was still amazed at how much of him there was to stand up.

"Still hitting on the unmarried mothers?" I laughed.

"Yep, a new one everyday," he replied, heading back to the counter just as Jill arrived. At least there'd be one night off from my miserable musings.

* * *

I sat in my room until I saw the headlights glide up the driveway.

Grabbing my purse, I ran downstairs calling, "See you

later—should be home by 11," as I ran out the door. The fewer questions the better. I'd already told Jill about my "date" with Brad on the way home in the car.

It was drizzling as I dived into the front seat.

"Thanks, Brad," I said, clicking the seatbelt into place. Noticing a pair of knees between the seats, I glanced up and was shocked to see a familiar face.

"Sol . . . is that you?" I asked incredulously.

"Hey, Heaven," he beamed. "Small world!"

"What are you doing here?" I continued.

"I should ask you the same thing. Last time I saw you, we were all slumming it in Queensland!"

Life had been a lot less complicated then— at the beginning of the trip anyway!

Brad leapt in to save me. "She's over visiting Jill and Ricky for awhile. She's their cousin." I was grateful he didn't add any further details.

"I'm Jay," cut in the curly headed blonde guy sitting next to Sol, "and this is Fee," he added, pointing to the girl occupying the other window seat. She smiled and nodded. But my stomach lurched. I flicked my head around and focused on the road as we travelled past the entrance to the gardens. I shut my eyes for a moment, then tried to focus.

"You alright?" Brad asked, flicking his eyes from the road for a moment.

I took a deep breath, "Just a bit . . . carsick," I replied.

"Ahhh, the upholstery," shrieked Sol laughing.

The boys continued to chat until we pulled into the theatre car park. I didn't pay attention to what they were saying. I was too busy trying not to barf all over the dashboard. As soon as Brad's tyres rolled to a stop, I leapt out of the car and took several deep breaths.

"You sure you're alright?" Brad grinned, placing a protective hand on my shoulder. "You look a little pale," he added.

I nodded. "Just need some popcorn—and since it's our first date, you're buying?" I winked.

Out of the corner of my eye I noticed Fee's eyes narrow at my flippant comment. Clearly I was stepping onto someone else's territory. I made a mental note to make no further jokes on the matter.

"A *date*, huh?" Sol added with a waggle of his eyebrow. He slapped Brad on the left shoulder.

"Ahh, yeah . . . it's a private joke." Brad reddened.

"Like a private *date* joke?" Sol pushed as Brad's flush deepened.

I glanced around at Fee, almost feeling the knives embed in my back as the conversation continued. I needed to back out of this quickly. "So, what are we seeing Fee?" I asked, trying to change the subject.

She forced her lips into a smile. "Since it's my pick, it's gonna be . . . a chick flick." She paused for impact. The guys immediately began making gagging noises and deep groans of pain.

"Hmmm, I wonder if I can get a two-for-one deal?" I asked, rubbing my chin with feigned concern.

Three pairs of eyebrows shot up in confusion. Brad shook his head slightly as if to say, "I've not said anything!" I smiled and shrugged. They'd find out sooner or later.

"One for me"—I pulled my shirt tightly over my stomach to reveal my steadily growing bulge—"and one for bub."

I smirked but inside I was dying. I hoped it didn't show too much yet.

There was an intake of breath. Fee was the first to recover.

"Ummm, congratulations!" Her smile was genuine. It was enough to make her relax. She was obviously convinced I was no longer a threat. I glanced up at Brad with a slight tinge of regret.

"Wow, Brad—and you haven't even had a first date yet?" Sol laughed.

"Funny—ha ha—I'm laughing my head off, Simpson!" Brad said, rolling his eyes. "Now let's get inside before we have to wait for the 8.30 session to start."

* * *

The movie was fine, but I was too distracted to give it my full attention. The plot line was the same old-same old. Boy meets girl, boy falls in love with girl, boy overcomes major obstacle and snatches girl back from the arms of another and they live happily ever after. If only there was a "happily-ever-after" in the real world.

Fee managed to grab the seat on the other side of Brad. Her hand lay expectantly on the armrest for the entire movie, while Brad appeared blissfully unaware. I felt sorry for Fee, as it seemed Brad had few feelings in return.

"Let's get some food—I'm starved!" Jay urged as soon as the credits began to roll.

"You're always starving, man!" Sol replied. "Where do you put it all in the skinny body of yours?" he added, jabbing Jay in several ribs.

"Burgerfuel?" Brad asked with an arch of the eyebrow.

"Umm, I'm vegetarian," I began.

"Me, too," piped in Fee.

"And me," Brad added.

"Wow, I'm used to being the minority . . ." I began.

"Well, we're not but that's OK. Burgerfuel will provide for all our culinary requirements," Jay said, spreading his fingers sagely.

"Come on, I'll race you to the car!" Sol said, taking off.

The boys shot off and Fee and I walked together more sedately.

"Sevo?" Fee inquired with a raised eyebrow.

"Se-what?" I replied.

"You know, are you like a Seventh-day Adventist, too?"

I had no idea what she was talking about. I let my mind tick over the past few days. My cousins went to church on Saturday with Brad. Perhaps it was like a religion.

"Because you don't eat meat—like us," she continued.

"No, I'm not a Seven-day-ventist. . . . My mum's just an environmentalist—you know, 'Meat is murder' . . . ra ra!" I added a couple of punches in the air to punctuate the remark.

"I guess that's why your preg . . ." She stopped and reddened.

I could see where she was going.

"Yep, that's the one. We atheists are all for the free love, 'Nothing but mammals' thing . . ." I grinned—but deep down it hurt like crazy. I guess it could have been a fair assumption on her part.

"Oh no, that's not what I meant," she said, obviously horrified at herself.

"It's OK, Fee—truly." I smiled.

"No, it's not. I always say dumb stuff like that. It runs through my head, then just rolls out my mouth. I need to install some kind of filter system. I'm so sorry, Heaven." She seemed sincerely sorry.

"S'OK, don't worry," I replied.

We rounded the corner and the guys were already beating each other up against the car. Well, Sol and Jay were. Brad was standing by, watching and laughing. He glanced up when we arrived. His eyes darted between us and he frowned. He was perceptive. I was going to get questions about this later, I just knew it.

Brad opened the doors of the car for us and I jumped in the back seat this time.

"No, Heaven, you hop in the front. You've already gotten carsick," Fee begged.

"I'll be fine. Your turn."

* * *

The burgers were great and with three vegetarian options to choose from, it was hard to pick. The V-Twin was good and the chips—again, Kiwis know their fries!

The guys goofed around for a while, but Jay had to work early so we dropped him back first. Since everyone knew of my "delicate situation", I got the front seat without argument. As soon as Fee got out of the car and we pulled away from the kerb, it began. "OK, what happened with Fee?" he sighed. "Whatever it was, I know she wouldn't have meant it the way it sounded . . ."

"Wow, you're the guy with all the girl genes. How did you get so perceptive?" I smirked.

Brad just glanced across and raised both eyebrows waiting for me to continue. I repeated the exchange to him. He just shook his head.

"And before you say anything else, it's OK. I know she didn't mean it," I finished.

Brad just groaned and rubbed his eyes. "I'm sorry, Heaven," he said, shaking his head.

"It's just 'cause she likes you, you know." I shrugged.

"Yes, I know that," he replied quietly. "Unfortunately, it doesn't change things now, does it?"

Wow, that seemed a loaded statement. Did he mean that he knew Fee liked him but it didn't change anything or that I was pregnant and what she said didn't change anything?

"Don't say anything to her," I added as we pulled up the driveway. "I'm fine, OK?"

I hopped out of the car.

"This wasn't what I had planned for you tonight. I was hoping you'd get a break from . . ."

"No, thanks, Brad. It was a lovely evening. I really enjoyed myself—truly!"

"Coming to church on Sabbath?" he asked, absently glancing up at the front door.

"Why, Brad, are you asking me to your church?" I grinned.

"What—sorry." His eyes widened. "I wasn't trying to . . ."

I knew he'd asked it more out of habit than as a considered question.

"Ha!" I laughed throwing my head back in amusement. "Well since you asked so nicely—sure I will. You gonna pick me up or should I get a lift with the fam?"

He winced and scratched his ear. "Pick you up for Life Group at 9.30?"

"Like Sunday school, right?"

He nodded.

"Do you think we could just try the Mass first?" I asked.

"Yep . . ." he began

"OK then, see you at . . . ?" I left the question hanging.

"10.30," he replied, banging the car into reverse.

"It's a date," I called after him. I knew he heard as the window was still rolled down. I could just make out the flash of white teeth through the windscreen.

EIGHTEEN

I'd changed six times. Pregnancy clothes were so unflattering. I couldn't wear my jeans anymore, even with the button undone. My swelling belly was now encased in a huge band of elastic material. It was set on the second-tightest gather, which sadly meant my waistline still had a lot more expanding to do, if the amount of space allowed in my new "preggy pants" was any indication.

I pulled on a pretty electric-blue maternity top and slung on a jacket. Looking at my reflection in the mirror, I was glad Mum hadn't bought me all those shape-hugging tops so many pregnant women wear. I had no desire to advertise that I was multiplying.

Brad's car pulled into the driveway at 10.25. The nerves kicked in—it had been years since I'd been in a church. All I had was fuzzy recall of a man standing up the front speaking what seemed like a foreign language dressed in graduation robes. I checked my reflection in the mirror one more time with a frown. Not like it mattered how my face looked, in a few weeks I'd be the size of a houseboat less the crew.

"Hi," Brad said, smiling widely as I slid into the passenger seat. He slapped the car into reverse. The butterflies in my stomach rapidly changed formation, flooding me with nausea. Why did the action of a car in reverse have such an impact on my stomach? The rest of the time I was totally fine.

The church building didn't look much different from any of the other factories surrounding it. I'd imagined steeples and a large wooden cross over the entrance, but there was neither. Although he didn't try to rush me, Brad looked like he was in a hurry. He retrieved a guitar case from the back of the car and I followed him up the steps and into the building.

Two smiling church attendees flanked a large semi-circular table in the entrance. The table was covered in brochures and flyers I assumed were for other programs the church offered. The welcomers waved a greeting to Brad and smiled at me warmly.

"You playing today, Brad?" one of them asked, tapping a handful of brochures in his palm.

"Yep—and I'm running late. Oh, this is Heaven by the way." He indicated to me. "Heaven, this is Zack and Shelly."

I nodded.

"Nice to meet you, Heaven. Can I offer you a bulletin?" Shelly asked, thrusting a folded piece of paper into my hand with a smile.

"Ummm, thanks." I'd slowed to look around but Brad took my arm.

"Sorry to rush you, Heaven, but I'd like to find you a seat before I have to go up front."

I froze. "What—you're leaving me?"

Brad grinned as he pulled me toward the double doors that led into what I assumed would be the main auditorium.

"Just for the singing. I'll try and find Sol and Jay for you to sit with. It's OK, I won't be long and you'll be able to see me the whole time," he emphasised with a smile, as if trying to sound like he was addressing a small child. I sighed and stopped baulking.

* * *

It was a larger room than I had expected. Hundreds of chairs strung in long lines faced the large black backlit stage. Spotlights and other coloured lighting hung from a bar above the first row of chairs. There was a keyboard and drum kit behind a huge tinted Perspex shield.

Brad spotted Sol, who was furiously waving to us from a bank of seats near the front. Jay was with him and so was Fee. She smiled widely when she spotted Brad and, to her credit, the smile only faltered momentarily when her eyes fastened on me. I waved back and Brad steered me over to them.

"I've gotta go. I'll be back soon. Jay, scoot over and make some room for Heaven, would you?" Brad asked, then shot through a door at the end of the row, which obviously led to the stage.

"Hey, Heaven, welcome to church. Brad told us you were coming today," Jay said warmly.

"You been before?" Sol asked, pulling a tube of Mentos from his pocket and offering me one. I took it gratefully. The minty flavour hunted off the last of the nausea.

"Not since I was a kid. What's all this?" I indicated to the room. "It looks more like a concert venue than a church."

"Funny you should say that. It used to be—but the company went broke or something. The church was able to buy it all, lighting, sound . . . the lot. It's got speakers all through the house. The guy who set it up was a serious sound nut," Jay explained.

There wasn't time for any more questions. The band

179

walked onto the stage. Brad had two other guitarists with him. They both looked very young—and nervous.

"They're his students," Fee said leaning across Jay's knees. I looked at her blankly.

"He teaches guitar," sh explained. "They're his students. It's their first time up front." She turned to smile up at Brad with just a hint of hero worship on her face.

I didn't know any of the songs, but I stood up and sat down when everyone else did. I spent most of the music time watching Brad interact with his students. He would smile and nod encouragingly to them and he counted them in to each song. The boys made mistakes a couple of times, obvious even to me by the look of horror that crossed their faces. Their hands would immediately jump back from the strings as if they'd been hit with an electric shock. But Brad would smile and coax them back in after a couple of bars. The music ended and Brad slapped both boys on the shoulder. A voice boomed out across the PA system. A young woman had replaced the singers.

"Thank you, Damien and Joel. That was their first time leading us in worship today. Thank you for sharing your talents with us." The audience burst into applause and a smattering of enthusiastic "Amens" echoed around the auditorium.

Brad shooed Sol over and slid into the seat next to me just as the woman at the front added, "Thanks to you too, Brad, for mentoring these young fellows."

I held my breath. It felt like there was a spotlight on me. Every eye in the congregation turned in my direction. I glued my eyes on Brad and wondered if everyone was also now staring at the pregnant girl sitting next to the church hero.

After what seemed like ages, the woman at the front began speaking again. I settled back into my chair, concealing my belly with the oversized bag I'd brought with me.

"Are you done now?" I asked almost apprehensively.

"Yeah, Tracey's got one of her students playing for offering. It's their first time, too," he whispered.

* * *

I watched with interest as the program proceeded. Young men jumped up with what looked like inside-out vacuum cleaner bags to collect everyone's money. I managed to find a few coins in my bag to throw in as they passed.

Then there was an interview with a couple who had been overseas doing some kind of mission project and another couple were welcomed back from their honeymoon in Queensland. I drifted off at that point, thinking about my visit to the pharmacy. I was jerked back to the present day by a squeeze of my arm.

"This is our senior pastor," Brad pointed to the youngish man who had just stepped onto the stage.

"Senior pastor?" I queried. "I thought senior pastors were like . . . old or something."

The pastor's eyes swivelled our way. He smiled at Brad, then his eyes seemed to fasten on me.

"I told him I was bringing you today," Brad added.

The man's smile seemed to widen and he nodded slightly in my direction.

"Oh, dear God," I whispered to myself, "please help him not to say my name."

His eyes travelled on and I sighed with relief.

Suddenly I felt perplexed. *Had the pastor been going to say my name or had he only jumped over me because I'd asked his God for help?* I shook my head. Of course, it was a coincidence. I nodded and straightened my shoulders. All these Christians were just trying to confuse me.

I looked around at the people. They all seemed captivated by the young preacher with the animated hands that ducked and dived about as he spoke. He moved from side to side, addressing all the different sections of the audience. My cousins were sitting on the far side. Aroha had been waiting for me to notice them. She looked at Brad sitting beside me and forced an exaggerated wink, then waved.

* * *

The talk was interesting, as far as talks go. He spoke about grace and it being unmerited favour, like when you get a cool gift from someone even after you've trashed them on Facebook just the week before and you don't deserve it.

He told a story about a woman who's whole family had been killed in a German concentration camp. She'd managed to survive but one day she was talking at a meeting and recognised this old man in the audience. At the end, he'd come up and explained to her that he had been a soldier in one of the camps. He had witnessed and assisted in the murder of hundreds of Jewish men, women and children. She had been in that very camp. That was how she recognised him.

The soldier went on to say how riddled with guilt he was about what he had done. He knew she had been incarcerated in one of the many camps. He knew she'd suffered and lost loved ones, but he'd also just heard her talk about the importance of forgiveness. He now stood before her asking her for forgiveness, not realising the full extent of his involvement in her own family's demise.

I imagined the pain and anguish this woman, Corrie ten Boom, would have gone through as she saw the lost faces of her family reflected in this man's eyes. But then she'd prayed and her God gave her the strength to raise her hand and offer it to this undeserving man. I didn't hear any more of the sermon, I was too busy thinking about Corrie ten Boom and her act of unmerited favour. I wondered if I was capable of that kind of forgiveness—I really didn't think so.

* * *

Before I knew it everyone was standing for a last song. Brad had disappeared through the stage doors again and reappeared by the keyboard, without his students. He led the musicians in a guitar-driven acoustic version of a song that sounded vaguely familiar to me, though I couldn't quite put my finger on it. It was a beautiful song and the crowd sang it ever so gently and respectfully. Glancing around, I saw a few tears glistening in the eyes of people sitting close by. The pastor prayed while the musicians continued the song quietly in the background.

When he finished, I leaned over to Jay and asked, "That was pretty, it sounded familiar?"

"It's by Brooke Fraser," he said. "She's a Kiwi, you know?" he added.

As soon as the pastor left the stage, the hum of people's chatter began. Everyone around me seemed consumed in conversation. I watched the door intently, waiting for Brad to reappear. I didn't really want to chat to any of these people I didn't know. In fact, I wanted to get out of here right now. I thought about making a bolt for his car but worried someone might try to talk to me before I made it out. I needed Brad to hide behind.

Finally he came through the door, guitar case in hand. Fee made a beeline for him, so I followed them up the aisle and out of the auditorium. Several people made eye contact and smiled at me. I politely smiled back, then quickly looked the other way. They were just trying to be friendly, but they didn't know my condition. After all, these were all good Christian people—not like me.

Brad and Fee stopped to chat to a couple of people along the way. I chose to hide behind Brad's bulky frame. Sensing my desire for anonymity, he'd just introduce me quickly then move the conversation on. We inched toward the main exit. The pastor was chatting with people as they left.

As we drew closer, I tried to cut in between Fee and Brad but she made it impossible. I was being channelled in. Shaking hands with the pastor would be unavoidable.

"This is Heaven, Pastor Dan," Brad said, gesturing in my direction.

He had warm eyes and there was something about this man, something calm and confident . . . even safe. He offered me his hand and I took it.

"I have been looking forward to meeting you, Heaven. I'm so glad you could make it." He smiled. His handshake was warm and firm and his eyes didn't suggest anything but genuine pleasure to meet me.

"That story . . . about Corrie—ummm—ten Boom, was it true?" I blurted.

"It most certainly is. The book is in the church library, if you'd like to borrow it," he said, placing his hand lightly on my shoulder.

"It was good—your talk . . . I liked it, I mean,"

"Thanks, Heaven," he smiled. "I'm glad you enjoyed it. You have a fantastic week."

Brad guided me out the door but I stopped. The couple behind me almost crashed straight into me.

"The book—I'd like to read it if I'm allowed to borrow it." I glanced up at Brad.

"S'alright. I'm pretty sure Mrs D's got a copy at home. If not, I'll drop it round to you. Let's go now, I'm starved!" he said, taking my arm. Fee reluctantly went the other way, offering Brad one last wave goodbye. He grinned back and led me to his car.

"What did you think?" Brad asked as he opened the door for me.

"You play really well. I really liked the last song," I said as I hopped in.

"Thanks—but I more meant about the whole program, not just me," he replied modestly.

Pausing for a moment to reflect, I waited for him to get into the driver's seat. "It was . . . interesting," I said, clicking my seatbelt into place.

"Interesting, ay?" He nodded as he put the car into reverse. "Well, that's a good start."

And that was all I knew for the next five minutes as the nausea engulfed me—and we'd only just backed out of the car space. I groaned and rested my head on the dashboard. I heard Brad's rapid intake of breath, as he tried not to laugh.

* * *

Brad leapt out of the car carrying a bottle of drink and a bag of snacks.

"What are you doing?" I asked as I rummaged for my keys to the front door.

"Coming for lunch. Mrs D invited me." He grinned triumphantly.

I didn't need to keep digging. Aroha swung the door open wide. "Hi, Brad," she beamed. "Give you a game of Connect Four later?"

"No worries—prepare to lose!" he said.

"You know Mum hates it that you bring stuff," she said, rolling her eyes as he thrust the food and drink into her hands.

"Tell her it's not me—it's Mum," he grinned. He smiled a lot. Without doubt, Brad was the smiliest person I'd ever met. It was nice.

And it was a yummy lunch. Jill seemed to indulge Brad like one of her own children. She'd apparently cooked all his favourites and they joked around with one another like it was a regular occurrence.

Brad played game after game of Connect Four with Aroha, letting her win several games before she finally won a game for real. At that point, she jumped up and crowed like she'd just won an event at the Olympics.

Brad rolled around on the floor with Billy and chatted comfortably with Jill and Ricky. The only thing that seemed to be missing was a reason for him to be here. *This surely didn't have anything to do with me, did it?*

"It's time for 3D, Mum. Are we going this week?" Aroha asked after glancing at the clock in the kitchen.

"Oh, is it that time already? You coming, Brad? . . . Heaven?" Jill asked, hesitating when she arrived at my name.

Glancing across at Brad, I shrugged.

"Sure, let's go. Aroha, did you want to come with us?" Brad asked casually.

"I get the front," she crowed.

"Ahhh, you better let Heaven. She's not the best at car travel," Brad explained.

Aroha's face dropped. I felt bad but it was true. I didn't know how I'd go in the back on a longer ride.

"Yep, fat chick in the front. I'll just get my bag," I added, running up stairs—well, sort of running.

I glanced back as I rounded the banister at the top of the stairs. Jill's face was set in a sad frown. She was thinking something she wasn't saying.

"3D" turned out to be quite an event. There were about eight families, all crammed into the two living areas. I was offered several different options of hot drinks by the host.

"Do you have chai?" I asked when I realised I wasn't going to get away without having a hot drink.

"Certainly," he beamed triumphantly. "Syrup or powder?"

"Whatever Brad uses will be fine." I smiled back.

Brad's head shot up from the other side of the room at the sound of his name.

"So you like my hot drinks, hey Heaven? You think there's a career in it for me?" He winked.

I felt my face redden. Aroha shoved his shoulder. She'd been following him everywhere but he didn't seem to mind. In fact, I think he enjoyed her company.

The front door opened. A man and woman entered. Her eyes were red and he looked like he'd been crying, too. The room was suddenly quiet. Something had obviously happened. Jill ran over to the woman and threw an arm around her shoulder. She slumped into them and Jill led her up the hall.

Now was probably a good time to inspect the garden. The day had shaped up quite nicely and a walk outside in the rare sunshine would be welcome.

* * *

The grass felt lovely and soft underfoot. There was a paddock of white woolly sheep over the back fence, which dropped away to the next house. The hill kept on a downward slope until it reached a drop off and a beach in the distance below. Nowhere in New Zealand was far from the beach. Shame the weather wasn't better so it could be appreciated more. But the views were breathtaking.

"Too many people for you?" Brad inquired.

I hadn't heard him come. I jumped and the baby swished. He'd scared us both.

I shrugged. "It's nice out here and . . . that lady looked pretty upset. I don't know them and I felt . . . out of place."

Brad nodded. "Yeah, it's kinda sad really, considering . . ."

He looked down at my stomach. Instinctively, I covered it. I didn't like the fact that every day it swelled a bit more.

"Considering what?" I asked to distract him from my growing waistline.

"They've been having IVF. That was the last one they had and it didn't take. They will have to begin the process all over again now."

I shook my head. *It seemed incomprehensible that I could be pregnant from just one time and she was paying big money to get what I'd gotten from a night of drunken . . .* I let the thought trail off. We needed a change of subject. I suddenly felt guilty about not wanting my baby.

"So what's with you and my cousins? It seems odd you should all be so close . . ." I stopped when I noticed a flash of pain in Brad's eyes.

"How much do you know about your New Zealand relatives?" he asked quietly.

"Ummm, very little actually. I didn't even know we had relatives here until my mother suggested I come stay with them. Sorry, tell me to mind my own business if . . ." I began.

Brad sighed heavily, dropped down onto the grass and stared out to the ocean.

"It's because of Will," he said sadly.

"Will?" I queried.

Brad sighed again. He was quiet for a long moment before he rolled his shoulders and began a story I never expected to hear from these happy-looking people.

CHAPTER NINETEEN

Will was my best friend. We'd been friends since forever. Jill and Ricky were really young when they had him. Probably not much older than you are, actually." He eyed my bump again, then went on.

"Our mums met at the church playgroup. Will and I went through school together. We were always at each other's house. Mum knew if I wasn't home to call Jill's . . ." Brad paused for a moment and took a shuddery breath.

I waited for him to continue and made the mistake of looking up. Tears were collecting in the corners of his eyes. I felt terrible. I wished I hadn't made him start. I didn't know what to do.

Tentatively I reached across to pat his hand but he misunderstood and slipped his fingers through mine. He smiled across at me for a moment but didn't let go. In fact, he settled my hand in his lap. My hand looked completely lost in his huge ones.

My heart leapt involuntarily at his acceptance of my touch. I growled at myself. This was no time for romantic thoughts. It had to be the pregnancy hormones.

"Anyway, you get your driver's license at 15 in New Zealand. I was a few months older than Will so I got mine first. Even after we both had our full licences, our mums always felt better when I drove. Will used to be a bit heavy on the gas." Brad sighed again.

"One night, we watched a movie at a friend's house. It

wasn't even late when we left. We were almost home. This guy was coming round the corner and he was on our side of the road. I swerved to miss him. He was coming so fast . . . he . . ."

I watched a tear break from his lower lid and slide down his cheek. He stopped to compose himself wiping it with his free hand.

"He hit the passenger-side door so hard. When I came to, Will was unconscious. I called an ambulance . . . but I guess I already knew he was gone. He was so quiet, so still, . . . so, so broken."

We sat there for a long time, my hand in his. He didn't say anything more and I didn't know what to ask. I'd looked at all those Christians this morning, thinking everything was probably so perfect for them all—so simple.

"But I thought," I cleared my throat, "I thought since you believe in God that . . . you know, He'd like look after you better than the rest of us." My voice sounded different in my own head, like from a long way off.

He wiped away another tear. "God doesn't promise to make our lives any easier than anyone else's, Heaven," he said quietly.

I shrugged. "Then what's the point?"

"He just promises to be there when the tough stuff comes. And He will be, Heaven. He'll be with you—if you want Him. He was there for me and Mum and Jill. It was hard but God helped us. He showed me that . . . even though Will was gone, I could live for the both of us.

"Then God gave Jill and Ricky a surprise. They didn't think they would have any more children, so they named

191

him in Will's memory—but they call him Billy. I think it would be too hard to do it any different. I like to be with them. I love them, too, you know—and Aroha is a great kid. She still misses Will a lot.

"But the thing is, we all know one day we'll get to see him again. One day, God'll make Will again, only a better version. A perfect version. A perfect version of all of us . . ."

"So, you say He helped you guys through it—how?" I asked.

He squeezed my hand. "He was with us—we were never alone. When the pain got to be too much, I could pray and He'd give me . . . peace."

"Peace, we could all use a little peace," I whispered.

He nodded and we continued to just sit.

* * *

"Brad, Brad? Are you out there?" It was Aroha.

I pulled my hand from Brad's grasp. I didn't want her to get the wrong idea. Brad was destined for much better girls than me. But part of me was a little disappointed that he didn't put up any protest when I let go. Maybe he just needed me for support while he shared the story. That made sense.

"There you guys are!" she said when she spotted us. "Mum and Dad are leaving now. They said I had to go with them."

Brad nodded. "OK kid, I'll catch you next time."

"What about Heaven?" she pressed.

"S'OK, I'll bring her home later. There's something I want to show her."

Aroha nodded. "OK, see you later, Heaven . . . Brad."

192

She skipped away. Fortunately, she was too young to take the temperature of the situation she'd just walked into. We heard the sliding door slam and, a few minutes later, the sound of a car backing down the driveway.

"Right," said Brad, jumping to his feet. He reached down, pulled me up, led me to the sliding door and poked his head inside.

"We're off now, guys. Thanks for the drink. We'll see you later."

I let him lead me to the car. I wondered if he realised he was holding my hand again, maybe it was because he felt sad after our conversation. My head was so busy with all Brad had told me that I scarcely noticed him back down the driveway and was relieved to realise I was completely free of my usual reversing sickness.

"Where are we going?" I finally asked, as we turned out onto the Great South Road.

"To visit Will. It's been a while," he replied simply.

A big green service station was coming up on our left.

"Can you pull over here? I'd like to stop," I asked.

Guess he figured I wanted to use the ladies room—which I did—but it wasn't the main reason to stop. After I returned the toilet key, I grabbed the biggest and brightest bunch of flowers sitting in the plastic buckets by the "Gas and Go" stand. There was plenty of time to find the correct change while I waited in line. I trotted back to the car with my flowers. Brad smiled as I heaved myself back into the front seat.

"For my cousin," I indicated to the flowers.

"Thanks, Heaven. That's really nice," he whispered sincerely.

* * *

The cemetery was near the airport. Seemed strange such a quiet stillness existed in such close proximity to the hurried bustle of an airport. Hundreds of jets took off every day travelling to every part of the world. Businessmen raced to make million-dollar deals, while in the cemetery none of it mattered. All that remained were the memories held by those who visited and few of them would be reflecting on the deceased's mergers and acquisitions.

Brad took my hand again as he helped me out of the car. He didn't let it go as he led me down the silent rows of cold, grey stones. I'd been brought up to believe it was disrespectful to walk on graves. It was clear Brad had, too. We walk past each grave slowly and in silence as an additional sign of respect.

I read the names and calculated the ages of the occupant as we passed. Some had lived long full lives, but a particularly beautiful grave belonged to a young woman who'd only been in her early 20s when she'd died. Like Jill and Ricky, her parents must have been heart broken. Funny how I was starting to look at things from a parent's perspective—and my child wasn't even born yet. To lose a child must be so, so sad.

"Here he is," Brad whispered, as he dropped to his knees to pull away a few blades of grass that hadn't been caught by the recent visit from the groundskeeper.

I liked graveyards, though I couldn't remember anyone in our family ever dying. Mum used to visit her grandmother's grave from time to time. She wasn't Catholic or anything but she always used to cross herself when we arrived. I didn't know what was expected when you visited a graveyard with Christians, so I copied her gesture after arranging the flowers in Will's vase.

There was a picture of Will on the gravestone. He looked a lot like Ricky but with Jill's nose and smile. I could see a resemblance to Aroha and Billy, too. It must be hard for them to look at Billy every day. He would be a constant reminder of what they'd lost. Absently, I reached down and began caressing my bump.

Brad was completely silent throughout our visit. I watched his eyes. So many emotions ebbed and flowed there, like the ocean. I said nothing. This was his moment with his friend. I backed away and left them together and continued down the row reading the other stones.

A few stones later, I found a grave occupied by Stella and James Colquhoun. It was her name that caught my eye.

In loving memory of
Stella Marie Colquhoun
Died July 11, 1986, aged 78
Dearly loved wife of
James Douglas
Died May 10, 1993, aged 85
Loved mother and father of
Judith, Colin, Peter, Ann and Jennifer.
Asleep waiting for Jesus' call.

They'd been the same age but died seven years apart. All those years together, it must have been hard for James to visit her and look at the space on the stone waiting for him—but harder still to be without her.

"Asleep waiting for Jesus' call," I whispered aloud.

How nice it was for him to believe he'd see her again—his Stella. It was a pretty name. I looked down at my bump again and smiled. There was a little star growing inside of my belly. *A star in the Heavens,* I grinned to myself.

Brad was dusting the dirt from his knees. It was probably time to go. I waved goodbye to Stella and James, and went back to join Brad. Not wanting to disturb him, I hung back and waited. He didn't notice me immediately. He just kept staring at Will's grave, except his eyes were closed.

Finally, he opened them and turned to smile at me. "Come on, time to go," he said reaching for my hand again. I watched as his giant-sized hand engulfed my much smaller one. It was funny, I'd never held hands with anyone else but Jarrod—and Mum, of course, but she didn't count. I'd never felt so safe and comfortable holding Jarrod's hand. It was always like I couldn't fully trust him. The obvious answer to that was that I couldn't. After all, look at the state he'd left me in.

* * *

Brad opened the door for me again. It was very considerate of him. I'd been finding it more and more difficult to reach across and shut the door past the ever-increasing bulge of my mid-section.

"So that was Will," Brad smiled sadly.

"It was nice to meet him." I nodded respectfully.

Brad arched an eyebrow as he slid the car into reverse. I moaned inwardly.

Once I'd gained composure and we were travelling in a forward direction again, I added, "What I meant was, it was nice to put a face to a name. Now that I think of it, there are a few pictures of him around the house. I just didn't know who he was.

"I met some other people while you and Will were 'talking.' I was thinking about a name for the baby . . ." I continued.

"So, Heaven," he asked carefully, "you say you are thinking about a name. Does that mean you have decided what you are going to do when she is born?"

I let the words hang in the air for a while. I hadn't decided. I hadn't thought about anything beyond the abortion clinic. Even Mum had stepped up and bought my maternity wear and it was Jill who packed me off to the midwife for each appointment. I knew I was left with two options—to keep her or not to keep her.

"I don't know," I said, clutching my stomach. I felt the sobs burst from my lips as I spoke. "I just don't know."

I barely noticed Brad pull off to the side of the road. The next thing I knew was I was engulfed in his arms. They were gentle and safe. There was no judgment, only empathy and sadness for me. I cried myself out and wiped my face on his hanky. When I offered it back to him, he grimaced.

"I think you can keep it." He smiled. "Now maybe you should tell me the rest of the story. I think there is some stuff you've left out."

TWENTY

I told Brad the rest of the story, not missing a detail. He didn't interrupt me, but I felt his arm tighten across my shoulders when I explained my drunken mistake. His eyes boiled when I told him about the day in the library. He opened his mouth to speak, but stopped and nodded for me to continue.

When I finally finished, he hugged me again because the tears had returned. He stroked my hair. "I'm so sorry, Heaven. What has happened to you . . . it's so unfair. But we can work it out. It can be OK," he hushed.

I pulled back. I couldn't manipulate this sweet guy into my mess. "No," I wiped my eyes on the back of my hand, "Brad, this is not your problem—it's mine, you don't have to . . ."

"Yes, I don't have to—but you are here all by yourself and I'm not going to make you face this alone," he began.

"I'm not alone! I've got Jill and Ricky . . ."

"Yeah and that's heaps. You couldn't possibly make room for me then—is that what you are saying, ay?" Brad asked raising both eyebrows.

"Well, no—and why do you Kiwi's always end sentences with a question?" I giggled through my tears.

"We don't, do we?" He winked. We both laughed.

* * *

Twenty-five weeks. My pregnancy was now obvious to all. I didn't think I could get much larger but there were still 15 weeks to go. Brad had picked me up for church each Saturday morning—or should I say, Sabbath morning. I was feeling almost comfortable there and we were regulars at "3D."

Brad's long legs were tangled around the plastic chair legs he was perched on and he was flicking through a car magazine as I exited Bev's office.

"See you again next week, Heaven," she called after me.

Brad flipped the magazine shut and smiled. "All good?" he asked.

"Yep, she's growing like a weed." I smiled.

Tinsel mistletoe dangled above his head, an image of Brad and me together flashed into my mind. I dismissed it immediately, such a silly thought and totally impractical.

Brad loped along next to me as we left the medical centre. Christmas decorations were everywhere and, strangely, they made me homesick. Though my family lay in tatters, I'd never been apart from them at Christmas time. Katie had promised to Skype me on Christmas day—but that wasn't the same as being there.

"So what do you want to do for the rest of the morning?" Brad asked, swatting a hanging bauble out of his face as we headed for the door. "I'm not starting work until two, so we've a few hours to kill if you want."

"Good, then let's go shopping," I smiled.

"Shopping!?" His face dropped. "Maybe I'll just . . ."

"Christmas shopping," I cut in. "Surely you haven't finished all yours yet?"

"Well," he frowned scratching his collar.

"I'll take that as a no."

"How about I lend you my car?" He brightened.

"Sorry, no licence," I smiled triumphantly.

Brad was rooted to the spot. "What!? You've got no licence—but you're 17!" he squeaked. His face reddened, it had obviously been a while since his voice had jumped an octave like that.

"Well," I countered, "my mum's old and she hasn't got a licence. In fact she considers it some kind of achievement—like it's her environmental duty to be car free."

"But how do you get around?" Brad asked, regaining his composure.

"Train or bus—but usually train. My dad has a car that he uses though," I added.

"I could give you lessons," Brad offered as he opened the car door for me.

"That would be great—but can we just go buy presents for the moment?"

Brad's shoulders sagged in defeat.

* * *

We relocated the car across the road to the Manukau Shopping Centre car park. I really liked the art shop I'd seen on my first visit, so clutching my new credit card—attached to Dad's bank account—I went in. There was a particularly nice print of a painting by deSotogi. His pohutukawa trees were beautiful but I wondered why he painted the ocean green, it would look so much prettier if it were blue.

Shrugging, I asked, "So what are you going to get your family for Christmas?"

"Well, I thought I'd buy Mum a gift voucher from Farmers," he replied absently.

"That's not very inventive," I frowned as I picked up a koru paperweight. "Who else?"

"Well, that's it really—but I usually get something for Ricky and Jill."

"So what about the rest of your family?" I had a sudden sinking feeling as the words escaped my mouth. I wished I could reel them back in somehow.

"There isn't anybody else—just me and Mum. It's been that way as long as I can remember."

I waited for him to continue—but he didn't. How could I have been hanging around with Brad for more than a month and know so little about his family? It was probably because I'd been so busy bemoaning my own, I had no time to worry about anyone else's.

I settled on the deSotogi picture, despite his green water. It really was a lovely painting. The shop assistant got it down and wrapped it first in bubble wrap, then Christmas paper.

"Do you deliver overseas?" I asked, offering her my shiny credit card.

"Yes, we do. What's the address?" she replied, handing me a sheet of paper to complete the details. I swiped Dad's credit card and we left the shop.

The credit card had arrived in the mail last week. Dad had obviously gotten an attack of the guilts after what he'd said before I left. This was his way of making amends. "Sorry" never passed his lips but apology provisions readily flowed from his pockets and this was a big—a no-limits credit card! He must feel really bad.

"Let's choose something great for your mum—my shout . . . well, Dad's shout, anyway." I grinned, waving the card.

"You don't need to do that, Heaven," Brad replied.

"I know that, but my dad's sorry, so I'm gonna make sure he's very sorry!" My grin widened.

"What about your mum and sister?"

"Ah, Mum will just get some third-world family a goat or something, like she did last year. She prides herself on claiming Christmas is just a materialistic holiday, although I've never noticed her refuse the jewellery Dad buys her every year. Bet it will be a huge something this year on the account of his playing around and getting caught," I added, as we stepped into Steven's Homeware.

"How about something nice for the kitchen? Does your Mum like to cook? That's really pretty." I pointed to a large stainless steel vase on the top shelf. I could see Brad was becoming uncomfortable but couldn't work out why.

"So what will you buy your mum?" he asked steering me out of the shop again.

"I'll make her a donation to the Salvos, maybe."

"Well how about Katie then?" he pressed.

"Probably iTunes gift cards. I don't know—but what about you? You've never told me anything about your family. We always talk about my stuff—and that's not very fair. What kind of a friend does that make me, if all I do is go on about my stuff?" We were standing next to Muffin Break.

"Fancy something to eat? I'll get you a muffin," he suggested.

"After the shopping," I said heading off down the western wing. Brad's shoulder's sagged but he followed.

The muffin was great. Double chocolate filled with white and dark chocolate pieces. He bought me a chai, too, skim with no sugar. He sat nervously spinning a thick shake round and round in his hands. I'd never seen him like this. I knew I shouldn't press but just couldn't help myself.

"So tell me about your family," I said, wiping the chocolate from the corners of my mouth with a napkin.

Brad sighed. "Look, there's just me and my mum. I never knew my dad." He probably hoped that would be enough.

"So where did your dad run off to?" I assumed it would be something like my family's situation, only his dad obviously made it away.

"He didn't. He died before I was born."

I cut him off with a volley of coughs brought on by choking on my muffin. Brad got me a glass of water.

"Wow, sorry, Brad—your best friend . . . and your Dad." I coughed again.

"It's OK, truly. I don't remember him. But Christmas is not something we focus on. Usually I just have lunch with Jill and Ricky," he replied, taking his chair again.

"But what about your . . . ooooh." I hunched forward. My stomach tightened. It felt like someone had just stabbed me in both ovaries.

"You alright?" Brad leapt up in concern.

"Just Braxton Hicks, I guess," I replied, breathing through the cramps.

"Braxton whats?" he asked with an arched eyebrow.

"They're like early contractions, practice for labour—or

maybe she just shoved her foot into one of my organs." I smiled. I had to make light of this. He looked genuinely worried. "Brad, I'm fine!" I added firmly.

"Maybe I should take you home," he said, helping me out of the chair. He was handling me like I was an old woman. But I was feeling kind of tired.

I bought $100 worth of iTunes gift cards for Katie and made a donation to WSPA as I left—they helped moon bears in China. It came with a huge picture of a free bear cub and its mother wrestling happily in the mountains, in China probably. I knew Mum wouldn't be too interested in where they were, just that they were free.

I dropped into the post office on the way back to the car. At least my family was out of the way. I wanted to get something for Jill and her family, too, but there would be time for that later.

"You still running?" Brad asked as we turned on to the motorway.

"Yes," I replied, almost guiltily. It was a pretty slow jog but I didn't want to completely lose my fitness. I couldn't remember a time I'd not loved to run. But I knew stopping was inevitable. "Perhaps it's time to stop."

"You can still walk in the gardens, you know . . . everything doesn't have to move fast all the time Heaven," he added. There was a pause.

"Have you thought any more about what you're going to do? You know, after she's born," he asked.

This was the third time he'd asked me this question. I needed to think about the answer.

"I . . . I can't decide," I conceded.

TWENTY-ONE

Brad parked in the driveway and put his hand on my arm. "Look, I can't imagine how tough this must be for you—but the sooner you make your mind up, the sooner you'll be able to begin accepting your decision. No matter what you choose, there is going to be some serious downsides for you."

I nodded.

"Do you need some help—you know—to work through your options?" he asked.

"Help? You mean like a counsellor or something, like family planning?" I frowned. My mind was filled with memories of the abortion clinic—and Kelly and the lady chasing me out the front door.

"No, I was thinking more along the lines of . . . well, spiritual guidance. Our senior pastor . . ." he began.

"You mean like confession. Do you guys have confession?" I grimaced.

"No, no, just someone to talk to. You aren't a stand-alone situation, you know. There are others in our church who have faced similar situations. I know he's helped them arrive at a decision," Brad explained.

I had a vision in my head of the Christians of old taking babies away from unwed mothers.

Suddenly I felt wary. "What—is he going to manipulate me into giving away my baby?"

My eyes narrowed.

"No . . ." I could see he was becoming flustered, "No, some have but others have kept theirs . . ."

I cut him off. "I'm not talking about my stuff to some perfect man who's probably never done a thing wrong in his entire life. How could he possibly know what to tell me? He's like the next in line to Jesus, isn't he? You know, like the pope or something."

I was feeling angry, like the moon bear in the picture would be if one of those Chinese poachers came to take her cub away.

Brad shook his head, he could see he wasn't going to get anywhere with this conversation. He sighed again.

"Look, Heaven, I don't understand where you got the idea that Christians are all perfect. We're not—we're far from it. What makes the church beautiful is all the broken pieces coming together. We're like a mosaic, Heaven. All of us are broken and God takes those broken bits and forms them into a masterpiece. In supporting and loving each other, God makes us into a beautiful picture of His love."

I retreated to the door handle and closed my eyes. Maybe this was just some strange ploy to get my baby. Send in a hot guy to be nice, then make her give it away. I had to hold it together.

He held his breath. "Would you . . . would you like me to pray for you . . . now?"

Pray? To a God I don't even know if I believe in?

"No," I said, leaping out of the car faster than a pregnant girl should have been able to. "No, thank you, I wouldn't. I don't want your God telling me what to do. This is my life! My decision and my body!" I slammed the door.

Brad leapt out after me. "No, wait, Heaven. You've got it all wrong. I'm not trying to . . ."

I ran to the front door, not wanting to hear his excuses. I dropped the keys and cursed my fat stomach as I scrambled around trying to pick them up.

It was Brad who offered them to me. To be fair, there wasn't an ounce of guile in his face. He was being sincere and I didn't know why I was reacting this way. I just didn't want to feel manipulated.

"Thanks for the lift, Brad. I'll . . . I'll see you later."

I took the keys and went inside, closing the door in Brad's very confused face.

* * *

My lungs burnt as I ran through the trail of blossom trees. Of course, the blossoms were long gone now but it was still pretty. The sun filtered through the lush green leaves, dappling the path in light and shade. It would be my last run before I had to resort to a fast walk. I must've looked funny running along with my pregnant belly bouncing up and down as I moved. A fast walk would probably not be much slower than the jog I was achieving now.

My mind was flooded with regret. I had no idea why I'd spoken to Brad that way. I knew he was trying to help and I couldn't work out why I'd been so abrasive.

There was a mosaic in the children's garden in the middle of the park. I thought about what Brad had said about Christians—how they were really just people with problems like me, not the perfect specimens I imagined. Brad's background was less than perfect and Jill and Ricky's and the woman at 3D, who couldn't have a baby. All of them were suffering.

The driveway was in sight. I put on a last burst of speed, enjoying the burning it produced in my tiring muscles. I felt my stomach tighten in protest at the added speed. *Yep, it was time to give the running away for a while.* Gasping, I clutched the door handle and took a long swig from my water bottle. I could hear Jill on the phone in the kitchen.

"Look, I'm sure she didn't mean it that way, Brad."

My ears pricked up. She was talking to Brad.

"She's got a lot going on . . . no, no, you haven't blown it. Just give it a while, she'll come round . . . Don't be embarrassed, Brad. You were only trying to help. It was just too soon for her to consider. . . . Yes, I'll tell her you're sorry, but I'm sure she'll . . . OK, you get back to work, but stop worrying. . . . OK, bye, Brad, bye."

The talking ended, and the kitchen was filled with the sounds of banging pots and clattering cutlery. I opened the door, there was no point waiting for her to leave the kitchen now. Jill would be in there for the long haul now until dinner.

"Hi, Heaven, did you have a nice run?" she asked, while wiping down the chopping board.

"Yes, thanks, Jill. But I think it will be the last one. I'm feeling a bit sore." I rubbed the sides of my bulging belly.

"Why don't you go up and have a shower? Dinner won't be ready for a while yet." She smiled.

"OK, thanks, Jill," I said, reaching for the stairs.

"Ummm, Brad called while you were out," she added hesitantly.

"Oh." I pretended to be surprised.

"Yeah, ummm, he said to say he was . . . sorry—and he didn't mean to upset you. Is everything OK between the two of you? You've spent so much time together lately . . ." She let her voice trail off. She must have been torn about who to worry about most—the pregnant girl or her almost son.

"Yeah, think I'm a bit hormonal, that's all." Being hormonal seemed to explain away everything when you were pregnant.

She nodded. "OK, I'll see you at dinner."

* * *

The shower had been my refuge since all this began. With the water pouring over my head and my eyes glued shut, I could pretend most things weren't really happening. All except pregnancy, that is. As soon as I opened them, there it was, bulging out like someone had inflated a balloon under my skin. I dropped onto the shower floor.

How could everything have gone so wrong? My future was ruined. My plans to be a doctor were in tatters. I'd lost Jarrod, my family was thousand of kilometres away, I barely spoke to my best friend anymore and now I'd managed to alienate Brad as well, all because I was too freaked out by the thought of him praying for me.

Was prayer really so bad? But, no, I'd never done anything for God. I had no right to ask anything from him now.

After I dried off and dressed, I checked my emails and Facebook. There was nothing in either that interested me. I was gone and my friends had moved on. I looked at my phone on the chest of drawers. It was probably time to text Brad and apologise. But I wasn't ready for where he wanted to take me.

I flicked again to my emails. There was one from the education board informing all senior students that our results were now available online. With everything that was going on, I'd forgotten about my marks. My marks should have been what I was living for but Jarrod had derailed all of that. Sighing, I clicked on the link. While waiting for the page to load, I rummaged through my bag looking for my student number and access code. I filled in my details and took a deep breath. My hand shook as I clicked and waited for my results.

I smiled sadly. I'd done it: 98.6. It was more than enough to get into Sydney University's medical school. It was enough to get into any course I wanted. I imagined the whole thing play out before me: my first cadaver dissection, sitting my last exams, graduation, me in a white coat with my stethoscope, seeing patients.

I heard Jill's voice from downstairs. It was time for dinner. My vision faded and I sighed. It would probably never happen now.

* * *

A whole week! That's how long it took me to talk to Brad. I don't know why I waited so long. The stupid thing was when I did call him, he just kept apologising to me. He said he was going to call me several times himself, but he didn't want to risk upsetting me again.

Jill was going to do the grocery shopping so I decided to catch a lift with her. I wanted to buy Brad a Christmas present. If he was going to have Christmas with us, it was only fair I put something under the tree for him, but in reality it was probably more a "sorry" gift.

It was an All Blacks jumper, perfect actually. All Kiwi blokes liked rugby or so I assumed. This had to be a winner. The bonus was there were two members of the All Blacks in the sports store doing a signing, so I had them sign the jumper. It said "To Brad, you're a legend, bro," but I couldn't read the signatures and was far too embarrassed to show my ignorance by asking them who they were.

I headed down to the gift-wrapping table and waited in line. I could keep an eye on the exit from the supermarket from here. I still had to come up with something for Jill, maybe a day spa or something. I could certainly use one of those.

Then I gasped for breath. The woman in front turned around. She looked concerned when she realised my condition.

"Are you alright, dear?" she asked warily.

I lent on my knees for a moment until the pain passed. "It's fine—just a Braxton Hicks," I replied.

"How many weeks are you?" she pressed, slipping an arm around my waist.

"Twenty-six," I smiled.

"Excuse me," the woman called to the lady at the gift-wrapping counter. "Can this young lady go next? She's pregnant and in pain."

I flushed violet. "It's fine. I can wait . . ."

"Nonsense, dear, you're as white as a sheet . . .well, you were a moment ago. Now you look decidedly flushed. Can I get you a chair?" She didn't wait for me to reply.

"Have you got a chair up there this girl can sit on?" she called to the counter ladies. There was a scraping on the floor as one of the girls pushed a chair out for me to sit on. She waved her head toward it and kept wrapping. The woman marched me up to the seat and sat me down.

"I used to be a midwife before I retired you know," she said. "You are carrying very low for 26 weeks. I'd be watching that if I were you. Has your midwife mentioned it?"

"No," I said, falling into the seat. It did feel better to sit down.

"Heaven! Heaven—are you alright?"

I looked around to see Jill running toward me with a cartload of groceries bobbing along in front of her.

"Here, wrap this one next," said the woman pushing my All Blacks jumper in front of the next woman in the cue. I winced at the imposition but the woman just smiled and said it was OK. Then Jill arrived.

"Heaven, what's the matter?" she asked breathlessly.

"Just Braxton Hicks—but she's carrying very low for 26 weeks," the woman answered.

"Sorry, you've been so helpful and I haven't asked your name," I cut in.

"It's Stella, love." She turned back to Jill and they continued to discuss my medical state.

Another pain rolled through like a freight train but I bit my lip and covered it well. I didn't want to cause any further trouble. I caught my breath.

"Her name's Stella," I said to myself.

"What was that, love?" Stella asked, pulling herself from the conversation with Jill. They'd just moved onto dilation.

"My baby—I'm going to call her Stella . . . because my name's Heaven," I added.

Stella's eyes misted. "Why, darling, that's . . . that's beautiful. I don't think anyone's ever named their baby after me!" She wrapped her arms round me with more force than I thought a woman of her stature could muster.

I didn't have the heart to tell her I'd named my baby from a gravestone and her name being Stella was merely a coincidence. The gift wrapper dropped a beautifully boxed and ribbon-garnished gift on the table in front of me.

"That'll be $5, thanks."

I offered her a bill. She bounced her teeth on a blob of chewing gum while searching for the right change.

"Will you be right to get out to the car?" Stella asked, still concerned.

"I'll be fine, thanks so much," I said, dropping the gift into the trolley with the groceries.

* * *

"Do you think you should call Bev?" Jill asked as she loaded the groceries into the car.

"Nah, I'm fine. It was just a Braxton Hicks. I get them all the time. It was just a little stronger than usual, that's all," I replied, finally giving up on offering to help. Jill had slapped my hand away each time I reached for a bag. I lowered myself into the car seat. It was good to sit down again.

213

"Stella's right, you are carrying very low. Are you sure?" Jill asked.

"No really, I'm fine. I just need to sit down." I waved dismissively.

Jill looked guilty.

"What's wrong?" I asked.

"Well . . . I had planned to drop into the church for a bit. I'm leading the kids' Sabbath school this week and I just wanted to make sure everything was ready."

"I'll be fine. I can find a chair somewhere while you get everything sorted."

Jill looked at me again, like she wasn't sure whether to believe me or not.

"It will be fine—let's go," I said, patting her knee.

"Well, OK, I won't be long, promise."

TWENTY-TWO

The church was very quiet during the week. A few people worked in the front office but the church itself was so . . . peaceful. Jill let herself into the children's room and I wandered around in the foyer for a while. I straightened a few piles of brochures, then ambled into the empty auditorium. I dropped heavily into one of the plastic chairs near the front.

It was so still. I closed my eyes and breathed in the tranquillity. But somehow even though the room was empty, I sensed I wasn't alone. I could feel something—a calming peaceful presence. Perhaps Brad was right. Somewhere a door banged and I could hear footsteps. Now there really was someone here.

"Hello, Heaven." It was the senior pastor.

"Hi, ummm, Pastor Dan. How did you know there was someone in here?" I looked around. *Did God tell him?*

Pastor Dan pointed up at a small camera in the corner of the stage roof.

"No, only CCTV—no divine intervention." He laughed at his own joke.

"Oh . . . well, that's good then." I felt embarrassed for the second time in two hours.

"Jill's setting up in the children's room, so I had some time to kill." I shrugged, answering his unasked question.

Not waiting for an invitation, Pastor Dan sat down in the seat beside me. "So how are you, Heaven?" He had a way of asking like he actually wanted an answer other than "Fine, thanks—how are you?" He waited while I decided on a response.

"Have you been talking to Brad?" I asked warily.

"Well, actually I have—but not about anything I thought would be of that much interest to you," he replied, scratching his head as if trying to work out if Brad might have mentioned what I was referring to.

"Good." I nodded my head.

"Good?" Pastor Dan asked leaning forward on his chair. "So what is so good that Brad shouldn't share it with me?" He grinned. "I like good stories."

Stella chose that moment to kick. I saw the vibration through my shirt. It was like she was saying, "Go on tell him." I rubbed the spot where her little foot had been and sighed.

"He wants me to make a decision about what to do with Stella," I said.

Pastor Dan's eyes narrowed a little. "Is he pressing you one way or another?"

"No . . ."

"That's good then. It didn't sound like something he would do." Pastor Dan nodded.

"He's right though. I do need to decide," I added quietly.

"What do you think you want to do?" he asked. "When you think forward into the future. How do you see it working out?" He looked at me intently.

"Do you think I should give my baby up?" I asked suspiciously.

"Do you?" he replied.

My shoulders slumped. I felt the tears stinging the back of my eyes. Now I had her, I couldn't imagine my life without her—trouble was I also couldn't imagine being a single mum either.

Pastor Dan put his hand on my shoulder. I could feel his sincerity. He wasn't trying to make me decide one way or the other. Just like Brad, he was only trying to help.

"Do you think it would be alright if I prayed for you, Heaven? I know you may not be convinced it will help, but it can't hurt to try now can it?" He smiled again.

"I guess," I whispered in a small voice. It wasn't like a bolt of lightning was going to shoot out of the sky because someone who wasn't sure whether she believed in God or not was trying to pray to Him.

Pastor Dan left his hand on my shoulder and took a deep breath.

"Dear Lord, we come to you now to ask for your guidance. Heaven has a weighty decision to make, Lord. Things have not quite worked out as she planned and now she has to decide what is best for her and her little one.

"Lord, please guide Heaven as she chooses. Give her wisdom and help her make not only the best choice for her child but for herself also. Then, once her decision is made, give her the peace of Your presence, Lord—peace in the knowledge that You work all things together for good for those who love You. Amen."

"Amen," I repeated.

Pastor Dan left his hand on my shoulder a moment longer,

then opened his eyes and smiled at me. It was strange. Suddenly the peace I had felt dwelling on the outside, in this room, felt like it was now inside me, too. The weight of the decision was lighter somehow and there seemed to be almost a glimmer of hope. Hope, now that was something I hadn't felt in a long time.

* * *

Pastor Dan rose to leave.

"Pastor Dan?" I grabbed his arm.

"Yes, Heaven," he said, sitting back down.

"You know what you said in the prayer—about all things working together for good—what did you mean by that?"

I was clutching his arm, like I was trying to grasp the possibility of things being . . . good.

"Well, just that. No-one is perfect, you understand that don't you, Heaven?" he asked.

I nodded, but this man was pretty close to perfect from what I could tell.

"No-one is perfect," he repeated. "We all make mistakes, even when God is with us. The beauty of having God at the wheel of your life is when we invariably rip the wheel back and have a go and mess things up, we can say, 'God, please help!' And because He loves us, He will take the wheel again, swing our life around and get us back on course. The truly wonderful thing is that the messes we make along the way—He uses them for His glory."

I was confused. Pastor Dan could see this. He added another illustration.

"Have you ever seen the back of a tapestry?" I nodded. My mum had gone through a tapestry phase—and the back of a tapestry was always a mess. There were knotted threads, crossed-over colours and bits of hanging cotton.

"Well imagine that is what we hand to God. It is full of our mistakes . . ."

"Like getting pregnant at 17?" I suggested.

"Yes, you could say that, I guess. But there are so many other things we all do—betrayal, theft, infidelity, dishonesty and gossip."

"Gossip!? Where did that come from?" I laughed.

"Gossip is no laughing matter, Heaven. It is listed among all the sins you would consider worst. The Bible has plenty to say about the evils of a loose tongue."

I forced my giggles into a smirk. "OK, gossip—very bad. Do go on."

He nodded, "Well, God takes that tapestry and through His grace he turns our lives into something beautiful."

"Like a mosaic—all the broken pieces . . ."

"Yes, just like a mosaic," he smiled.

"So what you are saying is that it doesn't matter what I choose. If I trust in God, He will make it work out for the best?" I smiled.

"Yes, but don't be fooled into thinking it will make your path easier. That's not what He promises. But if you trust Him, then let Him give you guidance. One day you will look back on this time and realise He helped you and you did make the best decision you could make for you and your baby," he said.

"So what usually happens now? Is this when I say, 'OK,

who do I give the baby to?'" I asked, picking at the stitching of my maternity pants. I didn't want to look up.

The chair squeaked as Pastor Dan leaned back. "I'm not God—and I'm not you. You must choose."

"But what do girls usually do?" I pressed.

"Well, in most of the cases I have dealt with here"—I held my breath—"in most cases, the girls have kept them."

"Most—but not all?" I continued.

"That's right." He nodded.

"And have they all been happy with their decision—in general, I mean?" I felt Stella twist within me, like she was saying, "Give the guy a break!"

"All of them found the choice hard but I would say all were at peace with the decision they made. They all said they were confident it was the best one for them."

Pastor Dan stood up. I think he was ready for my interrogation to be over. It was over—the prayer had helped and I did feel much better.

"Thanks, Pastor Dan," I smiled.

"You're welcome, Heaven." He turned to leave, then turned back again.

"If you don't mind, I'll keep praying for you," he added.

I nodded. "I think I'd like that Pastor Dan."

He nodded in return, "That's good. God will be with you, Heaven."

"Thanks—I hope He is."

Pastor Dan left and I heard the auditorium door click behind him.

I sat there for the longest time, enjoying the absence of the strain I'd been feeling since the moment those two blue lines had turned up on the pregnancy test. As soon as I walked out into the daylight, the press of the decision would return but for now—in this place where I could actually believe God existed—I felt free.

It was a quiet ride home in the car. Things didn't quite go back the way they had before. I felt like I'd managed to souvenir a piece of God with me. It was like there was a small part of that church inside, a little bit of calm peacefulness remained. When I went to bed that night, I closed my eyes and went to the quiet place in my head and prayed. I can't remember the exact words but it was something like, "Ummm, God, if you are there and you can fix this . . . will you? Can you please help me to make this work out for Stella—and for me? Amen."

I had the best night's sleep that night—the best I'd had in ages.

* * *

I messaged Brad the following morning. I knew he'd be working. I wanted him to know I'd spoken with Pastor Dan, and I told him again how sorry I was for going off at him. My phone beeped as I clambered into the car with Jill. She glanced up at the sound.

I checked my phone—he'd said it was all fine. He was good like that.

"It's just Brad," I said, but didn't offer any additional information. She didn't need to know what had happened.

She smiled. "He's a good kid," she added sincerely.

If Brad hadn't told me what happened to her son, I

would scarcely have noticed the catch in her voice as she said those words, like he would always be connected to her grief somehow.

Silence hung in the car for the next few blocks. A quick study of her face told me she was somewhere years ago, reliving decisions she wished he'd made differently like, if only he'd stayed a bit longer or stopped for gas.

"So what's Brad studying at uni?" I asked, trying to shift Jill back from her sad musings.

"What . . . Brad? Oh, yes, hasn't he told you?" She laughed and shook her head. "That is so like him."

"And the answer is?" I asked, feeling suddenly very curious.

"Law—he's in his final year though I think they will probably ask him to do an honours year."

"Law! Honours?" I asked incredulously.

"Well, you didn't really think he was making a career at McCafé, did you?" she laughed.

"No, but . . . law? Maybe computer technology or something."

"Are you suggesting Brad's a geek?" Jill asked, shaking with amusement.

I reddened. "No, I . . . I just . . . can't see him in one of those funny wigs," I finished lamely.

"He wants to go into family law."

"Family law?" The vision of Brad surrounded by piles of cash disappeared. Knowing him, it would definitely be people-focused. In the end, it made perfect sense. But Jill was talking again.

"When Brad's father died, his dad's family didn't treat his

mum very well. When she'd finally pulled herself together enough to realise what was going on, everything was gone. I don't think they ever approved of Isabelle . . ."

"But what about Brad? He was their grandchild. Didn't they care about him?" I asked in surprise.

"They didn't know about him. No-one had been told because Isabelle and Phil had only just found out themselves. When she went to Phil's parents for help, they wouldn't believe her," Jill said sadly.

"That's terrible. How could they be so mean? Guess that explains the family law then," I frowned.

Jill pulled up outside the supermarket entrance.

"Thanks for the lift," I said heaving myself out of the car.

Jill gave me a helpful push. "I'll text you when I'm on my way back," she added as she slid the car into gear.

I waved as she pulled away from the kerb.

* * *

I didn't much feel like being back at the mall but my shopping trip had been cut short last time by the onset of those Braxton Hicks. I couldn't turn up on Christmas day with nothing for everyone else. I bought Ricky and Jill another deSotogi painting. I ordered it from the catalogue and they'd promised it would arrive in time for Christmas. The green water appealed to me after all. Like Katie, Aroha was getting iTunes gift cards and Billy was getting a "Finley the Fire Engine" DVD and a small race-car set.

It was still half an hour before Jill was due to arrive back. In the end, I gravitated back to McDonald's. Brad just happened to be outside, dumping a bag of garbage in the industrial bin. He smiled warmly when he saw me.

"Brad," I began, "I'm really sorry . . ."

"Ah, forget it," he said, enfolding me in a big hug. "I should have backed off when I realised you were feeling uncomfortable." It felt warm and safe in his arms. I shrugged off the feeling and him, as soon as was socially permissible.

"I'm just about finished. Can I give you a lift home?" he asked, leading me to a seat. "Did you want a chai? It's on me—well, McDonald's anyway."

"Yeah, sure," I accepted.

Jill sent me a text to tell me she'd been held up. I replied that Brad was dropping me home. I slid the phone back into my pocket just as Brad reappeared with his keys and jacket. He thrust a paper bag in my hand.

"What's this?" I asked as I opened it.

Inside was a copy of *The Road Code*. "It's not normal, not being able to drive," he explained, stopping to grab a couple of large fries and apple pies to go.

"Come on, we'll go to the beach and I'll quiz you on the first section."

"But it's freezing today," I frowned. I couldn't get used to the fact that it was the middle of summer, yet could be still as cold as a Sydney winter.

We sat in the car, eating fries while Brad explained the road rules to me. There were far too many of them. It made me wonder if anyone really thought about how close to a roundabout they were allowed to park or how many beers made a . . . whatever!

"I don't see why I need to know this. I'm never going

to drink again," I growled, thumping the book down on the dash.

"You have to know, it's on the test." He shrugged.

"I don't need a car in Sydney anyway. I can catch the train," I replied.

"So when are you going back?" he asked, suddenly serious.

"I . . . I don't really know," I began.

The same old question hung in the air, but he chose not to ask it. I knew he wanted to ask if I'd decided what I was going to do with Stella. Suddenly she kicked me really hard just under my left rib, like she knew we were talking about her. Then her foot trailed along my stomach.

"What was that?" Brad asked in surprise. He'd seen the ripple through my shirt.

"She was kicking. I guess she just shifted around to make herself more comfortable." I smiled and patted my stomach gently.

I don't know what made me ask, "Would you like to feel her? She's still moving."

Brad gingerly reached out his hand and I placed it on my stomach. His face was concentrating as if he were trying to hear if a train was coming before skipping over a line crossing. Typically, she'd stopped moving. She always did that when I wanted to show her off. I couldn't ignore how warm his hand was and how this connection with him would have been perfect if it were about 10 years from now and the baby was his.

"I felt it," he exclaimed. "I felt her move."

He increased the pressure slightly, hoping to feel Stella again and she obliged. Finally he removed his hand and I released the breath I'd been holding. I hoped holding my breath hadn't starved Stella of oxygen.

"That's amazing, Heaven." His face shone with excitement as he searched for the right words. "You're amazing, Heaven."

My heart flip-flopped in my chest. Everything went into slow motion as he leaned toward me. I knew what was about to happen. Three-quarters of me was screaming yes.

TWENTY-THREE

B ut the other quarter won. I opened the car door.
"Hey, lets go for a walk," I suggested, quickly hauling
my bulky frame through the opening.

I hoped he didn't notice the brush off from the wiser part
of me. The part that didn't want to trap this truly lovely,
sweet guy was now quietly satisfied, while the rest of me
was hurling abuse and curses so loud I thought Brad might
actually hear them. But I'd done the right thing, as much
as it hurt to admit it. There was a chance he just wanted to
give me a hug but better safe than sorry for his sake.

It was chilly outside but Stella kept us both warm. Growing
her was like having your own central heating system.

"So what did I buy the future expert family lawyer for
Christmas?" I asked, with a smile.

We had a fun hour or so walking on the beach. It always
was with Brad. I was convinced he hadn't noticed my duck-
ing to avoid his affection. Maybe he didn't even really know
what he'd been about to do himself.

We didn't see much of each other the following week.
He'd taken double shifts at McDonald's in the frantic lead
up to Christmas. I'd been busy at church, too, helping Jill
get the children's costumes and item ready for the Christmas
program. It had gone off without a hitch. The children had
sung "When a Child is Born" and four of the little girls had
done a ribbon routine to match. It was so cute.

I imagined watching Stella, a few years from now, do

something similar, with her wavy black hair bouncing as she moved. She would most certainly have Jarrod's coordination. I felt a stab of sadness as Jarrod's face flashed into my mind. But Brad's loud whistle echoed across the auditorium as the children finished, sweeping Jarrod's image from my mind.

* * *

Christmas itself was uneventful. It was a nice day but I felt strangely apart from everyone, like a silent observer rather than participant. I missed my family. They might be a dysfunctional bunch but they were still my family.

Mum had rung me just as Ricky was saying grace. I ducked out of the room to talk with her. It had probably taken her ages to get through.

"Happy Christmas, Mum. How's your day going?" I asked.

"Lovely. Your sister and I are helping out at the soup kitchen. We decided it just wasn't the same without you," she replied.

"How's Katie?"

"She's here, you can talk to her if you like. Katie, Katie—it's your sister on the phone. I think she's spent those vouchers already," Mum reported, laughing.

It was unusual to hear Mum so happy.

"Sounds like you are having a great time," I added.

"I've done a lot of thinking since you left. I guess the similarities in our situation have forced me to reflect on my choices—but we can talk about that when you get back with little Stella."

"Are you saying you want me to keep her, Mum? Wouldn't that look bad . . . for Dad?" I asked in surprise.

Mum was suddenly serious. "This isn't about him, Heaven, it's about Stella and you. I will help you, Heaven. You can study and I will care for Stella. I'm not doing anything important with my time. I just while it away with paintings no-one wants. I've learned a good deal raising you two. I know I can do a much better job this time if you give me the chance. Stella can have everything, Heaven—and so can you."

Mum kept talking while my mind wandered. This was it! This was what Pastor Dan had promised. Things would become clear and I would know what to do. I could keep Stella! This was the best present Mum could have ever given me and she sounded genuinely excited by the idea. She hadn't sounded this good in years.

"Heaven, Heaven? Are you still there?" my mother asked.

I pulled myself back to the present. "Oh yes, sorry, Mum—I missed some of that. What did you say?"

"I asked if you've booked to come home," she repeated.

"Ummm, no, not yet . . ."

"Well, you better allow enough time to organise Stella's birth certificate and passport. That will probably take you a month. I've already booked to come over . . ." I drifted away again.

Stella's toddler face was in my mind now. Her head was thrown back and she was giggling and laughing with abandon. Someone was swinging her round and round. Her hair was bouncing across her face and she was flicking it away with chubby hands. The image pulled out a little and I could see the man swinging her—it was Brad.

Immediately I shut the image down. It was one thing to daydream about possible futures, but I would not subject my heart to something I could never allow. Brad deserved someone much better than me and I would never entertain the idea of asking him to help raise a child that wasn't even his. I shook my head with determination.

How did the saying go? You can have anything you want, but you can't have everything you want. Expecting Brad to be part of my dream, even if he was willing, was too much to ask. I couldn't live with it if one day he regretted . . .

But I was getting too far ahead of myself. It was enough to know that Stella and I could still be together. With Mum on my side, Dad would have to back down.

The next month consisted of getting everything organised for Stella's arrival. I was nesting and there were so many things I needed before I left. I collected the forms I'd need to register Stella's birth and apply for a passport. Then I bought all the things I'd need before I took her home.

I also did one more thing that was probably a waste of time: I applied to medical school. I would need to defer to the following year, as there wouldn't be any chance of me starting by the beginning of March. Stella would have only just been born.

* * *

"Come with us for Waitangi weekend, Heaven," Sol urged.

"But look at me, Sol, I'm the size of a house. I can't come out with you!"

My feet had been lost to me for some time now. I'd completely given up on lace-ups and even gone so far as buying slip-on runners, not that I had been doing any running, more like a slow waddle. The back pain had been growing steadily worse over the past few days.

"Come on, Heaven, it will be fun," added Fee who was holding so tightly to Sol's hand they could have been permanently fused.

Apparently it had happened over Christmas. Fee had finally given up on Brad returning her interest and Sol had been waiting for the moment to strike. They both seemed pleased with themselves.

"Brad's coming," Fee added slyly, as if this would be enough to push me over the line.

"Come on, it'll be fun. Sharon and Greg are coming along to make sure we all behave ourselves," Sol pressed.

I bit my lip. I was 30 weeks and didn't feel comfortable flaunting my pregnant body in front of Sharon. She'd recently gone in to have more eggs harvested and the doctors had come up empty handed. It was looking like their dream for a family was going to have to go down an another route.

She'd explained all this with a big smile over a cup of peppermint tea at the last "3D" I'd attended. I remember trying to suck Stella in but all that did was encourage her to roll over making my stomach move like a great bowl of jelly, apparent to everyone within a mile radius.

Sharon had screeched with delight and asked to have a "feel." Stella had been very obliging but I'd felt wretched.

"Don't worry about it," Brad had said later. "She doesn't blame you."

But that didn't make me feel any better.

Brad returned from picking up our tickets. "I forgot to ask, did you want popcorn? I know you've been craving it lately." He handed me my ticket.

"No, thanks . . ."

"Heaven says she's coming to the lake,'" Fee interrupted.

Brad eyed me with surprise. "That's great, Heaven." He turned to Fee. "I'd already asked her but she kept saying no. She was worried about going into labour down there."

From where they were staying, it would be at least an hour back to the hospital in Rotorua. I didn't want to go into early labour and have Stella on the side of the road.

"Look, it's unlikely—and if you do, Heaven, I'm a third-year student nurse and just finished a rotation in the maternity ward. You won't be without medical support," Fee added.

"Just not any pain relief," Sol piped in with a laugh.

That was a worrying thought. I didn't want Stella's first sounds from outside the womb to be of her mother screaming for mercy.

Well, this probably would be my last hurrah. It would be all breastfeeding, nappies and sleep deprivation after this.

I sighed, "OK, so long as it isn't a windy drive in. I don't want to have to stop every five minutes to barf."

"Nah, it's fine. Smooth as," beamed Sol.

* * *

"Stop!" I shrieked, reaching for the door handle and covering my mouth. Brad pulled over and I lunged for the grassy verge. I had no idea where it was all coming from. This was the third time and I'd already seen my lunch and most of my breakfast. I heaved myself back into the car.

"I was only going 40—honest," Brad pleaded.

Sol and Fee looked blissfully unaware as I apologised again for the delay. Through the windscreen, all I could see over the crest was a hairpin coming up. I could only imagine how many more were buried in the trees ahead. Brad rested his hand on mine.

"Only another 20 minutes max," he soothed.

"Or perhaps 40 minutes at my pace." I forced a smile.

Brad gathered the hair hanging in my eyes and tucked it behind my ear. I just didn't have the energy to do it myself. He patted my cheek then slid the car into D and slowly edged toward the hairpin.

What school did hot guys go to that taught them how to tuck hair like that? Jarrod used to do the same thing. My reaction was the same in both cases. I'd been fighting the attraction I felt for Brad, but feared the battle was almost lost. All the while, good sense told me this would only end badly with—at best—my heart in tatters.

* * *

The lake was breathtaking, bright blue against the pale blue sky and shiny green of the skirting forest. The camping ground was old but clean and comfortable. Fee and I were sharing a cabin with Sharon and another girl, Tammy.

"I bags the top bunk," Fee called throwing her sleeping bag over my head.

"Well, I don't think me and Stella are going to fight you for it," I replied.

"Is that what you're going to call her?" Sharon asked as she finished smoothing out her sleeping bag.

I held my breath.

"That's a lovely name," she continued, "—a star from Heaven."

The tension melted away. It seemed she truly meant it.

"Can I just say before this all gets uncomfortable, Heaven, don't feel bad for me. I've left it in God's hands. I will be a mother one way or another. He has promised me that. Now if it's not by . . . the usual means, then we'll adopt. So please don't feel bad. Now," she added, "I'm a nurse, too, so if you have any pains or questions, I work on the maternity ward at National Women's Hospital . . ."

"Wow, isn't that like really difficult for you? Seeing babies born every day?" Fee asked as she fluffed her pillow on the bunk above.

"Fee," I hissed.

Sharon smiled. "No, it's OK. I love seeing babies born and the bonding that takes place between a newborn and the mother. It's beautiful—another step in the miracle of life. The bonding is so complete and touching. I hope to experience it myself one day but, if not, at least I get to be part of this wonderful miracle every day."

It was a beautiful afternoon. Once we'd finished unpacking, we went canoeing on the lake, returning just as the sun was setting. I found myself watching Greg and Sharon. They had been together 10 years and still seemed to be as in love as any young couple. They held hands and laughed at each other's jokes. He offered her his coat when it got cold. They were so different from my parents. They were the kind of parents I wished I could have had. She seemed so convinced children were coming her way. I needed to find out more. *How could she be so sure?*

* * *

By the time we'd pulled the boats ashore and got the fire going, dusk was approaching. We made vegie burgers over the barbecue, then sat around the fire to eat them. I joined Sharon and Greg.

"Hey Sharon, could I ask you a personal question?" I broached, pulling over a chair to join them.

"Sure," she responded, offering me a marshmallow on a stick. I took it. Toasted marshmallows were my favourite—next to chocolate, anyway. I poked it into a hot place among the coals and began.

"In our room before, you said God had promised you a child. How do you know that's just not you wanting it so bad you've decided that's what God intended?"

I shifted uncomfortably, now the question was out I felt like I was mocking her beliefs. The rest of the group went silent. Now, I really wished I'd kept my mouth shut. But she was very perceptive.

"It's OK, Heaven, I'd be happy to share that with you. I can even understand your scepticism." She paused to collect her thoughts then began.

"When Greg and I had been trying for about five years, I was getting really down. I remember crying out to God one night. I asked—no, begged—Him to tell me why this was happening to me. There was no obvious reason why we were infertile. I had completely baffled the doctors. Originally they had been convinced I'd conceive quickly. I felt like God was stopping it somehow . . . I was so angry.

"Well, I cried myself to sleep and that night I had a dream. I dreamed about these two dark-haired babies, one boy and one girl. I couldn't make out their faces, but I felt God whisper to me that these twin babies would be mine and, like Sarah and Isaac in the Bible, we just needed to be patient.

"When I woke up, I was so excited. I was convinced I'd be pregnant in the next round of IVF. But it hasn't worked out that way. I still believe my twins are coming. It's not like He said I'd have them myself, He just said they would be mine. We applied for international adoption three years ago, but it can take a long time, too. Now we just have to keep waiting and keep trusting that He will provide." She smiled.

I looked at my marshmallow, now a blackened lump on the end of my stick. I'd been deeply touched by Sharon's conviction and her acceptance of what she couldn't change. I wished I'd had God on my side when I'd first found out about my pregnancy. I don't think I would have felt as alone.

Since the day Pastor Dan had prayed for me, I'd felt like something peaceful, Someone wise, was with me all the time—and I guessed it was God. When I felt overwhelmed, like I so often did, I felt Him whisper to me, "I am with you, you will be safe, you are not alone." Like the guy on the DVD whispered to his son when they were in the storm.

Stella chose that moment to kick me hard in the back. My whole belly shuddered. It took my breath away. Suddenly, there were spots before my eyes.

"Heaven, are you alright? You've gone all pale."

I opened my eyes and Brad was on his knees in front of me. Sharon leapt to my side.

"I think maybe you should lie down. Brad, why don't you help her back to the cabin. I'll make her a warm cup of chamomile tea and bring it up in a minute. That should help settle her and the baby."

I nodded and Brad helped me to my feet, slipping his arm around my waist.

"Come on, Heaven. It's been a long day with all the vomiting now, hasn't it?" he encouraged me.

* * *

It was cold away from the fire. Even with my baby incubator on board, I was shivering by the time I got back to the cabin.

"Did you bring a hot-water bottle?" Brad asked.

"I wasn't going to, but Jill made me throw it in *just in case*," I said with a weak smile.

"Here, I'll fill it for you while you get changed." He took the bottle and was gone.

I brushed my teeth and got into my pyjamas. On the toilet, I noticed an unusual substance in my underwear. I dismissed it as I'd had occasional spotting throughout the pregnancy. The midwife had said it was normal. Besides, my due date was still 10 weeks off. I was feeling a bit crampy in the lower abdomen, probably from all the vomiting. I just needed to lie down.

I climbed into bed and Brad brought back the hot-water bottle. He'd wrapped it in a towel.

"I made it a bit too hot, so Sharon told me to wrap it. We don't want to scald Stella now, do we?"

I curled onto my side and tucked the bottle under my stomach. It immediately felt much better and I sighed and closed my eyes. I was already drifting off when I felt Brad brush my hair back across my forehead. "Good night, Heaven," he whispered.

I heard the door click open.

"I've brought up the tea," Sharon whispered.

"I think she's already asleep," Brad whispered in reply.

"She's a lovely girl, Brad . . ." Sharon began but Brad cut her off.

"It's OK, Sharon, it's not like that—well, not for her anyway." He sounded sad.

"Come on. She'll feel much better in the morning. Let's go—and, Brad, if you're interested in her, I wasn't suggesting it was a mistake. Just, it would be best if you left it until after the baby is born."

The door squeaked open.

"She has so much going on . . ."

And the door closed and I went to sleep.

TWENTY-FOUR

It was a bizarre dream. I was in labour. Stella was on her way but our delivery suite was full of people. Not really how I would have planned it! My mum and dad were there and so was Dad's entire family. Appallingly, Brad and Jarrod were on either side of me, encouraging me to push but neither of them seemed bothered by the other. Sharon and Fee were both dressed in scrubs at the end of the bed supporting my legs. Not pleasant but the pain was too intense for me to care . . . much!

"I can see her head," Fee exclaimed in excitement, but I still couldn't see the doctor who was delivering Stella.

"She's here, Heaven. Our baby is here. Oh, she's so beautiful," Sharon cried.

"Our baby? What do you mean 'our baby'?" I gasped.

The doctor held Stella up for me to see. Though still covered in blood, she was beautiful and perfect. But instead of handing my baby to me, the doctor passed my Stella to Sharon. Suddenly Greg was with her and they were looking at Stella with such love it took my breath away.

"But she's mine!" I sobbed.

"And she always will be." The voice of the doctor was so familiar but I couldn't place it.

Suddenly a shaky old home movie began rolling on the ceiling of the delivery suite. It was of Dad pushing me on the swing in the backyard when I was a little girl.

"You can have anything you want, Heaven," he said,

pushing me again, "just not everything you want."

I was giggling as the swing flew higher and higher. He used to say that all the time.

"But she's mine!" I screamed as Sharon and Greg turned to leave the delivery room.

"Thank you, Heaven," Sharon was saying, "thank you, so much." Then they were gone and the doors closed behind them. But strangely the umbilical cord hadn't been cut. Somehow we were still connected.

"Stella!" I sobbed.

The doctor took my hand and spoke gently. It was such a familiar voice. "Stella will always be a part of us."

I looked up and was stunned to see that she was me!

"We are her mother," she smiled.

She was me, only older. There were wisps of grey and a few soft wrinkles but the eyes were unmistakable.

I grasped the doctor's arm. "Are we happy? Did we do the right thing?" I had to know.

Suddenly the room was full of light. I blinked and shaded my eyes. I could just make out the shape of someone but it was more the feeling, a completeness, a warmth. I closed my eyes and let it envelope me.

When I opened them again, Brad was standing next to me, holding my hand. He was smiling—everyone was.

"All things work together for good," he began.

But his voice was drowned out by another. "The choice is still yours, Heaven," I heard the voice say.

Suddenly Sharon and Greg were back in the room, offering Stella to me. The older doctor me was standing next to them but she was fading. Then the whole room was fading.

* * *

I woke with a gasp. It was early morning. The birds were singing their morning chorus with abandon.

"That was disturbing," I thought, rubbing my eyes.

I slid out of bed, slipped into the clothes I'd dumped on the bed the night before and stepped into the morning. Mist curled off the lake and hung from the trees. Hardly anyone was up but I caught sight of Brad down by the water's edge. He had a tackle box and a long fishing pole. If I was going to talk to him, I needed to hurry.

"Brad," I called, waddling toward him.

He turned. "Heaven, what are you doing up?" But he was smiling as always.

"Could we talk?" I asked.

"Sure," he said, leading me over to the stumps by the fire. "Are you cold?" he asked, offering me his coat. He draped it over my shoulders as I sat down.

"I just had the strangest dream . . ." I began.

"It must have been those marshmallows you ate before you went to bed," he said, dismissing it with a wave of his hand.

"Usually I would agree with you. But . . . maybe I'll just tell you what happened."

And I began relaying my dream to him.

He didn't interrupt once, even though it even sounded weird to me and I'd been the one to dream it. He sat silently for some time after I finished.

"So what do you think it means, Heaven?" he finally asked.

"Well, I think it means I have to choose—either I'm a doctor or a mum," I suggested.

"Is that what you really think? There are plenty of women out there who are both doctors and mums," he interjected. He paused for a moment to grab a stick off the woodpile. "'Cause I think that might be a bit simplistic, that's all."

"You think I'm wrong?" I asked, creasing my forehead.

"Look, if you've retold it correctly—and I think a dream like this is really just your subconscious working through decisions you are trying to make during waking hours—" He arched an eyebrow and I nodded for him to continue.

"Well, I think it's saying you will always be Stella's mum, no matter what. The whole weird thing with the umbilical cord . . ." He threw a piece of kindling on the fire. "It seems more like you either choose to raise Stella or become a doctor."

I was getting angry. "But why would God make me choose between the two?" I growled.

"I don't think He is," Brad countered. "This is your subconscious, remember?" Up went his eyebrow again.

I took a deep breath and calmed a little.

"Look, let's stop and think about your personality type for a moment. I've known you for only a few months but it seems to me you are an all-in or all-out type of person. You want to achieve the best results at whatever you choose, would that be right?" Brad asked.

I nodded.

He went on. "Do you think perhaps if you were to choose to raise Stella you would throw yourself into being the best parent you could be, finding it too hard to split yourself between studying and Stella? That you might possibly think, 'I'll do medicine later'?"

"But plenty of people do that . . ." I began.

Brad struck a match and placed it in the newspaper. "Yes—but the question is," he asked as he huffed out the flame, "will you?"

"Look, Heaven," he said, getting to his feet, "no-one ever said this was prophetic. In the end, the choice is yours. You had a hard day. Sharon and Greg are here and they are nice people. It's obviously entered your mind at some stage that you should or could give Stella to them. But in the end, the only part of the dream you should really pay attention to is: 'All things do work together for good for those who love God.' If you choose to keep Stella, God will bless you; but if you choose to give her to someone else to raise, He'll bless you, too."

"So you really don't think this dream was a vision from . . . God?" I asked weakly.

Brad shrugged. "Do you?"

I shrugged in reply. I really didn't know.

He grasped my shoulders and dipped down to my eye level. "The question remains the same—what are *you* going to do?"

I looked into his earnest eyes. He wasn't trying to pressure me either way. He just wanted me to stop torturing myself and choose. Suddenly the tension of the moment changed. Brad reached up and stroked my face gently, his eyes softened.

"I wish . . ." he whispered.

But I never found out what he wished.

The front door to our cabin crashed open and Fee stepped through. "Hi, guys!" she called. "Beautiful morning, isn't it?"

I looked up. The mist was gone.

* * *

The pains started mid-morning. I dismissed them as more Braxton Hicks but, while we were preparing lunch, Sharon began watching me intently. I paused and closed my eyes and waited for the latest one to pass.

"That's 30 minutes apart, Heaven." I looked up. Sharon was looking at her watch. Everyone froze.

I laughed. "It's just Braxton Hicks. I'm fine . . ."

"No, I've been watching you now for two hours. They are steady, lasting at least one minute and coming at 30-minute intervals. Now they might stop, but I think it would be best if someone took you home. It's likely you're in labour."

"Labour? I can't be. I'm not due and I've not even packed my bag yet . . ." I began.

"All the same, I think you should go pack. Better still, you sit down and I'll pack for you." She turned and marched up to the cabin.

Brad got to his feet.

"And where are you going?" I shot in his direction.

He looked a little bewildered. "To pack, of course. I'm taking you home."

"Oh, I knew I'd go into false labour and ruin everyone's holiday." I pounded my feet on the concrete slab. Stella replied with an elbow jab to my right ovary. I winced.

"See, we're going. If Sharon thinks we should go, we are going!" He left in the direction of his cabin. *Yep, I was wrecking everything!*

About half an hour later, we waved goodbye to the others and were off through the winding hills back to Auckland.

244

Two hours later, the contractions stopped.

"How long ago was the last one?" Brad asked tensely, watching the road to avoid potholes.

"45 minutes ago. See, I told you they would stop. Stella moved and it just . . ."

"Better safe than delivering Stella in the bush," Brad cut in.

He had a point. I wanted drugs—and lots of them. I'd even toyed with the idea of having a "Caesar" but then Bev wouldn't be there and I loved my midwife.

"We could go back," I suggested.

"If it's OK with you, I think I'd rather have you closer to a hospital," he replied, flicking his eyes away from the road long enough to let them linger with concern on my stomach. "I'd hate for something bad to happen to Stella. I shouldn't have suggested you come—it was selfish."

Selfish? What did he mean by that? Suddenly he seemed to be concentrating very hard on the road ahead. We didn't talk for a while, but I was wrapped up with the thrill of him wanting me around. I was being juvenile and probably just hurting myself imagining us together but I couldn't help myself. The more time I spent with Brad, the more time I wanted to spend with him. He made my relationship with Jarrod seem so superficial.

With Jarrod it had all been about looks, status and attention. I was good for his image. With Brad, something deeper existed. Like it wasn't all just about what he wanted and needed. Like he truly cared about my needs and what made me happy. I could never imagine Brad ever trying to make me do something I didn't want to do.

But I had to stop thinking like this, it was non-productive.

I could never let Brad get messed up with me and if I kept thinking about him, eventually I would have to come to terms with the fact that I was—I gulped—*falling in love with him. There, I'd admitted it, stupid idiot that I was. Why did I have to go and do that?*

Facing my feelings was only going to make it worse. I bit my lip and felt the tears burn behind my eyes. I couldn't let them fall. *What would I say? "Brad, I love you. Can I please trap you in a relationship with me and a child who doesn't even belong to you"? That would make me the worst type of person.* No, Brad deserved so much better.

* * *

"You're quiet. Are you OK?" Brad asked with concern.

I pushed the teary feeling down. "Yeah, I'm fine—just maybe a little tired. Being this big is not really helping the whole sleep thing." I forced a smile.

"Why don't you try to sleep a little?" He glanced across and patted my arm.

My body pulsed with electricity. *Oh dear, in the past when he touched me, it hadn't felt this strong. Facing up to my feelings for Brad was obviously affecting me worse than I thought.* I tried to come up with a list of things I didn't like about Brad but nothing substantial came to mind. That wasn't helpful!

"So Brad, what would you say was your worst character flaw?" I asked so suddenly he jumped.

"I thought you were asleep? Ummm, I don't know. There are lots . . ." He shrugged.

"Name one," I challenged, leaning forward hopefully.

"Ummm," he scratched his head. "I'm often late . . ."

"I've never seen you arrive late for anything!" I said defensively.

"That could have something to do with the fact that time-challenged people usually aren't late for things they are looking forward to," he explained.

I felt myself redden. *OK, that didn't help.*

"I'm bad at math," he offered, "I only just passed . . ."

"Good enough to get into law school? That's hardly failing!" I interjected.

"I killed my best friend," he whispered.

The pain was clearly always only just below the surface.

"It was an accident and it was the other guy's fault, not yours," I began.

But he just shrugged again. "That's not how I see it," he replied. "I should have . . ."

"Should have what? Should have control of every car on the road? Should make sure every bar is closed before you go driving with your friends?"

"Should have made sure you were near a hospital? What if Stella had come? What if she'd died?" His voice was filled with anguish. I didn't know what to say.

* * *

"Brad . . . have, you know, have you like . . . have you prayed about what happened that night?" *Eeesh, what was I now? Some kind of preacher, pastor-type person?* I didn't even really know God and here I was suggesting prayer?

"Of course, I pray. I pray for Jill and Ricky every day. I pray I can be the kind of brother to Aroha that Will would have been. I pray other young people will never have to . . ."

Suddenly an epiphany, "But Brad, do you pray for God to help you forgive yourself?"

He looked shocked. So shocked he pulled over. I let my words sink in for a moment before adding.

"I don't know much about this God business . . . but it seems, from what I've heard of Him, that He probably forgave you already—am I right?" Brad nodded blankly. He was still shocked by what I'd said.

"And I know Jill and Ricky never blamed you. They know it wasn't your fault." He didn't move.

"Well, to me . . . it looks like the only person yet to forgive you . . . is you!" I said, reaching over to squeeze his arm.

I could see he was hurting and I wanted to ease his pain, but each time I touched him, it was only going to make separating from him later more difficult. But I could see I'd hit the nail right on the head. Brad was consumed with guilt.

"Look, Brad, ummm, I know I have no right to suggest this. And I don't know how to do this properly. But it really helped when Pastor Dan . . . Could I—could I . . . pray for you?"

I bit my lip. The words were out and I had no idea where they'd come from.

Brad's face broke into a hopeful smile. "Would you?" he asked, taking my hands in his.

He closed his eyes and bowed his head. I closed my eyes and hoped God would give me the right words to say to make Brad feel better because I had nothing. I felt Brad's forehead come to rest on mine. I took a deep breath.

TWENTY-FIVE

U mmm, God, ummm, thanks for hearing me. I'm glad You listen to us when we talk to You. You know my friend Brad. He's hurting. He can't forgive himself for the accident. Could You please give him some of that peace You gave me? Could You please show him that Will's death wasn't his fault and help him forgive himself? Guilt is such a crippling emotion. I've watched it cripple my family for years and Brad's is so unwarranted. And he has been such a great friend to me. I wish . . . I wish . . . him the best. Ummm, thanks God. Amen."

I couldn't stop him then. He wrapped his arms around my neck and hugged me for a long time. It hurt to be this close to him—but he needed me. I could feel his shoulders shaking with sobs, until they finally subsided.

He pulled away from me a little. His eyes were wet with tears. Our faces were so close together that I could hardly breathe.

"Thanks, Heaven. I can't believe you just did that for me. For some reason, I could never bring myself to pray that prayer. I lived through the accident and felt guilt was a small price to pay for being alive. But it was wearing me down. God did it—He lifted it from me. Thank you so much!" And he wrapped himself around me again.

"I'm so lucky to have you . . . for a friend."

I was dumbfounded. *He was lucky to have me? Now there was a strange thought!*

"Ummm, I don't think it is quite that way round," I offered, with a look of surprise.

He reached up, touched my cheek gently and whispered, "You sell yourself too short, Heaven—way too short."

This had to stop. I had spots before my eyes. I needed more regular oxygen and I couldn't take it in with him so close to me. I knew in these few minutes I'd done irreparable damage to myself. But it would be worth the pain if it helped him.

"Ummm, do you think we could . . . you know, drive? I'd like to find a town. I need to use the facilities, if you know what I mean," I smiled shyly.

Brad leapt back to the business of driving. "Sure, 10 minutes—tops."

He smiled back at me. And we were off again.

* * *

Having stopped at Matamata for burgers and kumara chips—a tasty local delicacy—it was late when we arrived home. I was so tired I scarcely noticed the rental car in the driveway. The Braxton Hicks were back, but I hadn't mentioned them to Brad. He'd only have been worried again.

It wasn't until I got inside that I realised who was there. I froze in stunned silence as the familiar voice drifted in from the lounge room.

TWENTY-SIX

Brad let the door bang behind him as he followed a few moments later with my bags. He just about knocked me flying with the door when he opened it.

"Heaven," he laughed, "what are you still doing hiding behind the door?"

"Heaven! Heaven? Honey, is that you?"

It was my mother's voice. I barely had a moment to breathe before she hurtled around the corner and engulfed me in an unexpected and intense hug. I was left lost for words. This display of affection was not the kind of thing our family usually did.

My mother cooed supportive words and "I've missed you" repeatedly in my ear, while I stood straight-backed, awaiting the arrival of the second voice.

Jarrod stepped round the corner moments later. He stood silently watching my mother's outburst. Our eyes met over her bobbing, blubbering head. I was surprised by my reaction actually. I'd been expecting some kind of heart response when he came into view but there was nothing. My mind had flicked momentarily to "I can't believe they are going to see me fat like this!"—but that was it.

I went into self-analysis mode, trying to evaluate what had changed. But all-too-soon Mum had let go of me in search of the hanky she kept in the purse she'd bought at Fashion 360. She didn't believe in tissues—they were bad for the environment.

I shifted my hands subconsciously to protect Stella. The last time I had seen Jarrod, he had wanted her dead. Stella seemed to sense my distrust. I felt her slither downward, kicking as she went.

"Hello, Heaven," he said, using his handsome crooked smile that had always melted me from any mood in the past. However, my time in New Zealand had somehow inoculated me against him. I felt like there was some kind of protective shield between us. Like he couldn't hurt me any more. Could it have been . . . God?

"Jarrod." I said his name in an even tone.

I felt Brad's arm stiffen next to me. He was still holding the suitcase. I looked down at his white knuckles gripping the bag handle and wondered how it could possibly withstand that kind of pressure.

Jarrod was nothing, if not perceptive. I could see him sizing up Brad and calculating the potential risks involved with getting closer to me. Jarrod took a step forward, at which point my bag slapped loudly on the tiles.

I'd barely noticed the silence around us but no-one had spoken. They were all holding their breath, waiting. Jarrod's eyes narrowed as they flicked toward Brad. He wouldn't enjoy the distance they had to travel upward in order to make eye contact.

"Heaven, could we talk please?" Jarrod asked, without taking his eyes off Brad.

"He wants to apologise, Heaven," my mother cut in as she dabbed her eyes. "He's missed you terribly. Your father's gotten him a job—it's a good one. He'll be able to support you."

Mum stopped speaking as I shot a silencing look in her direction. Her expression of triumph evaporated into confusion. I could see what she'd done in an instant. Jarrod was here to propose. To make us into a happy family, a family just like mine. Destined to repeat the same mistakes, leading us in the same deadly cycle of dissatisfaction. We wouldn't be passing that legacy onto Stella. I caressed my stomach gently. No, she would have something so much better!

"Heaven?" Jarrod risked another step, like he was approaching a savage leopard rather than an oversized teenager with a precarious centre of gravity.

"Can we have some privacy?" He pointed a warning finger, like somehow he held all the cards! Was he really expecting I'd just fall into his arms and forget . . . forget how Stella had gotten here in the first place?

My mind strayed back to *that* night and I shuddered with disappointment—disappointment at myself for getting into such a drunken state and disappointment at Jarrod for taking advantage of it. I should have been angry with him, but somehow I was just too tired.

I placed a hand on Brad's arm, feeling the knotted muscles beneath his skin. He was strung like a bow. I had to get hold of this situation somehow or it could turn nasty. I'd never seen Brad like this and I knew the kind of taunting Jarrod was capable of.

"It's OK, Brad. Let's see what he has to say, OK?"

Jarrod's eyes darted between us, still sizing up the situation in his usual calculating style. I hoped he had enough sense to gauge the intensity of the moment. Unfortunately, he didn't.

"So is this your new baby-daddy?" he scoffed. In that

moment, I wondered how I'd ever thought I'd loved him.

"No, Brad and I are friends," I replied evenly, my eyes bounced between them like a ball in a tennis match. We were getting close to deuce.

"Friends," Jarrod snorted, "—he wants to be way more than just your friend!" He arched an eyebrow. "Now you tell him to get his keys and take a hike." He gestured toward the door.

The tension deepened. I sensed Ricky step into the hallway. My grip tightened on Brad's arm as Jarrod took a step closer. Brad hadn't moved a muscle, apart from the ones rippling in his upper arm as his hands clenched and unclenched by his sides.

"Why don't we all go and sit down in the lounge?" Mum suggested. "Perhaps we could get everyone a drink, Jill?"

Jarrod rolled his eyes and turned to Mum with a smirk. "Isn't that how all this got started in the first place?"

Perhaps he thought it would lighten the mood and everyone would laugh. I don't know—but it really stung!

I couldn't help it. I swallowed the sob but wasn't able to stop the tears welling up. They hadn't even breached my lower lashes before Brad moved.

It was silent, deliberate and conversation-concluding. As he stepped forward, he lowered his shoulder. Jarrod glanced around a moment too late.

His hands flew up just as Brad's wrist twisted to connect with his nose. There was a horrible crunching and an arch of blood spritzed the air as Jarrod hit the floor.

* * *

There was a flurry of activity. Jill and Mum raced to Jarrod's side as Ricky moved to the space between. He placed his hands on Brad's shoulders. I knew he was trying to calm him down. Brad was still frozen in position, fist clenched with a drip of Jarrod's blood clinging to the knuckle of his index finger. I felt like I was in the eye of a storm, calm and disconnected.

Aroha turned on the tap in the sink and began soaking the hand towel which hung on the back of the oven. She rushed over to Jarrod, offering it to Jill's outreached hand. Aroha was just going back when I heard Jill call for ice.

I felt a tugging then a snap, like someone had flicked a rubber band inside me. My pants were wet. *Great—with all the tension I'd just wet myself.* I clenched my muscles to stop but I couldn't.

A flood of water erupted down my legs. I jammed my hands between them fruitlessly, trying to stem the flow. The taut stretch inside my stomach relaxed for a moment and I was able to take in a full breath. But the pleasant feeling only lasted a fraction of a second. In the following instant, my ovaries burst into flame as a dozen carving knives twisted in my lower back. I clutched my stomach and gasped. "Brad—help me!" I whimpered.

The room froze in suspended animation as five pairs of eyes turned toward me.

"Aroha," Jill called from the floor, "get the towels—now!"

Instantly, Brad was back from wherever Jarrod's comments had sent him. He was by my side, his eyes filled with concern and confusion.

"Stella, she's coming . . . now!" I gasped between

contractions. I couldn't count the distance they were apart. It was too painful. Aroha was back with the towels.

"Take them to the car," Jill directed, while Mum glanced around helplessly stroking Jarrod's forehead. Aroha nodded and ran out the front door after thrusting a towel into my arms.

Another contraction wracked my body. I felt another gush of liquid run down my leg. It wasn't as dramatic this time but clearly Stella was coming, ready or not. Brad picked me up and carried me to his car. It wasn't quite how I'd imagined him sweeping me off my feet but under the circumstances it was the best I could expect.

"I haven't got my bag packed yet," I wailed as Brad lowered me into the passenger seat and buckled me in.

"I'll ruin your upholstery," I moaned.

Brad snorted, "Upholstery? You're in labour and you're worried about my upholstery? It's only a car, Heaven." He closed my door and raced around to jump in the driver's side.

"Don't worry about the bag," Jill called from the front door. "I'll bring it down just as soon as I've gotten everything sorted here."

* * *

Moments later, we were speeding up Hill Road.

"I'm sorry," Brad said, glancing across at me.

"Sorry! It's not your fault Stella's decided to come early." I smiled weakly before being wracked by another contraction. I could feel pressure. If we didn't get there soon . . .

"No, I'm sorry for hitting Jarrod. That was really bad . . ."

"Oh, Jarrod," I grimaced. I'd already forgotten about him. "Don't worry, he had it coming." I ground my teeth.

"Yeah, but it wasn't my place . . ."

"Can we not talk about Jarrod now, please Brad," I cut in with a gasp. "I'm in agony and if you don't hurry up Stella is going to be born right here on your front seat."

I howled as the next contraction quaked through my body. I was exhausted already!

"Is she coming? . . . do you want to push?" he asked nervously.

"NO," I spat. "I need a pedicure and a chai latte—of course, she's coming, you idiot. Now drive." That was mean—but I couldn't help it!

Brad thumped his foot on the accelerator. I cursed him as he bounced us through several more potholes and convinced him to run a red light.

"There's no-one coming—just go!" I screamed. I wanted to push.

Lights and a police siren burst into our rear vision mirror.

"I have to pull over, Heaven," Brad began.

"Brad, you can't. We are almost there. I swear she's going to be here any second. Don't make me have her in the car, please Brad . . . we are almost there. I don't want to have my baby without a doctor. What if she dies?" I sobbed. The pain was unbearable and the urge to push was becoming impossible to ignore.

"Please, Brad, hurry!" I buried my fingernails into his arm as another contraction exploded. He picked up the pace with the police car still in hot pursuit.

Moments later, we burst into the lit area of Middlemore

Hospital's emergency entrance. Brad had barely slid on the handbrake when he leapt from the car screaming toward the door.

"Help, quick, the baby's coming. I don't think she'll make it inside!"

Moments later, two pairs of arms reached into the passenger seat and pulled me onto a gurney. The pain was excruciating.

"I wanna push," I moaned through clenched teeth.

They wheeled me through the doors and straight onto the waiting elevator. A cool hand was placed on my forehead. "I just need to check, OK?" a kind voice said.

"She's early—she's not due for another two months." It was Brad's voice. He hadn't left me. But I couldn't see anyone now. The pain had blurred my vision.

"Brad," I called weakly, grasping with my hand. Suddenly his huge hand enveloped mine. It was almost unbearably warm but I needed him.

"I'm here, Heaven, I'm here. I promise I won't leave you, OK? You'll be fine. You're not going to have Stella in the car," he whispered earnestly in my ear, stroking my face with his free hand.

I smiled briefly.

Then I grunted, "Urrrgghhh."

"Don't push yet, Heaven, OK?" The kind woman said. I heard an edge in her voice.

"She's fully dilated, Doctor," the midwife said.

The elevator dinged to a stop and the doors opened.

"Right then," the doctor said cheerily, "let's go have a baby."

"Her name's Stella," I said weakly.

"OK," she said as we rushed down the corridor, "let's have Stella!"

* * *

I don't remember much after that. The pain was so intense. I remember grabbing someone's coat and begging for drugs as they wheeled me in—but it was too late.

Someone offered me a cup of ice chips and a nurse shoved a gas mask in my hand. It could have been the same woman but the faces were too blurry.

"Now, Heaven, it's time to push. When the next contraction comes we need to make the most of it."

I nodded and grimaced.

"Is one coming now?"

I nodded again.

"OK, let's go!" The doctor disappeared between my legs. I thought it odd for only a millisecond, then the pain arrived again.

"Push!" the doctor demanded.

I pushed so hard I saw stars. I heard Brad gasp beside me and realised he was still holding my hand. I smiled up at him. I noticed he looked pale.

"Are you sure you want me in here, Heaven?" he asked. "I think I can hear your mum outside now."

"No, please don't leave me," I begged.

I didn't have time to hear his reply because another contraction was on its way.

"Ready, Heaven? OK now, push!"

I pushed and felt something shift. She was coming down. I wanted to push again.

"Wait for the next contraction now," the doctor warned.

I could feel it coming.

"Are you ready?" the doctor asked again.

"Yes," I replied through gritted teeth.

I pushed and pushed for what seemed like ages. Suddenly I felt something give and slip through.

"OK, that's great, Heaven. Now don't push for a moment. Just hold on . . . OK, we've got the head." She smiled. Brad couldn't help himself—he took a peek.

"Right, Heaven, the next push and we'll have her . . . ready?" I nodded. The thought of her being out was wonderful. I gave one final push and felt the rest of her slither out. Next thing the doctor was holding a tiny, bluey-red slimy mass in her hands. I forced myself to focus, then realised it was Stella. She opened her little mouth and cried. My heart melted. My baby was alive. Her little legs were moving and she was still connected to me when they lifted her up onto my chest.

"Would you like to cut the cord?" the doctor asked Brad.

Brad looked at me and I nodded. I was too wrapped up in Stella to worry about what else was going on.

"Hello, Stella," I said, looking deeply into her tiny blue eyes.

"I'm sorry, Heaven, but we need to clean her up and get her into a humidicrib. She's too early to be out here on her own for long," the nurse said, reaching for my daughter.

I took one last look at her and patted her tiny head before nodding for them to take her. The nurse rushed her over to the humidicrib and then they were gone. Just like that, one moment she was completely a part of me, my constant companion—next moment, she was gone.

I was about to say something to Brad when another contraction hit me. Another nurse came over and began pushing on my stomach.

Hey, what's going on? Stella's here! I thought.

"I'm sorry, Heaven, but we still need to deliver the placenta. So let's just have one last push." I halfheartedly obliged and soon we were all done.

* * *

I lay back on the bed still clinging to Brad's hand.

"You were amazing, Heaven," he smiled. "That was just amazing." He shook his head. "I don't know what to say. Would you like me to call everyone in now?"

"If you don't mind, could that wait a bit, I'm kinda tired," I sighed.

"I'll go then," he said, patting my hand.

I clutched tighter and Brad winced. "OK, I'll stay—but do you think we could swap hands now? I know you just had a baby and everything, but you've all but cut the circulation off in this hand," he said apologetically.

I released his hand and carefully wriggled over, pointing to the vacant space.

"Can you fit there then?" I asked weakly.

"Sure," he replied, slipping gently onto the bed. We said nothing for a few minutes. I felt light, like I was floating. The room was swimming in a silvery haze. I closed my eyes and began slipping off to sleep while he stroked my hair.

"Don't go to sleep. The doctors will be back to move you in a minute," he whispered.

"Yeah," I mumbled.

He rested his head on mine. It felt so comfortable. I wished I could stay awake to appreciate it.

"You did really well today, Heaven." I knew he was right next to me but his voice seemed so far away. I was slipping somewhere nice and peaceful. He was still talking in the background. He'd just asked a question. *What was the answer?*

"I love you, Brad," I mumbled. *Was that the right answer?*

TWENTY-SEVEN

I woke up to an annoying beep. I remembered trying to shoo it away but it wouldn't go. Finally, I opened my eyes.

Brad was fast sleep with his fingers laced through mine and his head resting on my bed. Mum was curled up on the chair under the window.

I looked around. I was in a completely different room. I tried to sit up but felt too weak. Trying to move had caused a throbbing pain in my arm. A long tube was running down from a bag of blood on an IV pole and into my arm.

Brad felt me stir and looked up in concern. "How are you feeling?" he whispered.

"Ummm, fine, I think. Maybe tired still . . . what happened?" I croaked.

"You had a major bleed of some kind," he said, running his fingers through his hair.

"Is Stella OK?" I asked in concern.

He smiled. "Yeah, she's great—pick of the nursery." He looked like a proud father. Then his face dropped. "I thought we'd lost you," he said seriously, taking my hand again. He paused as if he was checking I was really awake.

"Do you remember what you said just before you lost consciousness?" he asked earnestly.

I thought hard, but couldn't quite put my finger on it.

"Well, I do," he moved in closer, "and I almost never . . ."

The door swung open and a nurse came in. Brad backed up to give her room. She checked my eyes, temperature and pulse.

"Looks like everything is getting back to normal now, Heaven," she smiled. "You gave us quite a scare."

She checked my IV, then disappeared out the door again. Mum stirred on the couch. Brad glanced over, grimaced, then took my hand again.

"She'll be awake soon." He turned back to me. "I'm sorry I hit Jarrod," he whispered.

Wow, I'd just about died and we were talking about Jarrod.

"Forget it, he had it coming," I reiterated.

"Maybe, but it wasn't my job to dish it out—and I'm sorry."

I rolled my eyes and looked back at Mum again. She was stirring some more.

He hooked himself up close to me, placing his hand on my cheek.

"I don't know if you remember what you said when you . . . Anyway, I just wanted to say . . ."

It all flooded back. I blushed all the way to the tips of my ears.

"Brad—I'm . . ." I began, but he placed his finger on my lips.

"It's OK, Heaven. I . . . I have feelings for you, too, and when you are ready and the time is right . . . perhaps you would consider letting me be . . . the special person in your life," he whispered.

I giggled. "The special person?"

"Well, 'boyfriend' seemed a lame title after I just held your hand while you gave birth." He grinned.

My smile faded. "But I'm not good enough for you."

"Not good enough?" he repeated in surprise.

"No, I'm not. You deserve . . . a nice girl," I argued.

"But I've got one—that's if you'll have me, that is. I think you're fantastic," he whispered just as Mum stirred a third time and woke up.

"Heaven, you're awake—I was so worried," she said as she rushed over.

* * *

Brad wheeled me into the special care nursery a few hours later. Stella was fast asleep in her crib. She looked like a tiny baby doll with her pink woolly hat and huge nappy. Her name was spelt out in big letters above her head so she could see it if she opened her eyes.

I placed my hands on the side of the humidicrib and looked in. The nurse came over, I had no idea if she'd been the one who helped deliver her or not.

"She's doing really well, Heaven—she's strong. I don't think it will be more than a few weeks and you'll be able to take her home," she said after checking all her vitals again.

"I know all this"—she waved her hand—"can look pretty frightening but don't be . . . She's doing great. Would you like to hold her?" she asked.

I looked at my tiny daughter and thought about her life. I imagined her at three or four dressed in a fairy costume, dancing about in some kind of end-of-year play. I imagined her first day at school, her first athletics meet . . .

"Did you want to hold your daughter, Heaven?" she prompted.

"Ummm, no. She's probably pretty tired. I think . . . I'll

265

just watch her sleep for a while, if that's OK." The nurse nodded and went away.

Brad shifted behind me. It had been a long day for him. "Did you want to go get something to eat, Brad. I'll be fine here while you're gone." I didn't take my eyes off Stella as I spoke. He needed a break.

"I'll stay with you," he yawned.

"It's OK, Brad. There are lots of people here. You go have something to eat." I sniffed, "—and maybe a shower."

He laughed. "OK. I'll be back in a couple of hours." Then his face turned serious. "You know Jarrod's here. He wants to see you." He reddened. "Jill told the doctors what happened just before we—you know—came to the hospital. They wouldn't let him in—in case he upset you . . ."

I nodded. "That's OK. I'm glad they didn't, but I think I'm ready to face him now."

"Did you want me to stay?" he asked, looking a little worried.

"No, I'll be fine. You go freshen up." He turned to leave.

"But you'll come back, won't you?" I felt my heart speed up. Was what he said before what he really meant—or was it all just the heat of the moment?

In one big step, he was back beside me. He took my face gently in his hands and patted my cheek. "I most definitely will be back, just as soon as I can be."

I heard my mother clear her throat at the door of the nursery. "Can we come in now?"

I was amazed she'd managed to stay out as long as she had.

* * *

266

My mother walked in. Jarrod was a couple of paces behind her. His eyes looked like a raccoon's and his nose was taped up. He'd obviously made use of the hospital while he'd been waiting and had his nose set.

"Can I talk with you a minute, please?" Brad asked.

Jarrod backed up a little. I think he thought Brad was going to take a second swing.

Brad held his hands up in a gesture of peace, "Nah, none of that, just want to talk."

Jarrod looked at me. He looked almost sad, like he'd lost something. But he followed Brad back into the hallway. I could see them through the door. Brad was apologising. A few seconds later, he clasped Jarrod's elbow as they shook hands.

"You're a lucky young woman," my mum finally said. I'd almost forgotten she was there. She'd been quietly watching her new grandchild sleep.

"She's beautiful, isn't she?" I beamed.

"Yes, but I was talking about Brad. He's . . . he's . . ." She couldn't find the words.

"Truly special!" I suggested.

She nodded. "Truly special! Not every young man would be willing to take on someone else's child."

"Yes, I know!"—which reminded me of something else. I called back to Brad. He was still talking to Jarrod at the door.

He stepped back into the room. "Did you need something?" he asked with concern.

"No, well, yes—you." I winked. The clouds rolled back and his eyes sparkled.

"That's good to hear . . . but I know you didn't call me back to just give my ego a boost," he said grinning.

"No," I replied seriously. "Could you please bring Sharon and Greg back with you? I wanted to have a chat with them."

"OK." He looked curious but didn't ask. "Will do." He squeezed my hand. "See you in an hour or so." Then strode out the door.

Stella chose that moment to wake up. Her little arms fluttered like a butterfly. She opened her mouth and let out a wail.

"Ohhh, come to grandma, you poor baby," Mum cooed from outside the humidicrib. The nurse came over.

"Would you like to feed her, Heaven?" I nodded.

The nurse put Stella in my arms. She was so tiny. I imagined Brad trying to hold her. He'd only need one hand. The nurse gave me a small bottle.

"Is this all she drinks?" I asked in surprise.

"She's only really small, Heaven. Most babies her age would still be drinking from a syringe but she's going so well we thought we'd try a bottle. She's got a great sucking reflex for one so young." The nurse seemed proud of Stella, so I was, too.

I watched her alternately chew and suck for a moment before settling in to suck contentedly.

"Are you planning to breastfeed?" she asked me.

It was probably time I thought of her in some other way than just the nurse. I glanced at her name badge. "Umm, no thanks, Pam," I smiled.

"OK, you'll need the doctor to prescribe you some Parlodel so your milk won't come in." I nodded. I didn't hear much more. Mum's green roots were showing. I could hear her going off about breast being best and the importance of bonding with your baby, but it all took second place to Stella.

"Mum, you're stressing Stella. We can discuss this later. We don't want any negative energy in this room now, do we?"

Her mouth snapped shut. She couldn't argue with that. My mother's religious beliefs were extremely eclectic.

Stella finished the bottle.

"Well done, Stella!" the nurse said as she took the bottle from me.

"Jarrod," I asked, "would you like to hold her?"

"Could I?" he asked in wonder.

Jarrod eagerly sat down in the chair and Pam lowered Stella into his arms. He waved her little feet and touched her dainty hands. Stella reached for his finger and wrapped her hand around it.

"She's so strong," he gasped. Then his eyes filled with tears and he began to sob. The nurse helped Stella back into the humidicrib.

We all watched as Jarrod crumbled. I didn't know what to do. I turned to Mum for advice but she was too wrapped up in Stella. I rolled my chair over closer to him. He calmed enough to speak.

"I'm so sorry, Heaven. I've been so . . . so terrible in all of this. I don't deserve you. You are better off with Brad. He's a good guy—and Stella . . ." The tears erupted again and I waited for them to subside.

"What I did to you was inexcusable, Heaven. I don't even expect you to forgive me— I'll never forgive myself. I just want you to know . . . I'm sorry." He looked so full of anguish and regret, amazingly I felt sorry for him.

"Yes, Jarrod, what you did wasn't OK but—look at her!" But he'd started crying again.

"No, Jarrod, stop. Look at her!" He sniffed several times, dabbed his broken nose, then turned. He couldn't help but smile. Mum was singing to our tiny baby through the glass.

"She's perfect. She's the good to come out of the bad—the sunshine after the rain. Let's not dwell on the past, OK?" I smiled.

He nodded.

"But Jarrod, promise me one thing, OK?"

He nodded eagerly. "Anything, Heaven—anything!"

"Promise me you will never do anything like that again." My eyes filled with tears. "Promise me you'll never do what you did . . . to anyone else, OK?"

I watched his face fall but he held it together. "I promise," he whispered.

Then we both just sat there and watched her for the longest while.

"I've lost you, haven't I?" he said suddenly, turning to me.

His eyes were clear. The pain was no longer apparent, just maybe a little haunted around the edges.

I sighed. "Yes Jarrod, we can't be together again. Some things just can't be recovered."

He nodded. "Brad's a good guy. He deserves you much more than I ever did."

He paused. "But . . . how are we going to work things out. I know it's just early days yet, but I have a financial responsibility and I would like to see her . . ."

"Please stop, Jarrod. There's something I'd like to discuss with you—but not here. Could we take a walk?" I asked.

"Sure." He got up to leave and turned to wait for me.

"Ummm, I can't walk yet, do you think you could . . ."
I eyed the wheels on my chair.

"Oh, of course, sure," he said, a little embarrassed.

"Mum, we'll be back in a little while, OK?" I called.

"OK, sure darling," she said, not taking her eyes off Stella.

This was going to be harder than I thought.

TWENTY-EIGHT

Brad was back in a few hours with Sharon and Greg. Jarrod was holding the baby, cooing at her like an idiot.

"Sorry I took so long," he said stroking my hair.

"That's fine." I bit my lip.

"Now where is this baby?" Sharon asked excitedly.

Jarrod looked at me and I nodded. Sharon walked over to take a peek at Stella.

"Oh, Heaven, she's beautiful," she smiled, her eyes a little misty. I nodded for Jarrod to take Stella to bed.

"There's a reason why I asked Brad to bring you here today," I said, looking at them both. "Would you mind taking a seat?"

Sharon and Greg both looked at each other in surprise, but they duly sat down and waited.

"Jarrod over there is Stella's . . . father. And we talked today about something. I never really wanted to be a mum, though I am one. But I'm not ready for the responsibility that goes with raising a child. And I was wondering . . . if you would consider adopting Stella?"

All three mouths dropped open and Sharon's eyes filled with tears.

"There would be a few conditions and I will only go through with this if you feel you can agree to meet them."

No-one spoke, so I went on.

"The first condition is that I always remain her mother. She can have two mums. Jarrod and I still want to be involved in her life. We want to be invited to every special occasion, birthday, first performance and school play. We want photos and regular updates. Though you will be raising her, we still want her to know us and know we love her."

Sharon and Greg both nodded, so I went on.

"The second condition is that you are never to get divorced or allow your marriage to degenerate." They both looked a little surprised.

"I grew up in a home where my mum and dad didn't really like each other, let alone love each other. I don't want that for Stella. I want her to be part of a loving, caring family where everyone loves each other unconditionally. Even if you don't feel like it."

"I can't see that being a problem," Greg said solemnly. "We promise to take care of our marriage. I love Sharon more now than when we met almost 20 years ago. We will keep that commitment to you."

"There are only two more conditions. The first is that no matter how many other children you have, your commitment to Stella will remain the same. I mean, if for some reason you are able to have your own children, you have to promise that you won't love Stella any less."

"Of course we won't, Heaven!" Sharon looked aghast, but I had to check.

"The last one probably sounds pretty strange coming from me but I want you to bring her up as a Christian. I know I've only known God for a little while, but I feel the difference. I want Stella to grow up with people who will teach her about Him. I want her to see and be a part of the beautiful mosaic God can make from those who allow

Him to be in their lives. For the first time in my life, I feel like I'm not alone. I feel part of something bigger. I want to know more and I want Stella to grow up in a home that lives the mosaic—not just on the weekends but every day."

"I can see you've really thought about this, Heaven . . ." Sharon began.

"Look, I don't want an answer right now. I would really appreciate it if you would talk this through together for a while. I want you to be sure of what you are agreeing to," I finished.

"OK, we'll be back after lunch," Greg said and they left the room.

* * *

Brad stood watching me for a while. His face flooded with a range of emotions. Finally he pulled up a chair beside me.

"I can see you've really considered this." He took my hand in his. "I hope your decision didn't have anything to do with . . . with me. I really like Stella," he said tentatively.

"No, no," I replied. "And I hope you don't think less of me for not wanting to raise my daughter. I'm just not ready. I know lots of girls do—but I want more for Stella . . . and more for me. This way, I feel we can have it all." I smiled.

"What did Jarrod say?" Brad frowned.

"He was willing to accept whatever decision I made."

He nodded and rubbed his chin thoughtfully.

"Well, if you are sure, would you like me to draw up the paperwork?" he asked.

"I didn't want it to get that formal," I grimaced.

"It has to be, Heaven—to protect all of you and especially Stella. I'll put in your requirements and get one of the partners at the firm where I have done work experience to look it over before I bring it in for you all to sign."

I nodded and stared down at the worn linoleum.

Brad reached out and gently turned my chin toward him. "If it's any consolation, I think if you want to share her with someone, you've picked the best people to raise Stella. They are wonderful people and are totally committed to one another."

"Thanks, Brad. That means a lot!"

"What you're doing for them, what you're giving up," he whispered, "I think you're amazing."

"Thank you for everything, Brad," I said, wrapping my arms around his neck, taking care not to knock the IV, and hugging him. "When I discovered I was pregnant, I thought my life was over. But in the end, it's like you say, God takes us where we are and makes the best of us, no matter what mess we're in."

Brad smiled. "Yes, 'cause if He didn't, we'd have never met."

* * *

Three weeks later, we all sat in a conference room at Middlemore Hospital. It wasn't a fancy room but it had a large table surrounded by plastic chairs. Brad and I sat on one side. I rocked Stella in her bassinet in a new pretty pink premmie outfit, complete with matching booties. It was her "going home" outfit but it would be a few weeks yet before she could leave. Directly across from us sat Sharon and Greg. They could barely suppress their excitement. The room was silent as Mr Garret, a partner from Brad's firm, reviewed the papers. I looked down at Stella—my daughter—and swallowed the lump in my throat. I was about to give my baby away.

A rustling of papers drew my attention back to the lawyer.

"Everything seems to be in order." He glanced over his spectacles. "Good work, Bradley—well done."

Brad nodded uncomfortably. He'd been nervous about getting it right.

He handed the documents across to Greg and Sharon to sign. The scratching of the pen across the paper almost made my heart stop. Then Mr Garret swung the paper toward me. I swallowed hard and my hands shook as I picked up the pen. I whispered a quick prayer—"God, please help this to be right. Please look after my Stella."

I took a deep breath and signed the flagged sections of the papers.

Mr Garret said a few more words but my heart was beating too loudly for me to hear. He collected up the documentation, nodded at both parties and left the room.

I picked up Stella and held her gently and watched Sharon's eyes fill with tears.

"Heaven, if you don't want to do this, we'll understand," she began.

I looked at the couple across the table from me. It was within my power to give them what they couldn't get for themselves, to offer them a chance to share in the miracle of creation. I looked down at Stella.

I heard a voice echo in my mind, "She'll always be yours."

It was true, Sharon and Greg had agreed to everything and it had been their suggestion that Stella come and stay with me as much as I needed her to.

I swallowed again. I was doing the right thing. I kissed Stella's hair-wisped head and whispered, "Now you be a good girl for your other mummy and daddy. I'll miss you lots—but I know they'll look after you really well."

I kissed Stella again as Sharon came to stand beside me. Reluctantly I handed my beautiful baby into her waiting arms.

"Thank you, Heaven," she said, her voice shaking. "God bless you for your wonderful gift. Greg and I will always think of Stella as being our little treasure sent to us straight from Heaven." She smiled.

Greg reached over to hug me. He was too choked up to say a word.

I smiled through my own tears as Brad slipped his arm around my shoulders. Watching them wheel Stella back up to the nursery without me that day was the hardest thing I'd ever had to do. But I felt it was the right decision. My pain was the back of life's tapestry. I held onto the fact that God would take those broken pieces and blend them all together into something beautiful. I just had to trust in his plan for my life.

TWENTY-NINE

E veryone had flown in—Mum, Dad, Katie, Kelly, all of Jarrod's family and a bunch of our extendeds. The church was buzzing with all our relatives. Dad had booked a restaurant for the Saturday night, even though I told him that wasn't how it worked. But he couldn't be dissuaded. Mum had bought a ridiculously ornate and expensive christening gown from a shop in Gordon. It hung almost a metre past Stella's feet but Sharon had graciously obliged.

I adjusted the bow on Stella's head. I couldn't believe how much she'd grown in three months.

"How's medical school going, Heaven?" Sharon asked trying to distract me from my nerves.

"Busy—I had no idea! Oh my, Stella's just chucked all down your back." I laughed at the long white streak that flooded down the back of Sharon's red dress.

"There are wet-wipes in my bag. Could you get them for me?" she asked turning around.

As I sponged my child's vomit from the back of her mother's dress, I smiled at just how well things had worked out. Stella was a beautiful, happy and loved baby. So many people cared about her. The contingent here from Australia was a testament to that. Suddenly another baby cried.

"Oh Stephen, you've woken. Can you get him for me, Heaven?" Sharon asked.

I reached into the baby capsule and lifted out Sharon and Greg's son. They'd gotten the adoption papers through for

278

their son just a month after I left. The even more amazing thing was—though they couldn't pinpoint the exact day—his birthday fell in the same month as Stella's. So they were almost twins. God had delivered two dark-haired little angels.

Greg's face popped around the corner of the door. "They're calling for us now."

I handed Stephen to Greg and he backed out. I was about to follow when Sharon stopped me.

"I just wanted to say thank you, Heaven. You have no idea—the joy you have given Greg and me. We are so blessed to have Stella and you in our lives." She smiled, handing me my daughter. "I think it only fitting you should hold her for the dedication. You are as much a part of this family as she is." Sharon's eyes welled with tears.

"Stop, Sharon, or we'll both be crying," I replied, wiping my eyes with the back of my free hand.

"God bless you, Heaven, for what you've done for us," she cried as we stepped out onto the stage.

"Don't worry," I whispered as I took it all in.

I glanced at Brad, who was playing the guitar with his students. He winked in reply. My eyes wandered to my friends and family grinning from the congregation below. Then lastly, they fell on the child in my arms. My beautiful Stella—my own perfect little star! Everything was wonderful. It was time. Pastor Dan was calling us.

"Trust me, Sharon," I added, my heart bursting with joy as we stepped forward to dedicate our children to God, "He already has!"

MEET THE AUTHOR

Amanda Bews always had a passion for stories. In high school, writing was always her favourite subject and after completing a Bachelor of Education, she enjoyed nothing more than enticing a passage or two out of her students. After marrying and leaving the shores of her native New Zealand, she settled in Sydney, Australia, with her husband, Brendan, and two sons. While at home with her third son, she decided it was time to have a crack at turning her dreams of becoming a writer into a reality.

She explained some of the process of how this happened.

What was the beginning moment of *Heaven Sent*?

My husband and I were driving and discussing a disturbing article we had read in the newspaper about the choices some young people were making, choices that were ending very badly for them and leaving them hurting in ways they hadn't foreseen. There was a map in the pocket of the car door and I said, "Wouldn't it be great if there was a map for life!" We began reflecting on some of our past choices and during this discussion the rough plan for a series of books was born, the first of which is *Heaven Sent*.

What inspired you to spend the time developing this story?

The high number of young women who are sexually assaulted while under the influence of alcohol. We do not live in a safe place. Our society is all about "me first" and unfortunately there are people who will prey on the unsuspecting—and sometimes those people can be closer to us than we think.

What did you learn or what most surprised you in the writing process?

I guess what shocked me the most was the number of people who, when I told them what I was writing about, could identify with Heaven's story. There are so many people who are our friends, colleagues and part of our church family that have suffered through soul-damaging experiences and say nothing. We can live alongside them unaware of their hurts. Stories give people an opening to share.

What of your life experiences have you drawn on in telling this story?

A collection of unwise choices that I and others have made. Sometimes watching other people fall can be more painful than stumbling yourself. I hope Heaven's story saves a few young people a grazed knee or two.

You address serious social issues in this book. Why do that in the form of a story, rather than a textbook for example?

I hope that *Heaven Sent* will be an entertaining story, while also allowing an opening for discussion, for the reader to ask the questions they have "through" Heaven and the other characters, making any potential discussions less sensitive and personal.

With a study guide available from the website <www. amandabewsbooks.com>, how would you suggest this book be best used?

I hope teen and youth small groups and school groups might consider reading this story and working through the study guides together. There are 13 discussion guides covering topical issues so leaders can run with it for an entire church quarter or school term—or pick and choose from the discussion what is most relevant to their situation.

What are the most important things you hope a young person might take away from reading this story?

Throughout the story, Heaven moves from a life where God is largely irrelevant to a place where she begins seeking His leadings in her decisions. I hope young people will think about what it means to be "with" God in everyday life choices because He wants to do life with them.

I also hope they ask themselves, "Is this wise?" Sometimes we spend time considering what we would and would not like to do. That is all nice but sometimes the things we feel we want to do are really not wise or safe. Life can pivot on what felt like one small choice. Since we cannot foresee the future, we need to play life like a game of chess and consider where our next move will take us.

"I was captivated by this story and had to keep reading to see what happened to this poor young girl. My heart ached for her as she made her tough decisions. Many young people are being confronted daily with these same issues. So I see huge value in the study guides that have been written as they will encourage discussion and support."

—*Julie Weslake, children's ministries leader, Sydney, Australia*

To purchase additional copies or class/group sets of *Heaven Sent*

or to access free study and discussion guides for *Heaven Sent*

visit

www.amandabewsbooks.com